MATING SEASON

VOLUME 1 | FIRST EDITION

LEXI SYLVER

MATING SEASON

EROTIC SHORT STORIES

BY LEXI SYLVER

MATING SEASON

EROTIC SHORT STORIES

VOLUME 1

Dedicated to

G.A.B, C.B.S., J.S., B.M.S. and E.A.L.

for your unconditional love and support

and

to all of you who dare

to shamelessly explore your Lexuality.

CONTENTS

A NOTE FROM LEXI

Welcome to my playground, friends and fiends.

Are you ready to explore your Lexuality?

Writing this book has been one of the greatest challenges of my life so far. Some of the stories in this specially curated collection were written many years ago. Through the editing process, I had to go back in time and get back in touch with the various phases of my sexual, emotional and psychological development. I traveled from my first awakening in my late teens as Lexi Sylver to my most recent erotic renaissance.

As I sifted through the hundreds of stories and journal entries that I've written to chronicle my sexcapades and fantasies, I rediscovered young Lexi.

I hadn't realized that even the earliest version of myself was fearless in her excitement to shamelessly discover her Lexuality, and didn't care about being judged for any of it. There was a purity about her — a willingness to delve into unpredictable, undiscovered territory. She was idealistic, with a desire to help others follow the same path and unapologetically explore themselves.

9

And I'm thrilled to report that not much has changed. I'm still that same open-minded libertine I always was, even if the ways in which I manifest my sexuality have evolved and become even wilder. I'm proud to be living my life authentically and have the freedom to express my sexuality any way I choose!

These days, I have the pleasure of educating others about sexuality in both my personal and professional lives. Whether through my articles, my podcast, or my travels around the world, I'm sharing my shameless perspective about sex with anyone willing to listen.

I feel extra strongly about leaving my mark through creative work, which has always been the foundation of my own sexual development. I want to encourage others to expand their own imagination in unique ways, to be brazen and remorseless about their own desires. I want to show you that your erotic possibilities are endless once you open your mind to new things and embrace your fantasies and your authentic self, rather than repressing them or feeling shameful about them.

Writing erotic literature has helped me form my identity and given me the space to delve into who I truly am and what I truly want for myself. Without this creative outlet, my imagination would not have flourished to the extent that it has. I'm also grateful for all of my lovers who have inspired me over the years, from my earliest sexual encounters to my more recent adventures.

Mating Season is the culmination of my experiences, thoughts and fantasies, and my ever-evolving understanding of sexuality. Through reading this book, you can follow along my transformation from my tamer days to my more recent and wilder exploits and BDSM experiences. Some of the tales in this collection are based on real life, infused with a few embellishments. Other stories are simply dirty fantasies that I wanted to share with you.

I've experimented with different narration styles, characters, and carnal connections. Every tale will seduce you deeper into my slutty, salacious world, and will reveal more to you about the inner workings of my dirty mind. Each story in this collection is ordered to entice, seduce and inspire all of you who dare to read them. You'll find my lighter, more fun tales at the beginning, with a gradual progression to more intense and darker stories towards the end.

Any writer who shares their work with the world bares themselves in a way that is even more profound and revealing than physical nakedness could ever be.

And now, in my newfound exhibitionism, I am willing and able to peel away the last of my inhibitions and reveal all of myself to you, just as I am.

Thank you for sharing this fantastic journey of erotic self-discovery with me, and for supporting me unconditionally.

Are you ready to get Lexual with me?

X X X

Lexi

TRICK SHOT

Max

The pool hall air buzzes with excitement. The energy of the crowd is electric as everyone watches the tournament, money changing hands with every game won and lost.

My senses are heightened as I soak up the intensity of everyone around me. Carefully aiming my pool cue at the last ball on the table, I sink it, finishing off my opponent to advance to the final round.

The crowd cheers — most of them my friends and colleagues and past tournament competitors, but with a few strangers thrown in. I've won multiple tourneys before, but the rush of winning never gets old.

I shake hands with my adversary and thank people who congratulate me as I meander through the crowd. Maybe I can check out the other game still going on and get a sense of who my next match will be.

There's a tall, voluptuous woman at the other table. She bends over to sight her shot, curves flowing like water. Judging from the gasps and shifts in the crowd, I'm not the only one affected. Her long black hair is pulled back into a tight ponytail, cascading down her back with a luster that mesmerizes me and those in proximity. Her tight jeans and black tank top look painted on.

She calls her shot, a nearly impossible combination of three balls in a row.

I choke back a dubious laugh and wait for her to shoot. Even *I* wouldn't try this. She exhales slowly, then draws her arm forward with precision. The cue ball smacks the five into the two and then into the four. Two balls sail into the same pocket and the other ricochets off the side band before sinking into the opposite corner.

Well, color me impressed. Applause rings out, and her adversary, an arrogant jerk I know from local competitions, has an outraged sneer on his face — like he can't believe he's losing. I revel in his misery.

Next, she jumps the eight ball over one of her opponent's, the cue ball safely steering clear of the pocket.

I'm riveted. How is it possible that I don't know the name of this talented pool player? I've never been starstruck before, but I'm beginning to understand how it might feel.

She shakes hands with her sour-looking opponent and the crowd swarms her, offering congratulations. I draw closer to her, wanting to get a better look at this intriguing woman. I need to meet her... especially before we head to the final round together.

She turns around suddenly, her eyes catching mine through the crowd. Their hypnotic amber color leaves me breathless, as does her luminous golden-brown skin.

"Congratulations," I say, moving forward, "That was pretty amazing." I speak loudly so she can hear me over the din of the fully packed pool hall.

"Thanks," she responds, blowing off the tip of her pool cue jokingly, like a Western cowgirl with a smoking gun. She smiles, catching me off guard with the dimple at the corner of her mouth.

"I'm Max." I introduce myself and extend my hand for her to shake.

"Kaila. With an i," she says. The skin of her hand is smooth, her grasp firm and warm. My dick stiffens, yearning to feel that grip around it. The look in my eyes must expose my attraction to her, because the corners of her eyes crinkle with amusement. It takes a moment for us to release each other, as though we're reluctant to break the physical connection. Or maybe it's just my imagination.

"Are you new to the circuit? I don't think I've seen you play before." I hold back all the other questions I have, not wanting to overwhelm her, or make her think I'm overly interested in her. I don't want to give her the upper hand.

"I just moved here from Hawaii. It's my first tournament in

this town." Well, that explains why I'd never seen her around before. She notices the cue in my hand and nods her head toward it. "So, how did you fare?"

Ah, she doesn't know me at all — yet. A grin threatens to slide across my face as the overwhelming urge to tell her how good I am at pool unfurls in my gut. I'm the five-time champion — basically a legend around here. Call it ego, but I've never wanted to impress someone so badly.

Unfortunately, I don't get the opportunity as the announcer's voice over the speakers declares it's time for the final round.

"You ready for this?" I ask her, my fingertips tingling with excitement at being immersed in the intimacy of one-on-one competition with her.

She looks at me, surprised. "You're my opponent?"

I nod and smile at her, my pulse starting to race as the adrenaline kicks in. "So, do you think you have what it takes?"

She shrugs. "I've picked up a few tricks here and there," she teases, a hint of flirtation in her voice. I can't quite tell yet if it's genuine or just meant to distract me.

"Enough to get yourself into the final showdown," I say, giving her some credit.

"I'm just here to have fun. I have nothing to lose," she says, but her eyes take on a competitive gleam, and my cock twitches again. Oh, great, a semi will *really* help me focus.

15

"Let's play," I say with a grin, casually gesturing for her to join me.

We take our places across the length of the green felt top table, staring each other down. I can't read the mysterious, playful look in her eyes. Is her heart beating as quickly as mine at the thrill of a real challenge? My blood stirs at the thought of conquering her... in every way.

"Heads or tails?" the announcer asks Kaila, trying to determine who gets the first shot.

"Heads," she calls, watching me from the corner of her eye.

The announcer flips the coin. "Tails," he says into the microphone.

Walking around the table, I try to ignore Kaila's intense gaze... and the painful strain of my dick pushing against my pants zipper.

Balls scatter evenly over the table as I break, sinking two solids.

When I look up, Kaila is watching me from across the table. My eyes are drawn to the small strip of bare golden flesh showing above her low-slung jeans.

I'm so tempted to touch her. What will her skin feel like under my fingertips? It looks so soft and flawless, hot with the blood pumping underneath. Breathing deeply to refocus, I manage to sink one more solid ball before scratching, distracted by thoughts of her like I'm a damn amateur.

"Your turn," I say, our fingers brushing together on the edge of the table as she walks past me to retrieve the cue ball from the corner pocket that I'd accidentally sunk it into.

It may be my imagination playing tricks on me, but out of the corner of my eye, I see her bite down on her bottom lip as she leans forward to take her shot.

* * *

Kaila

I can't quite decipher the expression on Max's face and it's infuriating. It's almost as though he knows his victory is imminent, but there's something else lurking behind it that I can't figure out. His smoothly shaved, strong jaw and confident swagger caught me off guard. So did his tanned body, which looks like it was sculpted out of marble then wrapped in a white T-shirt and tight-fitting jeans.

But I refuse to believe that's why I'm having trouble concentrating.

After all, I have no idea if Max has good reason to be so self-assured. Sure, he made it to the finals, but this is just a qualifying tournament for nationals. It's not *that* fancy. I've won bigger events than this.

So, I try not to pay any attention to him, but every time I look down the table at my next shot, there he is, watching me seductively with those dark eyes of his.

17

Except he keeps shifting, like he can't hold still or keep focused either. That brings me some relief, knowing he's unnerved in some way. That allows me to focus enough through this round, one shot at a time. I sink one but miss the next — really off my game. My pool coach would be so disappointed in me.

I fight off a looming sense of inferiority, like I'm not good enough to be here. But Max and I take turns having trouble playing, which reassures me somewhat.

The next few rounds pass in a haze, until only one of my solids and one of his stripes remain on the table. It's down to whoever can sink their final ball first. If either of us misses the eight right after, we'll lose.

I ignore Max, pretending he's not there, avoiding the heat of his gaze. My hands tremble with trepidation as I position my body and line up my shot. I take a deep breath to try and settle myself. I sink my last solid, but I have one last hurdle to overcome before I can claim victory.

The eight ball awaits, the black sphere taunting me. It's uncomfortably close to Max's last remaining stripe, and the angle of the shot, seems impossible, even with my skills.

Max sighs heavily as I calculate my shot and lean over the table. As I do, his eyes burn through my clothes as he stares at me. I exhale slowly and take aim.

My heart pounds as the eight ball almost falls into the pocket but stops at the edge. Defeat creeps in, because now Max has a chance. He's practically licking his chops with satisfaction.

I bite my lip and fidget, drumming my fingers on my thigh as Max ambles around the perimeter of the table, biding his time. He gives me a knowing look, then aims and sinks his remaining ball. Dread clenches in my belly as he eyes the eight ball like it's his next conquest. A sure thing.

My breath quickens when he looks up at me from the table, dark brown pools of mischief tormenting me. Frustration at my inability to read him gnaws at me, mingled with the distracting heat between my thighs. I soak up every drop of Max's physique as he bends over the table, admiring the sexy way his brow furrows as he concentrates on his next shot. THE shot.

All eyes around the table follow the eight ball as he sinks it into the corner pocket. I gasp along with the crowd as the cue ball keeps rolling... dangling on the edge of the pocket for a split second before slowly falling in.

Max's jaw drops, shoulders slumping in defeat. He's as surprised as the rest of us at what just happened. Scratching on the eight ball is an automatic loss.

I win — by default. Hands clamp down on my shoulders, whistles and applause ringing through the air to congratulate me. But this win bothers me immensely. Max should have made the shot. He was supposed to win. I didn't beat him properly and the taste of victory sours on my tongue.

"Congrats," Max says, rounding the table to shake hands. He looks like a wounded animal, but I can barely see him because of all the camera flashes around us, blinding me. I'm moving on to the next round of the tournament, with the best of the best from around the country.

I take Max's hand, squeezing hard, trying to convey my frustrated anger through my fingertips. My pulse races when I lean in closer and inadvertently catch a whiff of his musky scent. "You had the game," I say into his ear, letting go of his hand. He shakes out his fingers, surprised at my strength.

"Clearly, I didn't. I guess I wasn't concentrating hard enough," he replies, staring me straight in the eyes, unwavering. My belly clenches, heat pooling lower.

"Or maybe you just got lucky," he says, his tone challenging.

I place a hand on my hip, challenging him right back. "I'm not satisfied," I say, matter-of-factly with just a tinge of disappointment.

Max gives me an amused grin. "Why not? You won ten grand and your own top-of-the-line pool table and custom cue set. You're heading to the final rounds. What else do you want?" He casually leans back against the pool table, and my gaze is drawn to the considerable bulge in his jeans. He draws more attention to the area by hooking a finger into one of his belt loops.

I manage to peel my eyes away from the front of his pants and pause, contemplating the double entendre in his suggestive tone. I match his body language, also leaning one hip against the edge of the table, so close to him that I'm melting from the heat emanating from his body. I pick up a cue and start chalking the tip in preparation. "I want a rematch. You and me, best of three series."

Max laughs. "You've already won your prize." He's transfixed by my slow chalking of the pool cue, and he bites his lip. I hide my smug smile.

"This is for pride, not money," I point out. "I want to see if you have what it takes to beat me — and I'm going to beat you outright, and not by default."

Max cocks his eyebrow as he reflects on my challenge. If he's anything like me — and I've seen enough to know that we have a competitive streak in common — he's seething over his loss. Nobody likes losing because of an error like that.

"Fine. You're on," he says. "But we have to wait until everyone clears out of here and we have the place to ourselves."

My stomach knots in both anticipation and fear. How could I be alone with him here? I try to conceal my excitement and block the flood of erotic images that pass through my mind.

A young guy dressed in the staff uniform of all black sidles up to Max's side, trying to be inconspicuous. "Excuse me, Max, but we need you in the back before we close."

"Thanks, Liam," Max says. I'm momentarily perplexed by their exchange, but then Max turns to me and adds, "Oh, didn't I mention? I own this place." He gives me a cocky smirk before disappearing into the crowd, leaving me alone to be swallowed up by members of the press.

I glue a grin to my face for the reporters and take photos with the tournament's sponsor, all while trying not to think about the effect Max has on me.

* * *

Max

Resolving several minor issues in the back office takes me much longer than I'd anticipated. At least I know Kaila is still waiting, because her level of competitiveness outweighs any impatience she might be feeling. Finally, I make my way back into the main pool hall. Steve, my floor manager, is herding the last of the stragglers and staff members out the door.

"Are you leaving too, boss?" asks Steve as he takes out his keys, ready to close the place for the night.

"Not yet," I reply. "You can lock the door behind you." Steve glances at Kaila, and the jealousy is clear on his face when he realizes he's about to leave the two of us together. He nods at me and steps out into the night. "Thanks, Steve," I call after him, and he waves from the other side of the glass door.

Then I'm alone with Kaila. I turn back to see her practicing trick shots in the farthest corner of the pool hall, gearing up for our match. I approach from the side, observing her as she bends over and takes her shot. She moves with catlike grace. I could watch her for hours.

Despite my attempts at stealth, she sees me coming and looks at me as she takes her shot, magically sinking two balls into one pocket. The fact that she's seriously skilled, on top of her having a sharp tongue and an aura of mystery about her, awakens a spark in me that I long thought was dormant. My pulse races as she notices me watching her.

"It's about time," Kaila says, chalking up her cue as I walk up to her. "I thought you chickened out on me and left through a secret back door in the alley or something."

"Or something," I respond, flirting shamelessly. She smiles, and her eyes light up.

"Now I want to see what you've really got," she says, an edge of rivalry sneaking into her voice, "and then beat you properly."

"How can you be so sure you're going to win? After all, I'm a pro." I snatch her cue, turning my back to the table, and sink one of the balls she lined up to shoot without even looking at it. She arches an eyebrow, impressed, and my heart does a triumphant dance in my chest.

"You're a pro who scratched on the final table and lost," she sasses, moving around the table to collect all the balls from their pockets. "Let's let the score do the talking, shall we?"

I look Kaila straight in the eyes, trying to ignore her ample curves and the way they move under her tight clothes. "Fine. You can break."

She arranges the balls within the triangle for a fresh match and positions herself to break, all while staring me down. My dick stirs under her amber gaze, and a shiver runs down my spine. Fuck, her eyes are intense.

Everything moves like it's in slow motion. Kaila's breasts strain against her top as she takes her shot. I catch a brief flash of her belly folding slightly over the top of her jeans. Surely, she must know how gorgeous she is. She struts to the other end of the table with confidence, sinking two more balls as though I'm not even here.

"Your turn, Max." Kaila leans against the table and waits for me to take my shot. She eyes me appreciatively, her gaze traveling up and down my body. Does she realize how badly I want to reach out and touch her skin? My fingers itch to strip off her top and grab the dark waves of hair tumbling from her ponytail down her back.

I admire her style and watch her fall into a rhythm as we continue to battle for a hefty prize — pride. All while I feel like we're really playing for something more substantial.

* * *

Kaila

Time has blurred. I don't know how long we've been playing, but Max and I now have one win apiece in our three-game series. We haven't been talking much, but our intense eye contact hasn't wavered except for when we take our shots. It feels like it's a million degrees in here, despite the air conditioning still going strong.

It's been a struggle for me to focus. My clothes are tighter than usual around my body, and the heat between my thighs has gone from slow burn to nearly singeing my panties.

My only consolation is that I notice Max having similar difficulties, with his deep sighs and long pauses between shots, readjusting more than necessary to find the right angle and aim.

"This is the tiebreaker, the one for all the glory," Max says in a deep, theatrical voice. I smile and he hands me the rack to collect the balls from the pockets so we can start a new game. We're so close that his thigh presses lightly against mine, his heat transferring even through our pants. My desire to touch him is intense... and I sense chaos is about to wash over us.

I grab the triangle from him, then jab his chest with one rounded corner. Max smiles with amusement. "The question is, do you have the guts?" I retort, then turn to the table and start preparing our game. Not moving too much because I'm enjoying the feel of his body against mine — even if it's just his leg.

"No guts, no glory," he responds, playfully poking my thigh with the end of my pool cue.

"If you're so confident, why don't we raise the stakes?" I ask. Momentum is on my side — I just won the last round. And I'm emboldened since Max is clearly enjoying this flirtation as much as I am.

"What did you have in mind?" he asks, turning towards me so that our faces are only inches from each other. Everything snaps back into sharp focus at Max's audacious tone, adrenaline pumping through my system.

A hundred answers to his open-ended question pop into my mind, all of them filthy. Pool has always been a provocative game for me. Two people vying for control, trying to intimidate each other psychologically — that's the ultimate foreplay for a sapiosexual like me. Combined with the obvious physical chemistry and his proximity to me, this is a dangerous mix.

Max grins slyly at me. His arm brushes against me as he reaches for the chalk on the edge of the table, never breaking his gaze. I shudder when his warm breath ghosts over my ear. He trails his hand over my arm, down my side, my hip, coming to rest at the top of my thigh. If he were a few inches to the left...

"You enjoy a good challenge, don't you?" Max asks, his lips grazing the side of my neck. Goosebumps rise on my back and arms.

"I prefer a good win," I counter, barely recognizing the husky sound of my own voice.

Max presses his body into mine, pinning me between the side of the table and his body, so close to him that I can feel his hardness prodding through his clothes. My panties dampen anew at his nearness, craving his touch all over me.

"So... what kind of stakes are we talking about?" he asks as his lips hover dangerously close to mine. I summon the willpower to resist kissing him to discover if they're as soft as they look.

"Strip pool. If one of us misses our shot, that person has to remove one piece of clothing. If one of us sinks a ball, then the other person has to take something off. And jewelry doesn't count." My voice is surprisingly even, masking my tension.

Max groans approvingly. "At that rate, you're going to be

naked in no time." He sounds excited by that prospect.

"We'll see about that," I assert, then somehow pull myself away from him and the table — not because I don't want him to touch me, but because we have a game to finish — and my desire to win overrules my need for him.

I rack the balls, set aside the triangle and grab my cue to take my shot. I'm determined to get him naked. I want to see the body under all those clothes. Even if watching him undress is going to make it that much harder for me to win.

I sink my first ball easily, and smile as I look up at Max. "Strip," I command him.

"Lucky shot," he says, studying me as he unbuckles his belt, slowly sliding the leather out of the loops of his pants before he tosses it aside carelessly. His jeans look a little more low-slung than before he removed his belt, and I get a full look at the bulge at the front of his pants.

I mentally wipe the drool from the corner of my mouth and lean over the table to take aim. But I catch a glimpse of skin above the waistband of his underwear just as I shoot — and I miss.

"That was an easy shot," he says, approaching me, looking me up and down. "Now strip."

I slowly lift my tank top — a calculated move. I'm not wearing a bra. Max's eyes widen and he admires my breasts as my nipples harden. My hair feels too tight in my ponytail and I tug on the elastic to free my locks, shaking them out. My breasts sway with my movements and his gaze follows them.

"Your turn," I tell him. "Let's see you do better."

He peels his eyes away from me and rubs them as though trying to clear the image of me half-naked from his mind. Once I see how he's planning his shot, I strategically position myself at the pocket he's aiming at and just casually lean against the table, chalking up my cue and blowing the excess off the tip.

When he misses, I can't help but smirk.

"I'm off my game," he admits, slowly lifting his shirt from the bottom and up over his head. Holy hell. It was obvious even with his clothes on that he was in good shape — and what a shape. My eyes follow the treasure trail of dark hair from his navel as it disappears into the front of his jeans, and I swear I can see his bulge move. He tosses his shirt onto the empty table nearby, an amused grin on his lips. Fiery heat rages between my legs.

"You look distracted," he says, trying to throw me off my game — and I admit he's successful. But I don't want him to know that.

"And you look cockier than you should be," I argue, finding the perfect angle to do a three-shot combo. I sink two and then scratch the cue ball. "That's two things for you to take off." I smirk, trying to cover up my anticipation.

"And one for you," he points out. "You missed your last shot."

He removes his shoes one at a time, tossing them haphazardly to the floor, black socks still on. Damn. I'd been hoping his pants and underwear would have been next.

Hmmm. I can't remove only one of my stiletto boots because then I'll be hobbling around. Plus, the extra few inches give me a better stance when I bend over to shoot. He watches me unfasten my jeans, my fingertips nearly burning from the heat of the metal button and zipper.

I slowly bring the tight fabric down over my thighs and calves, then over each boot, until I'm standing in front of him wearing only a lacy black thong and my high heels. His lips part as he draws nearer to me, appraising me with lust. I don't feel exposed — I'm empowered. The cool air kisses my hot bare flesh but does nothing to lessen my rising body temperature, especially with Max standing a few inches in front of me. I ache for him to touch me.

"It's hard to tell who's winning here," he confesses, now so close that I can feel the tips of my nipples poke against his hard chest, his bulge grazing me.

"We're not done yet," I say breathlessly. "Your turn."

He pushes his body closer to mine. "You're blocking my shot," he says, not upset by that in the least.

I step to the side to give him access, my thigh still touching his, purposely leaning my breasts into his shooting arm. Still, it's hard to tell who's more preoccupied.

Neither of us are surprised that he misses again.

"You have an unfair advantage," he complains, locking eyes with me as he unbuttons his pants, slowly dragging the zipper down. Taunting me with a little striptease before sliding them down his legs and stepping out of them. To my dismay, he's still wearing black boxer-briefs, though they can't conceal the outline of his impressive dick. I quell the urge to tug his underwear down around his muscled thighs, to touch the dark hair on his legs and see how it feels under my fingertips.

I try to come up with a quip or barb in reply, but I can't think as he reveals more skin. My mouth opens and closes a few times without speaking before I manage, "Don't be a sore loser." His eyes narrow at my taunting use of the L word, but he smiles slowly.

Now it's my turn to lean over and take my shot. I know I'm giving him a full view of my round ass, the curves framed by the scant black lace of my thong. I can hear him muttering obscenities under his breath as he watches me take the easiest shot I can find on the table, motivated to see him fully naked. I sink my shot but then scratch the cue ball yet again.

"Strip," I tell him triumphantly, then realize that I'm also going to have to remove something.

I'm mesmerized by the sight of him hooking his fingers in the sides of his boxers, but he hesitates. I'm tempted to rip them off him.

"I'll show you mine if you show me yours," he says, his voice husky and his eyes twinkling with mischief. "Fair is fair."

I shrug, covering up my excitement at finally seeing his dick and start to lower my thong. He resumes peeling his boxers down his legs and the bulge I'd been admiring finally slides into view, tormenting me with his perfectly shaped package. His cock is mouthwateringly thick, its head curved for pleasure, just like my favorite dildo back home. I imagine trying to fit the entire length of him in both of my hands, end to end... he could split me apart if he were inside me.

My pussy drools liquid sex down the inside of my thigh and I remember I'm also bare, except for my stiletto boots. I can't recall where I threw my soaked underwear but I'm too riveted by the godlike creature in front of me to care.

I grab my cue and absentmindedly start chalking up the tip, just looking at Max's dick, hungering to devour him. I'm secretly ready to forfeit and conquer him instead.

Max approaches slowly until his hard cock is pressed against my thigh. "Are you sure you really want to take that shot?" he asks, one of his big hands sliding down the slope of my back to rest just above my ass. I gasp at the heat of his touch, my cue slipping from my grasp and clattering on the floor.

His arms slip around my waist and he pulls me up against his body, his dick sandwiched between us. My hips unconsciously push against him, craving contact.

Warm lips graze my neck and my shoulder, stealing my breath.

He groans when my trembling fingers snake up his muscled chest and stomach, then meander down until I'm holding his twitching cock in both my hands.

"We still have a game to finish," I remind us both, my voice barely a whisper.

His lips curl into a slow grin, his eyes darkening.

"Think of this as intermission," Max says, and his lips finally capture mine.

*   *   *

Max

Kaila's mouth is sweet and faintly minty, her lips pliant below mine, as thirsty for me as I am for her. My body responds to every point of contact as she presses against me, nipples rubbing against my chest as she strokes my cock.

I groan and run my hands over the small of her back, tracing the roundness of her ass. I can't resist squeezing, loving the way she feels in my hands. She moans against my lips, her legs parting in response to my touch. I lift her onto the edge of our pool table, and she winds her legs around my waist, my throbbing erection nudging between her thighs but not entering her. Her wet heat lures me in as I suck on her tongue, her nails digging into my shoulders with urgency.

God, I can't wait to get inside her.

Burying my hand in her thick, wavy hair, I pull her head to the side. She gasps as my lips move down to the curve of her jaw, nipping at her exposed throat. Her breath catches and she grabs my ass, searching for something to hold onto. The taste and musky scent of her fragrant skin intoxicate me, a primal sense of satisfaction and the need to conquer her running through me.

Her breasts crush against my chest, inviting me closer, her legs tightening like a vise around me. She's pushing her pussy up against my hard dick, inviting me to slip into her, but I'm going to make her wait. I dip my head to spend time worshipping her breasts, lathering them with the attention I'd been dying to give them since she first took off her tank top. The vibrations from Kaila's moans echo deeply in her chest so I can feel them in my mouth when I bite her hard little nipples and suck them into submission. She moans, her head arching backward to give me more access, her nails digging into my shoulders and the back of my head.

I look up and peer into Kaila's yellow-gold irises, the wild, dazed look in them driving me higher. I'm dying to possess this mysterious woman. I need to know all of her secrets — starting with her body. Our tongues tangle again as I run my hands up her thighs.

Her smooth, warm skin yields beneath my fingers, her supple muscles quivering with desire. I trace my way upward and she unhooks her legs from my waist to spread her thighs for me. My fingertips brush against the thin landing strip of hair between her thighs, her inner pink pussy lips glistening with her need. Kaila squirms against my touch, watching me as I look up at her and get to my knees on the floor. I ache to give her pleasure — and want to open her up more so she can take every inch of my dick squeezed inside her.

My fingers test her first, rubbing her juices over her clit. She tosses her head back and moans, balancing her hands on the pool table behind her. She shudders as I work her engorged clit, little noises wrenched from the back of her throat.

I glide two fingers into her scorching flesh, my cock throbbing as I can already imagine myself being buried inside of her. My other hand firmly spreads her legs further apart and I can see the juices drip from her swollen pink lips. My mouth waters — I have to taste her.

My fingers still moving inside of her, I drag my tongue from her juicy slit up to her clit, sucking on the sweet little nub. Her taste and her scent arouse me even more intensely, and I groan with delight at the privilege of drinking from her fount.

Kaila buries her hands in my hair, tugging and pulling as I lose myself in giving her pleasure. My cock aches with unbearable anticipation as she sighs, her entire body responding to me as I build her up to orgasm. Her thighs clenching around my ears, she shudders above me. Glancing up, I see her face twist in ecstasy, and satisfaction rolls through me just as her climax overtakes her, deep groans echoing in the empty pool hall and vibrating through her body and over my tongue.

Even with her in this position, legs spread in front of me and drunk with bliss, she's not my conquest; I'm hers. Rendered powerless by her brains and beauty. She's the one in control.

Famished for even more of her, I lap up her juices, my mouth wandering up again, over her neck and the tops of her breasts, lingering on her perfect nipples. Then she grabs the back of my head and pulls my mouth back to hers.

* * *

Kaila

I'm still reeling from the power of my orgasm and how quickly he'd made me come. Max is incredibly skilled with his tongue and fingers, and I'm dying to experience what he can do with his dick.

I bring Max's hand up to my lips and suck off my juices. His eyes widen in surprise when I slide my tongue around his fingers. My pussy aches, conscious of how empty I am as I yearn with impatience for his cock.

Grabbing him by his dick and pulling him closer, I rub his engorged head against my soaked opening, teasing both of us at the same time. I want him to stretch me apart and fill me. He groans and dips his head to kiss me again. I suck on his tongue for a moment before my mouth traipses over his neck and down his chest.

Eager to taste him, I peel myself off the pool table and drop to my knees in front of him. My mouth finally level with my prize — his cock.

His dick twitches, and I lick off the few drops of precum on his head. The stickiness extends from my lips as I pull away, obscene little strings dangling between us. He moans above me. His stare burns into me as I slip him into the heat of my mouth.

Max shifts, propping himself up against the side of the table, one hand cradling my head so that I don't bang into it. His fingers tangle in my hair as my tongue swirls around him, encouraged by his low, guttural moan. I throb with each stroke of my tongue against the silkiness of his hot flesh, mapping his shape for when he's inside me.

He tenses as I work him into a furor and I stare up at the blissful look on his face. His grip on my head tightens, his eyes clouding over while my tongue travels over the curves of his cock.

"Kaila," he says, nearly breathless, "I need to fuck you."

I mumble around his dick, "I need you inside me." He moans at the vibrations of my voice, and I lick him, working my way back up his cock, looking up at him.

He groans, pulling away from my mouth and dragging me to my feet. Recapturing my lips, he surprises me with a deep, succulent kiss. His cock presses against my belly, warm and pulsing, slick with my saliva.

Max slips his hand between my thighs, playing between my folds once again, and I inhale sharply.

Without warning, he grabs my ass with both of his strong hands and lifts me effortlessly, propping me up against the edge of the table, his eyes dancing with amusement.

"Are you afraid to lose to me?" he asks, voice teasing as his thumb rubs up against my clit again. Something fiery surges through me, his words sparking my fierce ambition.

I grab his shaft firmly in my hand, staring him in the eye. "I never lose," I say, and position his dick at the entrance of my sex.

* * *

Max

Kaila's hand guides me into the heat between her thighs. She's dripping so much that gliding into her is seamless. She groans as I penetrate her, echoing my satisfaction. I fully nestle my cock inside of her, basking in the intense heat of her pussy squeezing around me. I start to thrust slowly, deeply, but soon lose myself in her hips grinding against mine and speed up my pace.

She grabs me by the back of the neck and pulls me down to kiss her again, my tongue inside her mouth while my dick invades her pussy. Holding her in midair, I kiss and fuck her at the same time, the delectably wet sound of each thrust echoing in the pool hall.

Her hips roll into mine as we work ourselves into a rhythm, her soft breasts bouncing slightly with every movement. I lean back a bit to see more of her, transfixed by the fire in her amber eyes.

We moan together as I drive more fully into her, her pussy

clenching around me, gripping me from the inside as though she doesn't want me to leave.

I'm way too close to losing control and exploding inside of her, but I'm not done with her yet. I pull out of her and carefully set her down on the ground, grabbing her hair and kissing her.

Kaila gives me an evil grin and spins herself around with her back to me. She leans forward on the pool table, spreading her legs with her beautiful, rounded ass up in the air. Her wet pussy glimmers invitingly, waiting for my dick again.

I grip her hips and slip into her again, both of us groaning at the reconnection. I thrust long and deep, savoring the slick heat of her around me, her supple body laid out in front of me. Perfection.

Her juices trickle down my shaft and my balls, bathing me in her sex. I pound into her harder, faster. I listen for her moans and watch the twitches of her body to make sure she can take the size of me, but she's reaching behind me to grab my ass and pull me even closer, deeper.

I reach in front of her to rub her clit but her other hand is already there. Clearly, she doesn't need me for pleasure. That turns me on even more and I grab her mane of hair in my hand, twisting, and slowly pull her head towards me, groaning into her neck.

She arches backward to meet my hips, and I notice the knuckles of her free hand turning white from her grip on the edge of the pool table. Her ass quivers with each thrust, her moans deep, voice breaking as I stroke her G-spot from the inside.

My orgasm is getting close — but I want her to cum first. I slow down slightly, wanting to prolong this and drive her higher, but she turns around to look at me over her shoulder.

Smiling, she pushes me away and I slide out of her. She flips over to face me, her yellow-gold eyes blazing with passion.

"Is that the best you got?" she taunts, egging me on. And here I thought I was putting forth some of my best moves. The ferocity of my competitiveness overtakes me, and I grab her hand and lead her to a bar stool propped up against one of the pool tables nearby.

I stare at her intensely and hoist her ass up onto the edge of the stool, facing me with both of us at the perfect height. Kaila gasps in surprise as I spread her legs roughly. She smiles and grabs me by the dick again, raising her hips to guide me back inside of her in one stroke. I groan as I revel in her tight, wet heat. Our lips meet again, my tongue sliding against hers, my arm securing the small of her back.

I lose myself inside her again, every one of my senses alight. Kaila lifts her long legs until her calves are over my shoulders, her stiletto boots in the air.

Sliding my hand over her leg and up her thigh, I grab her ass to anchor her, and drive into her with abandon. She balances herself with one hand on the stool and the other on my shoulder as the back of the stool bumps against the side of the pool table over and over again.

I increase my frenzied pace, her breasts bouncing with each thrust as my hips pound against hers, the audible slap of skin mingling with the sounds of our ecstatic moans.

With my free hand, I slip my thumb over her clit and rub the engorged knot, in sync with my cock moving within her. Her pussy tightens around me in response, and I know she's close to the brink of exploding. As am I.

"Ohhhh fuuuuuuck," Kaila moans, her sounds of pleasure testing my limits of self-control. I pound into her over and over until she erupts with orgasm, her body racked with tremors as she clenches around my cock.

I don't stop until her body falters and the last of her spasms die down. Her climax fuels my pleasure, and the heat and pressure rise within my balls again. I slow down and remain buried within her, not moving, relishing the residual trembling of her pussy around every inch of me.

My hand slips behind the nape of her neck to bring her face up to mine, and I kiss her deeply and fully, reawakening her. I can't get enough of her. I never want to stop. I feel like I'm possessed by a sex demon with a singular focus.

My dick still inside her, Kaila pulls back from my mouth and smiles.

"My turn," she says, pushing me away from her and letting

me help her to her feet. She sways slightly as though drunk after her orgasm, taking an extra second to find her balance.

"Get over here and lie down," she instructs, tapping the green felt of the pool table as though gesturing that I should get horizontal.

The idea of anything but pool balls and hands touching the immaculate felt of my tables usually drives me insane — but right now, the sight of Kaila naked unhinges me.

I raise my body up onto the tabletop, lying down on my back, ready for her to do whatever she wants to me. Kaila joins me on the felt, turning her back to me, and straddles my face.

Her pussy and thighs are slick with her wetness, and I inhale her fragrant pussy, grateful to taste her again and be suffocated by her thighs. I grab her ass to pull her closer to me and lap up her juices as they drip into my mouth. Just as I'm relieved to take a break so that I don't cum too fast, she grabs my cock and starts to stroke me rhythmically, riding my face.

I can't see her playing with me, but I can feel every movement. Everything about her torments me. Her scent, the tightness of her fingers wrapped around my cock, the way her spit runs down my shaft as she eases herself comfortably into a sixty-nine position and starts to suck me again. I groan as she takes the entire length of me down her throat. I force myself to be patient and not explode inside her silky mouth yet.

My balls tighten when her hips move back and forth on my face, using my mouth as a sex toy. The muscles in her legs and ass start to tense in my hands as she moans around my cock. I struggle for composure and don't stop licking and sucking her pussy until she unclenches her thighs from around my face.

A sense of victory rolls through me when she lifts herself off of my mouth, slumping back to her knees behind my head, and looks down at me with a cum-drunk smile.

* * *

Kaila

I fight through the haze of the orgasm Max just gave me. I want to wipe that smug smile off his face and continue conquering him. I don't want this pleasure — and our connection — to end.

I crawl over his body and turn around to face him. I shimmy down him on the table and straddle his hips, his hands grabbing my ass before I even get started. His dark eyes are as clouded over with lust as mine, his gaze intense.

Grasping his cock in one hand, I coyly slip the head against the opening of my pussy a few times, unclear if I'm teasing myself or him. We lock eyes and I take him inside me, my wetness lubing him up. More of my juices drip down my thighs and make a mess between us.

Max runs his hands over my hips and ass, grabbing tightly as I start to grind myself on him, and I push down on his strong chest with one hand for stability. With the other hand, I squeeze each of my breasts and nipples, sending new sensations throughout my body.

I'm immersed in the way he fills me, his hips rising up from below. The pulse between my thighs pounds as he starts stroking my clit with the pad of his thumb. His expression turns from smugness to elation as I grind harder, faster, greedily taking as much pleasure from him as I want.

Max's breathing is uneven and ragged as his hips push upwards to meet my thrusts. He's coming undone and a wave of power rolls through me.

"I want to make you cum again," he groans, moving faster inside me, still in rhythm with my movements.

"I'm going to make myself cum," I respond, a little vicious tinge to my voice. He shivers at my malicious tone — clearly, he's as turned on by me being in control as I am.

I fuck him harder and faster until my mind goes blank. A growl rips from my throat, savage and shocking, but completely in line with my ferocity as I chase my orgasm to the end.

Max moans as I finish quivering around him, and just as his balls are tightening with the need for release, I slide off him. My mouth wraps over the head of his cock, and I can taste myself all over him.

He grunts deeply and erupts on my tongue, streams of his cum spurting out of him and trickling down my throat. I savor his taste and the heat of his juices as his body shakes and pulses with pleasure. I don't stop devouring him until I've sucked every drop, the same way he savored my pussy when I exploded on his tongue earlier.

Now it's my turn to be pleased with myself. We both try to catch our breaths, and I struggle to clear the fog in my mind. My hands find themselves on Max's chest, looking down at him, and delighting in the broad, exhausted smile on his lips.

Even though it's over, I'm hesitant to let him put clothes on again, wanting to admire his nakedness for as long as possible.

He pulls me down to him, kissing me almost drunkenly. "So, does this mean I win?" he asks.

"Not a chance," I reply with amusement, slapping his chest playfully. He laughs as I slide off the table, bending to grab the pool cue I'd dropped earlier. "We still have a game to finish."

Max groans and peels himself off the green felt to locate his pool cue. I pass him the chalk and eye the shot in front of us.

Somehow, I had thought that fucking him would alleviate the fire between us, but that possibility has long since evaporated. He's far too striking. I'm already aroused anew and ready for more. Insatiable for him. But I'll be generous and give him a break and a chance to recharge before I vanquish him again.

"Looks like it's my turn," he says, walking around to the other side of the pool table to visualize the ball's trajectory. "Prepare to be conquered," he warns, winking at me, and takes his best shot.

HEATED DEBATE

Danielle shifted in her seat at the front of the class, trying to get comfortable as she absorbed Professor Richard Davis's history lecture. It wasn't difficult for her, or for anyone else in her class, to pay attention to him. Besides his vibrant teaching style, he was the youngest and hottest faculty member.

The whole room watched Davis as he paced around the front of the auditorium, going on a heated diatribe about politics. Danielle was increasingly fired up as Davis's passion seeped into his voice, mesmerized by each velvety syllable.

"In the sixties, almost every American had a TV in their homes, and were exposed to vivid images of war, racism, poverty and political activism. This was all happening during the war in Vietnam, the insurgence of Civil Rights protests, the assassination of JFK and Martin Luther King, and later in the decade, the famous moon landing."

Even without Davis as a lecturer, Danielle loved this particular era of history, which was why she had taken the class in the first place. At the time, she had only heard about Davis through the rumor mill: He was fun, a tough grader, liberal with his office hours, and recently appointed as the University's Debate Team coach.

When she first registered for his class, she hadn't known that she'd spend two days a week, two hours at a time, crossing her legs trying to contain her lust for him. She continuously fought through a haze of lurid fantasies involving them and his messy desk at the front of the auditorium, trying instead to focus on the class. She badly needed an A as a final grade to maintain her excellent GPA and assure herself a spot in the exclusive post-graduate History program... and a chance to be mentored by world-renowned historian Campbell Woodyard.

Thankfully, she'd just handed in her midterm paper last class, meaning she only had to endure her sexual frustration for another six weeks or so. Her belly knotted with dread at the thought of her only connection with him ending at the end of the semester.

Davis paused his pacing directly in front of Danielle's desk, looking at her. "There were so many exceptional political moments during the sixties in the United States that reveal the far-reaching effects of that time, many of which are still felt today."

Danielle bit her lip, watching Davis push his glasses up the bridge of his nose, as he always did when he was deep in thought. She loved the way his straight sandy-brown hair fell into his face and he failed to brush it away. How the lack of a tan on his pale skin made her wonder if he was too busy working to travel somewhere warm and sunny. And she adored the charming way he wore checkered shirts and ill-fitting suits that seemed more appropriate for a professor twice his age.

"So how much of this media coverage was real? Which social issues were being highlighted and which were being obstructed? Who was controlling the media? And why?"

Answers to his questions raced through Danielle's mind and she almost raised her hand to reply, but a student behind her blurted out: "Skynet!" and the class erupted in laughter.

Danielle rolled her eyes at the Terminator reference, but only Davis could see her reaction. A bemused smile spread across his face. Was it directed at her? Danielle's pulse raced at the possibility of sharing this secret moment of intimacy with her Professor.

"Well, I hope that's not what you answer in your final paper, Charlie." Davis wagged his finger in mock discipline at his student, and the class laughed. He began pacing again. "I want each of you to really go deep into the sixties. Choose one major event or movement that stood out for you, and that's particularly meaningful for you. Explore the way the different media outlets represented this event and how they influenced popular opinion."

A few students around the auditorium grumbled and began talking to each other, so Davis raised his voice a few notches. "Relax, everyone. All the details are already in the class syllabus and online. You still have time until it's due. But get cracking on it, because it's worth 50% of your grade."

More grumbling rose from the audience and annoyed Danielle. She'd already written her thesis and outline for the paper and was going to run it by Davis today to hear what he thought about it. Hadn't anyone else bothered to read the course outline?

"If you need to see me during office hours, they're posted online and on my door. Class dismissed, everyone. Enjoy your weekend."

His students packed up their belongings, ready to leave and get started on their Friday night plans. Danielle needed to talk to Davis about her final paper, but he was already surrounded by a gaggle of smitten students. A twinge of jealousy shot through her as she watched those girls getting the Professor's attention.

Danielle fidgeted in her seat, forcing herself to be patient and wait her turn. A hot flush swept over her as she imagined having Davis focus his intense green eyes solely on her.

Seeking any distraction as she waited, she reached into her tote bag and pulled out the novel she had almost finished reading, *The Stranger.* But she couldn't resist glancing up at Davis every few moments, her attention pulled away from her book so she reread the same sentence several times.

She was finally finishing the chapter she was on when she realized that she and Davis were the only ones left in the classroom, and he was staring intently at her. Heat rose to her cheeks and chest as she slammed the book shut, feeling naked under his stare. What was he thinking as he looked at her? How would she even start this conversation? Her arousal was impeding her ability to think. She couldn't even move from her seat.

Her breathing almost stopped as Davis walked over to her.

"You looked so absorbed," he told her with a smile. "I didn't want to interrupt."

Davis scratched his beard, and Danielle longed to brush her fingers against the stubble of his five o'clock shadow. Yearning throbbed between her legs as she imagined the roughness of his face against the soft skin of her inner thighs.

"Yes, well, it's a great book," she replied, finally able to stand up, propping herself against the edge of her desk. She handed it to him, her fingers trembling slightly. Davis looked down at the cover and nodded approvingly before giving it back to her.

"Albert Camus, hmmm?" he inquired, leaning against her desk and looking at her with interest. "Very unexpected."

She shook herself from the trance brought on by his deeply melodic voice, sensing a note of condescension. "In all fairness, you don't know me well enough to make that assertion, Professor," she stated boldly, straightening her back and standing up.

He grinned. "I stand corrected," he said, and leaned back against her desk. "That book is not exactly what you would call light reading."

"Well, I'm up for the challenge," Danielle said, her tone unintentionally coquettish.

He didn't stop smiling at her, though he did quirk an eyebrow. Had she said something to pique his interest?

"Speaking of challenges, did you have a question for me, Danielle?" he asked, her name slipping off his tongue like silk.

Giddiness fluttered in her belly. He knew her name!

"There are over two hundred students in this class. How do you know my name?" She tilted her head curiously.

Davis laughed, the corners of his green eyes crinkling. "I make it a point to remember all of my students' names."

Just as quickly as her excitement had risen, it crashed down, realizing that maybe she wasn't as special to him as she hoped she was. "Oh. Right. That makes sense." She blushed, embarrassed by her own stupidity.

"I must confess, Danielle..." he hesitated, lowering his voice to a deep whisper. He leaned close enough to her so that she could breathe in his scent for the first time. The mixed aroma of coffee beans and leather dizzied her. "I read your midterm paper. And the way you answer your questions in class displays that same brilliance."

It was Danielle's turn to raise her eyebrows, caught off guard by his words and demeanor. This wasn't just academic praise from a Professor. He seemed genuinely captivated by her. Her stomach did gleeful somersaults, her ego inflating rapidly. It had been far too long since she'd felt truly attracted to someone on both a physical and intellectual level. Everything Davis said to her flattered her immensely.

"Thanks, Professor," she managed, fighting the blush that burned hot in her cheeks, wishing she could think of something more intelligent to say. His proximity flustered the hell out of her.

"Don't thank me yet," he laughed. "I have a serious proposal for you."

Serious? Proposal? Her mind raced through the dirty possibilities. "Go on," she said, about to explode with curiosity.

"You'd be a perfect candidate for the public debate against Lovey College next month. One of my students dropped out for medical reasons. So, if you're interested…"

She couldn't believe her ears. This was not what she had expected him to say at all. Being a candidate for that specific debate was so highly coveted that even some members of the Debate team didn't make it each year. A spot on that team, coupled with her stellar GPA, would basically guarantee her the scholarship to the post-graduate History program she was vying for.

Danielle was aware that Davis was in charge of the club, but never dreamed that such an incredible opportunity could be offered to her.

"Everyone wants that spot, and you know it," she said with a smirk.

He grinned at her boyishly. "That might be true," he conceded.

Danielle's knees weakened, charmed by the depth in his eyes and his unexpected compliments. She had to perch against the edge of her desk for balance, only inches away from Davis, who didn't move away from her. His gaze and smile were unwavering, and she struggled not to lean in and kiss him right then and there.

"You don't like admitting when other people are right, do you?" she asked.

"You ask a lot of questions, don't you?"

"And you don't answer many of them."

They stared at each other for a moment, feeling the chemistry between them, then started to laugh. She wasn't used to this level of repartee and how natural it felt.

The heavy auditorium doors clanged open, startling them and interrupting the moment. Davis jumped from where he was leaning against her desk, brushing off the front of his suit for some reason. As though just being here with Danielle was somehow inappropriate behavior or something to hide.

Dean Hanna Ball poked her head inside.

"Hey, Professor Davis. Can I borrow you for a few minutes?"

Davis cleared his throat. "Uh, right. Sure. Yes. I mean, no problem."

He turned back to Danielle as he walked towards his colleague and away from her, the spell between them broken.

Disappointment swept over her as she collected her bag, looking at him one last time before she opened the door to leave.

Davis called out, surprising her. "Danielle! I'll be in touch soon about the debate."

Danielle turned back and smiled at him, waving awkwardly, before she ducked her head in embarrassment and hurried from the auditorium.

Grinning from ear to ear, she reflected on his choice of words — I'll be in touch. Was that on purpose, or just a common cliché?

She made it halfway across the quad to her student apartment in a giddy haze before realizing she'd completely forgotten to ask Davis her original question.

* * *

Later that night, Danielle was working on her Philosophy paper for another class. She typed furiously, frowning at the way the words were coming out. She deleted the sentence, starting again.

I want to fuck Professor Davis, she found herself typing, then groaned at the frustration of her unrequited lust.

Her level of concentration was at an all-time low. Flashbacks of talking to Davis just a few hours ago popped into her head repeatedly. She could barely focus on anything else.

Just as she was feeling ready to smash her head against her desk in frustration, she saw she had an email waiting for her… from Davis. Her pulse pounded between her thighs, and the heat she'd felt in class with him came rushing back.

"Can't get enough of me, can you?" she laughed, sounding more confident than she felt. Her fingers trembled with anticipation as she opened his message.

Danielle,

Thank you for taking us up on our invitation to join the debate team. We're all looking forward to the insight and skills you have to offer our group.

Since we're midway through the semester, I'd like to coach you before we get started, to help prepare you for the debate in a few weeks.

Can you meet me Monday after class for our first practice?

Looking forward to seeing you.

Davis

Her stomach knotted up. She was thrilled at the prospect of seeing him alone. At least, that's what she deduced from his message. He was trying to be professional, but she suspected she knew what he meant by "looking forward to seeing you."

I'll be there with bells on, she wrote back. "And nothing else." She giggled to herself.

Realizing she might be alone with him again, she would have to find a way to quell her urges around him. He was her Professor, after all, and the semester wasn't over yet. She refused to get distracted by him when she had the possibility of a grad school scholarship riding on her getting straight As. She needed to spend more time acing her classes and the

54

upcoming debate and less fantasizing about Davis.

But would he make it easy for her not to flirt, not to touch him? Or would he tempt her to cross that line between teacher and student? Was that even something he wanted, or was she simply imagining that the chemistry she felt was reciprocated?

The pressure between her thighs intensified as she reread Davis's email. To her, his words insinuated that he was as excited as she was at the idea of spending time with him.

Danielle thought she would explode with desire for him. She lifted the hem of her silky nightgown and spread her thighs apart, masturbating to the words in his email.

She thought about what it would feel like to unbutton his shirt and brush her hands against the soft hair on his chest. To have his warm hands roaming the bare curves of her body until he'd memorized her form. He'd be so overcome with lust for her that he'd sweep everything off his teacher's desk and let it all clatter to the floor. They'd kiss with unfettered recklessness, not caring who would walk in to catch them together in the middle of the auditorium.

He'd hike up her dress and rip off her G-string, freeing his large cock from his pants. She'd guide him between her thighs and slip him into her wet pussy... finally. Their moans of ecstasy would echo in the large room as they moved together, connected on every level, fixated only on each other.

Her heart pounded erratically as her orgasm rose within her, and she called out his name as her climax overtook her.

As she caught her breath, she knew with even more certainty that it would be a serious feat to prevent herself from jumping Davis. Would she be able to control her behavior?

More importantly... did she even want to try?

* * *

Davis struggled more than his students to concentrate on his Monday afternoon lecture while a million thoughts raced through his head. All of them about Danielle.

As his students debated among themselves, Davis tried not to look at Danielle. She sat in the front row as usual, her eyes following him around the room. The heat of her stare burned through his clothes. He longed to know how her skin would feel under his fingertips. Her white dress covered her nearly to the knee, her sculpted calves and a hint of her upper thighs on display. His erection strained against his zipper and he forced himself to look at anyone but her.

As the class discussion escalated and Danielle interjected with a brilliant counterargument, Davis allowed himself to watch her. She radiated confidence and her words were impassioned and pragmatic. He couldn't have chosen a more suitable candidate for the debate team.

How could a young woman like her ever be interested in him? Even at 35 years old, the youngest professor in the faculty, he was almost fifteen years older than her. She could have anyone else her own age, anyone she wanted. Despite her intelligence, Danielle appeared to be oblivious to the awed way everyone looked at her, regardless of gender. Instead, she seemed to be focused on her academic performance, which stimulated Davis even more. That, and the way she looked at him, open and ready to learn, her glacier-blue eyes glittering with superior intellect.

He'd first noticed Danielle before she'd ever stepped into his class, although he'd never tell her that. He would watch her casually from afar as she walked down the school halls, conversing with other students, rebuffing some of their offers for dates. She was always laughing and engaging in animated discussions all around campus and wearing those little dresses — though they were never too tight or revealing. She exuded an undeniable sexiness that no one could overlook.

When he considered the ethics of dating a student, he chastised himself. He had to get a grip. Dating a student was explicitly against the University's rules. And he didn't want to lose his job or compromise his integrity. Granted, he'd never been in this situation before, because he'd never been attracted to one of his students... and he couldn't remember ever been so attracted to anyone else before.

Davis glanced at the clock on the wall and was flooded with relief that it was 6 PM and the class was coming to an end. He'd been so lost in thought these last few minutes that he'd regrettably paid zero attention to what anyone was actually saying.

"I won't be able to answer your questions after class today," Davis announced as students rustled around to leave class. "But I added some extra office hours tomorrow to make up for it. You can check the schedule online or on my door. Thank you."

Everyone filed out of the auditorium with apparent slowness, no one lingering this time to talk to him. Danielle waited attentively, book bag packed, sitting on top of her desk with her legs crossed elegantly to the side.

Davis was trying so hard not to stare at Danielle as he collected his belongings from his own desk that he lost his grasp on his papers. They spilled all over the floor.

"Dammit," he said, cursing himself as he knelt to scoop up the papers.

"Let me help you," Danielle said, coming to his rescue and kneeling in front of him. His breath caught as he noticed the U neckline of her white dress opening slightly, revealing the tops of her round breasts and the chain of her necklace dangling in between them. How warm would the gold be if he touched it? How soft would her young breasts feel if they were pressed up against him?

His cheeks burned hotly as his hand brushed against hers, a jolt of static electricity shocking him. He caught her eye as they picked up the same paper, both of them hesitating for a long moment before she released it so he could add it to the stack.

"Thank you, Danielle," he said as she rose to her feet and brushed off her bare knees.

"My pleasure," she replied in a deeper voice than he'd expected. Then she cleared her throat. "So, um... where are we headed to talk about the debate, Professor?"

He slid his papers into his leather briefcase and clasped it shut. "We could try the study rooms in the library." He figured it was a public enough space to not seem too indecent, while still giving them the privacy they needed to talk about the debate.

Davis's gaze lingered on Danielle's curves as she bent over to retrieve her bag. Was she wearing any panties under her dress? His cock pounded in his pants, and he willed himself to stop looking at her and reacting this way to her.

The idea of being close to Danielle thrilled him, no matter where it was. He already knew he would have to exercise self-restraint. If he crossed that line, he could lose everything he'd worked towards in his academic career. He'd be blacklisted from every University teaching staff in the country.

"We'd better get going," Danielle said, hooking her bag over her shoulder.

Davis grabbed his briefcase and followed her out of the auditorium, mesmerized by the way her hips swayed as she walked.

How the hell was he going to control himself with her?

* * *

Out in the cool autumn evening, the cold wind whistled against Danielle's bare legs as they walked across campus toward the library.

Danielle's nipples sprang to attention, and she wrapped her

leather jacket a bit more tightly around her. Her choice of wardrobe, chosen deliberately to entice Davis, was not designed for this blustery weather.

Even in the cold, the heat concentrated between her thighs built steadily as Davis began talking about the debate team. Danielle was increasingly aware that she was about to be extremely close to him in the tight quarters of those library study rooms.

Was he thinking the same thing as she was? Would he dare reveal it to her if he did? Was he afraid of the consequences of hooking up with a student? Or had he done this before and gotten away with it?

A sudden clap of thunder, followed by a blinding flash of lightning through the darkening sky, startled Danielle and stopped them both in their tracks.

Oh, shit. She'd left her umbrella at home and Davis didn't have one on him, either. She glanced at him with mild panic.

The rain began to pour down heavily, immediately soaking them both. They were still at least five minutes away from the library — three minutes if they ran there.

She could barely see through the sheet of rain, but felt Davis grab her by the hand. Her stomach did gymnastics as he laced his cool fingers with hers. "Come on," he said, breaking into a run with her, splashing through the water on the sidewalk.

They ran for only a minute or so, but they were already

drenched. Just as she was hoping they would find a spot to wait out the rain and dry off, Davis stopped running.

"Through here," he said, pulling her out of the downpour and into an old brick building that resembled one of the teachers' accommodations on campus. Once they were inside, he let go of her hand to unlock a second door.

She brushed her wet hair from her eyes and saw they were standing in the foyer of a walkup of several apartments. "Where are we?" she asked.

"I live here," he said. "I'm sorry — I just thought — well, it's closer than the library... We can just wait out the rain here before we head over. I should have brought an umbrella." Davis shook his head at his own absentmindedness. He removed his wet glasses, folding them up and putting them into the inside pocket of his coat. She could see his eyes more clearly, registering nervousness and something else...

"If only we had a crystal ball," she joked, glancing down at her soaked clothes and then at his.

"Or simply looked at the weather report."

They laughed, easing some of the tension she could feel between them. The storm raged loudly, thunder echoing in the high-ceilinged edifice.

Danielle was cold and her hair and clothes were dripping, but warmth flooded her as she realized they were alone and off school grounds. Her pulse raced at the unexpected invitation into his personal sanctuary. Were his intentions as impure as her own?

"Come with me." Davis took her hand to guide her up the wooden staircase. Her heart fluttered the instant he touched her hand and heat emanated from his palm. They walked up two flights before he stopped and looked down at their intertwined fingers.

"I'm sorry," he said, reluctantly slipping his hand from hers. "I don't know why I did that."

Danielle sensed he was conflicted. There was clearly a part of him that enjoyed the closeness and wanted to touch her in some way. He wanted her. But the fact that she was his student was stopping him. This was her chance to push him closer to her own desired ends.

"Yes, you do," she replied, meeting his gaze. "You know exactly why."

He didn't answer her, but his eyes revealed his inner turmoil. Was he debating whether he should allow a student into his apartment, and what might happen if anyone found out about it.

"Now are you going to invite me into your place to dry off, Professor, or are we just going to drip all over these stairs?" she asked, before he could change his mind and bring her back downstairs.

He smiled. "If I let you into my apartment, will you stop calling me Professor?" he asked.

"No promises," she replied, the hint of a smile at the corners of her lips.

He walked up the last set of stairs to the third floor of the building, creaking with every step. Danielle squeezed out her cold wet hair as she waited for him to find the right key.

His fumbling ended as he slid the key into the lock, turning it until they heard a click. The apartment door slowly swung open. "Go ahead," Davis said, gesturing for her to go first.

Danielle's stomach knotted in excitement. She was about to enter Professor Davis's apartment. She was doing what hundreds of students could only dream of doing with him. What she herself had dreamt of for weeks…

She stepped over the threshold, entering his private universe.

Davis walked in after her and closed the door behind them, dropping his dripping briefcase near the front door, and she followed suit with her own book bag.

Danielle slipped off her wet heels and placed them against the wall near the entrance, the wooden floor cool below her bare feet.

"Let me help you with your jacket," he offered.

Davis came up behind her. Her breath caught in her throat when he slid his hands over her shoulders as he helped her take off her jacket, sliding it off her slowly. Danielle's heart raced as his woodsy musk invaded her, intoxicating her with his scent.

She turned to face him and realized he was a head taller than her without her shoes on. His tempting mouth was only inches away. All he had to do was lean down slightly to kiss her…

Davis stepped backwards and into the hallway, looking nervous. He hung her jacket on the coat rack.

"I'll go get you some towels to dry off," he said. He padded down the hall in his socks, the old floorboards creaking under his steps, leaving her alone in the entrance.

Danielle's curiosity to see his inner sanctum spilled over, and she couldn't resist peeking into the adjacent room.

It was lined with ceiling-high bookcases filled with leather-bound books, except for where a large wooden desk imposed against one wall.

She felt at ease among all the books, in his personal space. She took several steps closer to one wall, checking out the titles on the shelves. She welcomed the aroma of old books and leather, which she was realizing was an aphrodisiac for her… or maybe it was just because those scents were now associated with her sexy Professor.

In front of a large bay window, a folded blanket and a pile of papers rested on the lone window seat.

Even more papers were stacked on the worn leather armchair in the corner near the fireplace. A soft-looking cinnamon-colored rug cozied up the space. Danielle pictured herself nestled there by a lit fire, sitting on Davis's lap as they took turns reading to each other, with only a small blanket to cover them.

She brushed her fingers over the polished wood of the desk and saw her midterm paper at the very top of a stack with a red A+ on it. She smiled, pleased at the grade, but made no move to touch it.

Danielle spied a copy of *Kingdom of Fear* by Hunter S. Thompson lying right next to the papers. Curious, she opened the front cover, and saw it was signed by the author himself. She squinted to read the scribbled inscription. *Davis, thanks for the talk and the rum. Mahalo.*

Holy shit. Thompson was one of her favorite writers of all time and she had all his books — unsigned — at home. And Davis had met him and even conversed with him! A twinge of envy shot through her, along with a rush of desire as she realized she was one degree closer to a legendary novelist.

Danielle felt a presence near her and turned to see Davis standing next to her. A blush rose to her cheeks — she'd been caught. Rain was pounding the windows of the apartment so loudly that she hadn't heard Davis come back down the hall. She removed her hand from the book as though she'd been burned.

An amused grin curled on his lips as he held out a plush towel for her, a light blue button-down shirt in his other hand. He still wore most of his wet clothes, clearly more concerned about getting her dry than himself. Without his blazer on, his shirt fit him like a second skin, and the view unnerved her more than getting caught.

"Snooping around your Professor's desk, hmmm?" he teased.

"I... um... well... I was just..." she stammered, grasping at any excuse. "Okay, yes. Yes, I was. I'm sorry." She accepted the towel from him and began drying her hair, watching his grin widen.

"Don't apologize. I'm flattered by your curiosity in me." *He* was *flattered*! Yet another confirmation of his interest in her. Her confidence level rose dramatically.

Davis lay the shirt he'd brought her onto the desk. "I figured you could wear this while I put our clothes in the dryer." When she looked down at herself, she saw that her white dress was so wet it was transparent — she could even see her white lingerie set underneath. Obviously, Davis could see it too.

Was he blushing? God, he was somehow even more attractive with a flushed face. His eyes moved from her body back up to her eyes. "I'll... I'll just go into the other room while you change." He turned on his heel to leave, but hesitated.

This was her chance. If she ever wanted to seduce her Professor, now was the most opportune time.

"Wait," she said, her towel slipping between her fingers and to the floor. Davis turned back towards her. "Can you help me with my dress?" She turned away from him, pushing her hair over one shoulder and pointing at the zipper that ran down the back. She could easily do it herself, but she relished the thought of him undressing her, of his hands uncovering her bare flesh.

A few seconds went by, and he didn't respond. Her heart

raced nervously, wondering if she should have asked him to do something so intimate. Then she heard the floor creak behind her as he approached. With her back turned to him, he couldn't see her satisfied smile.

His hot breath caressed the skin at the nape of her neck as he came up behind her. She gasped when his hand grazed her back, unfastening the clasp above her zipper. Her entire body vibrated under his touch, and she pressed her back against him, even though it made it harder for him to help her with her dress. She was stunned by the heat his body exuded, despite the coolness of his wet clothes.

Something hard pressed into Danielle's lower back, and her pussy twitched when she realized it was his cock. He stepped back slightly to unzip her dress, easing the zipper down slowly. Goosebumps rose on her flesh with every inch of skin he bared, exposing her body to the cool air. He lowered the zipper until the end, and she knew he could now see the top curve of her ass.

She sighed quietly as his big hands lingered on her skin, fingers tracing the edges of her bra. Was he going to take it off?

Her body hummed with anticipation, craving his touch and for him to undress her further, but it didn't come.

She turned around to face him, meeting his tormented gaze. She saw that he wanted her, too — but he was afraid to make the first move. This was her chance to fulfill the fantasies that had infiltrated her mind for these last few months.

"I'll just... go in the other room while you take that off..." his voice faltered, and he didn't move. He couldn't seem to tear his eyes away from her.

Boldness surged through Danielle, invigorating her. The ache between her thighs intensified, his nearness melting her core. She longed to reach out and grab the bulge at the front of his pants.

"You don't have to go." She met the intensity of his gaze, her pulse erratic. With deliberate slowness, she slid her arms through the sleeves of her dress, peeling the wet fabric off her body.

Davis's eyes dragged appreciatively over each expanse of her bared flesh as she let her dress fall to the floor in a soaked heap. She stepped out of it, now wearing only her lacy bra and panties. She might as well have been naked.

Her body flushed as she felt momentarily self-conscious, but her eyes didn't waver from his.

Davis exhaled slowly, running a hand through his hair. "Maybe I should give you some privacy..." he trailed off, clearly unconvinced by his own argument.

"Stay. I want you to see me. All of me." Danielle's pulse raced as she reached behind her to unsnap her bra. As it came loose, she slid the straps over her arms, freeing her naturally large breasts and her hard, dark pink nipples. She tossed her bra on the floor near her discarded dress, looking at Davis, amused.

"Danielle, you're my student... we really shouldn't..."

He stopped talking and watched her loop her fingers into her lacy panties, dragging them down her legs until they fell to the floor. She stepped out of them, kicking the small piece of white fabric to the side. Confidence flooded her, her pussy throbbing with impatience.

"I'm a student who's dying to fuck her professor. And you're a professor who clearly wants to fuck his student." Danielle slipped her hand down the front of his body, her palm rubbing against his still-wet pants. "Am I wrong?"

He groaned, his bulge twitching against her in response. "That's a solid argument," he admitted. He stepped forward, closing the gap between them. Her clit pulsed even harder at his nearness.

"We're the only ones who have to know about this," she said. "Do you trust me?" Never breaking eye contact, she slid her hands up his chest. She longed to feel his bare skin against hers, to expose him the way she was displayed to him — ripe for the taking.

He lowered his head, his lips now an inch from hers, his breath hot on her mouth. Her entire body begged for his touch.

"Yes, I trust you, Danielle."

She smiled up at him, taking his hand in hers, splaying his fingers. "Then stop protesting. There's nothing to debate here."

Danielle brought his hand to her breasts. Her nipples stiffened as his hot fingers brushed against them, a rush of heat overcoming her. She saw in his eyes the moment his restraint snapped. Lust darkened his green eyes and made him look wild.

Davis's lips captured hers, his strong arms encircling her waist, pressing her naked body against him. *Finally*. Danielle gasped with pleasure and kissed him back eagerly, savoring the sensual way his tongue slipped against hers. His stubble gently scratched her cheeks and chin, but she welcomed the new sensation.

Wetness trickled down her inner thigh, begging to be licked. Her hands ran up over his chest to the back of his neck, her fingers burying in his soft hair. Still kissing her, he gave her a gentle push backwards, cornering her between the bookcase and his body. His hands discovered the soft curve of her back, her hips, her ass, and then back up her belly to cup her breasts in his hands, rubbing the pad of his thumb against her nipple.

The combined scents of his musk, old books and leather made her dizzy. She moaned against his lips, standing on tiptoe to be closer to his height. His kisses grew hungrier, and she savored the silkiness of his tongue in her mouth. She needed more. She needed all of him.

Her hands slid under the hem of his wet shirt, her fingertips brushing against the hard planes of his chest and stomach. Davis pulled away from her briefly, pulling his shirt up over his head and tossing it carelessly aside. She smiled, smoothing her hands against his strong chest and abs in awe. She hadn't expected he would be so sculpted. God, he was so sexy. And so damn smart, too. The total package.

Her hands traced the trail of soft hair that led from his chest, down his belly and into his pants — just like she'd always fantasized. Her pussy squeezed with impatience. She pulled him close and kissed him again, exploring his broad chest.

Danielle's heartbeat quickened when he lifted her up easily, setting her down on the edge of his wooden desk.

His mouth traveled from her lips to her neck and down her chest, sending a jolt between her thighs as he captured her nipple between his teeth. He cupped her round breasts in his hands, his thumbs rubbing against her nipples as his mouth trailed lower. The faint scratch of his stubble gave her goosebumps.

He spread her legs and knelt on the floor in front of her, uncovering the slickness between her legs. Her pussy twitched at the feel of cool air on her swollen wet lips. He looked up at her, his hands grasping her thighs firmly. He dragged his hot tongue down the line of her belly, dipping into her navel before continuing its path down.

She groaned, squirming with pleasure under his grasp, raking her fingers through his soft hair. Her flesh tingled under the heat of his mouth, her hips involuntarily arching closer to his mouth. He traced his tongue up her inner thighs, slowly licking around the outside of her pussy. As he breathed on her clit, her pussy clenched and her hips pushed forward, desperate for him to devour her.

Davis looked up and gave her a lusty smile, then covered her pussy with his lips, enveloping her in silkiness of his mouth. Heat consumed her entire body, her thighs winding around his shoulders.

His tongue traced the pink lips of her sex and between them, easily reading her body language and the loudness of her moans. Her pussy tightened as he found his rhythm, already so close to exploding with her rising bliss.

Danielle leaned back on the desk with one hand, her free hand gripping the back of his head. She squirmed as he sucked her clit into his mouth, licking the swollen tip. He upped his tempo, moaning into her pussy, tireless in his hunger for her. His saliva mixed with her juices and dripped down her ass, pooling on the desk underneath her.

He grabbed her thighs and steadied her as she writhed under his attentions. She reveled in his strength, helpless to do anything but succumb to him.

She groaned deeply as he increased the pressure, sucking on her clit and lips, surprising her with the occasional light nibble on her engorged sex. Her pleasure built, her pulse pounded between her thighs, muscles tightening around Davis.

His hands slipped under her ass and pulled her even closer to savor her completely. Her eyes squeezed shut, her deep moans echoing in the room as her orgasm crashed over her in wave after wave of ecstasy. He didn't stop tonguing her, prolonging her pleasure until she was done trembling in his arms.

When she finally opened her eyes again, Davis had released her thighs and was kissing his way back up her body, a thick haze of lust clouding his eyes. He stood from his kneeling position on the floor, hovering over her on the desk. She pulled him towards her to taste the sweetness of her mess on his tongue.

Even after her powerful orgasm, she craved his dick inside her. She grabbed him by the waistband of his pants, looping her legs around his waist to draw him closer to her. She rubbed her hand over his throbbing bulge, then hurried to loosen the constraints of his pants without ripping them open. She unzipped and unbuttoned him, hooking her fingers into his navy-blue boxers. He helped her peel his boxers and pants off his legs, pulling his socks off in the process and tossing them on the floor.

Danielle was finally free to worship his nakedness. Her eyes fixated on his dick between those perfectly toned thighs. He was even thicker than she had fantasized about. How the hell was he going to fit inside of her? Her pussy throbbed at the challenge. She didn't care. She'd make him fit.

Davis groaned as Danielle's hands circled the base of his shaft. She admired the heaviness of his member as she squeezed, rewarded with his dick pounding between her fingers. Both of her hands couldn't cover him completely as she stroked him. His eyes slid shut with pleasure.

She longed to take him in her mouth and see how far she could take him down her throat, but the urge for him to stretch her apart overpowered her.

"I can't wait any longer," she groaned, tightening her grip to show him how serious she was. She spread her thighs even wider, shifting her hips closer to the edge of the desk.

His hand replaced hers on his shaft, and his cock approached the wet entrance of her sex. He teased her, sliding the tip of his cock up and down her pussy lips. Danielle moaned at the torture, lifting her hips to try and pull him into her.

He fed his thick shaft into her slick wetness, sliding into her, inch by glorious inch. She moaned as he carefully stretched her with each shallow thrust, until he'd filled her pussy to the brim. She'd never been so full of cock before and was amazed she'd been able to take all of him.

Every curve of his pulsing cock imprinted inside her as he stopped moving for a moment. He slid his hand around her neck and dipped his head closer to hers, meeting her eyes.

"It feels so incredible to be inside you," he sighed, covering her lips with his own before she could agree. Groaning with pleasure, she returned the intensity of his kiss, wrapping her legs around his waist and gripping his shoulders tightly. She was consumed by the feel of his hot flesh all over her, inside her… as filled up with Davis as she could possibly be.

He moved in long, deep thrusts, hypnotizing her with his rhythm. She delighted in the pressure of his dick inside her as he filled her over and over again. She grabbed his ass, digging her nails in to urge him to fuck her harder.

Her pussy squeezed him from the inside, spurring him to thrust faster and deeper. His pace intensified, her hips rising to meet his undulating rhythm.

Davis gripped her ass with his strong hands, taking control of her body and her pleasure. She grabbed hold of his taut shoulders to steady herself against his power. His eyes were feral, focused on her as he lost himself inside of her.

Pleasure coursed through her body, her core on fire. He slipped one hand behind her neck and grabbed her hair with careful strength, pulling her head back and covering her exposed throat with his mouth. He alternately kissed and nibbled his way down, then back up to her mouth. His breath was hot against her lips as he took her tongue captive between his lips again, sucking on it.

She moaned and pulled him closer, the vibrations reverberating through both of them. Without breaking their kiss, Davis lifted her from the desk and continued fucking her in midair. His strength aroused her even more, making her feel helplessly ravaged — especially as he used that power to push himself into her. Her breasts bounced slightly, her nipples rubbing up against his chest. Her pussy juices leaked all over them. She reveled in the slick sound as he fucked her faster. She'd never been this wet in her life.

Danielle clutched his shoulders for balance. Davis took a few steps towards the armchair by the fire, carelessly tossing the books and papers onto the rug. He seated himself in his leather desk chair with her on top of him, never pulling out of her in the process.

Now straddling his lap, Danielle rose a head above him, her breasts crushing Davis's face. He moaned against her sensitive nipples as he traced them with the hot tip of his tongue, sucking each in turn.

Her nerve endings afire, she glided herself over his dick, eased by the wetness that wouldn't stop dripping out of her. He ran his hands over her ass, pulling her to him and pushing himself deeper into her.

Completely pressed against him, she rode his shaft in sync with the rise and fall of his hips. Her body twitched as he slid a hand between them and stroked her swollen clit just lightly with his fingertips.

Danielle felt the heat surge within her, a force outside herself overtaking her. She moved faster, her blonde head dropping back, arching her breasts nearer to his face, unable to control the ecstasy of the continuous friction of his thumb on her clit.

She came hard, digging her fingers into the back of his head, his shoulder. A loud cry erupted from the pit of her belly. She shuddered against her Professor, and he smiled up at her in satisfaction.

He kept moving her hips back and forth to draw out the last of her throes, pleased with the power of her sexual response to him. When she stopped moving, he reached up to pull her face down to his, kissing her intently.

"You're even more beautiful when you're in ecstasy," he said. She laughed shyly and slid off his shaft, leaving behind a trail of her wet juices. Her pussy already missed his length inside of her. She couldn't get enough of him.

Her knees wobbled slightly as she lifted herself from Davis, weakened from the strength of her orgasm. She knelt on the floor between his legs, eyeing his glistening cock with thirst.

"I want to make you feel as amazing as you make me feel." Licking her lips, she wrapped her hands around the base of his shaft and stroked him, already lubricated with her juices. He throbbed between her fingers, and the urge to devour him overtook her. She lowered her mouth to the head of his dick.

The sweet taste and scent of her pussy were all over him. Her clit ached with need as he twitched on her tongue. She took him deeper into her mouth, rolling her tongue around his girth, fulfilling her oral fixation.

Davis groaned deeply, the sound resonating through his body and in her mouth. Danielle pulled him deep into her throat, as far as she could go without choking. Winding one hand around his shaft as she sucked, her other hand stroked his balls.

Glancing up at him, Davis's brow was furrowed in pleasure. She was working him up into a frenzy with her mouth, but her pussy ached anew with the need to have him inside her.

Slowing down and slurping on the way back up his shaft and off of him, she rose slowly from her knees and came face-to-face with him again. "Come here," she said, tugging his dick to denote the urgency.

He stood from the armchair as she pulled him towards her by his dick, turning her back to him and facing the nearby bookcase. She rose on her toes for extra height, spreading her legs for him.

She assumed the position for him to defile her again, the slope of her ass upturned and waiting for him.

She looked at him over her shoulder, watching Davis approach behind her. He held her around her slender waist, pressing her back against his hard body. Her skin burned where it came into contact with his.

His fingers twined in her hair and he brought her head back towards his body. His hot mouth brushed her ear, sending shivers down her spine before he released her.

Danielle hung on to the edges of the bookcase and let Davis's hands explore her. They traced the hourglass shape of her waist, her hips, her thighs, her breasts, covering every curve he could with his touch. His fingers slipped into the crest of her thighs, rubbing up against her swollen clit again.

She gasped as he seized her clit between his fingers, stroking her slowly as he pushed his body up against hers. His cock twitched against her ass and he moved his hips slightly in reaction to her moans. His hot dick probed between her legs, sliding against her soaked pussy lips but not venturing inside. The combination of sensations dizzied her, making her want to come again.

She clenched the bookcase for balance, her knuckles turning white. Fire shot through her and she ached for him to penetrate her again. She tried to angle her hips upward to slide him into her, but he wasn't allowing it. Her helplessness at taking the pleasure he gave her as she writhed under his touch only emboldened him more.

Davis seemed to sense that she was about to lose control again and guided the head of his cock into her pussy, thrusting deeply into her. His fingers still teased her clit as his dick found the perfect angle to massage her G-spot. He plunged into her, simultaneously caressing the most sensitive parts of her sex, sending her into a spiral of ecstasy that made her knees falter. His breathing came in uneven bursts and so did hers as he fucked her even more powerfully, almost lifting her feet off the floor with the strength of his thrusts.

Heat bubbled up and radiated throughout her core. She succumbed to the ferocity of her bliss, moaning uncontrollably as another climax crashed over her. Her head snapped back, pressing against his strong chest. His fingers teased out the entirety of her orgasm as he moved faster inside of her clenching pussy. He wrapped his other arm tightly around her waist to hold her in place as she struggled against the onslaught of her pleasure.

She gripped him inside her as she trembled against him. Spurred on by her tightness, Davis didn't stop, groaning as though her own orgasm catalyzed his climax. He throbbed more intensely inside of her, and he was almost breathless now. She suspected he was about to explode.

"Don't cum yet," she said in a warning tone and unwrapped his arm from her waist. She pushed him away from her and out of her and knelt in front of him, eye level with his cock. She stared up at him with her innocent blue eyes and grabbed his dick in her hands.

Sliding him into her mouth again, she stroked and sucked him with the same rhythm as he'd just been fucking her. Davis buried his hands in her hair while she worked her tongue in hypnotic circles. His groans came closer together, his knees buckling. She was thrilled he was close to the brink, eager to give him that release. She firmly tugged and sucked until he emitted a drawn-out moan, spilling into her mouth. His juices spurted hot down her throat, and she kept stroking his shaft and balls until he was completely emptied.

She looked up at her spent professor, licking her lips and smiling at him coyly. A sense of triumph flourished within her.

He rubbed his eyes as though waking up from a trance, then helped her to her feet. He wrapped his arms around her and covered her mouth with his, giving her a lingering, disorienting kiss.

"Mmm," she said with a grin, looking up at him as he held her body close to his. "So, are these the kinds of skills I'll need for the debate team?"

Davis laughed. "I'm not sure that's quite what the judges are looking for. But if they valued those skills, you'd win, hands down."

Danielle smiled and her insistent pussy pulsed again. She grabbed his hand and slipped it between her thighs to feel her liquefied sex. He groaned with appreciation, his eyes lighting up. "Well then, Professor, it'll be easy to convince you to go another round..."

ACCIDENTAL VOYEUR

Luca drove his battered truck through the open gates of the paved driveway, gazing at the mansion beyond the perfectly manicured hedges.

He rolled up to the front of the house, sighing deeply as he parked behind a red Porsche Boxster. What would it be like to live in such a palace and to own such a luxurious set of wheels? That kind of wealth was foreign to him, though he aspired to eventually be able to afford that kind of extravagance.

Toolbox in hand, Luca slammed the squeaky door of his truck and jogged up the front steps. This residence was home to Dr. Harry Watson, celebrity plastic surgeon, and his socialite wife, Charlotte. The two of them had been all over the Hollywood gossip columns lately — something to do with Dr. Watson having a secret mistress.

Luca's famous new clients had been referred to him by a local councilman, who'd loved Luca's recent work in renovating the politician's house. Wealthy clients like the Watsons were keeping Luca's cash flow steady and helping his business as a contractor and home repairman thrive.

He rang the doorbell and waited in front of the Watsons' tall double doors, seeing someone approaching through the frosted glass.

The housekeeper opened the door for him, a mop in one hand. "Yes?"

The woman was quite attractive, older than him, her milky skin barely touched by wrinkles. If he hadn't been working, he would definitely have flirted with her.

"Hi, I'm Luca. I'm here to fix the air conditioning unit." He smiled at her, trying to be friendly and professional.

"Mrs. Charlotte is expecting you," she said in a bored voice. She looked him up and down with a disapproving frown, her gaze lingering on his dirty work boots. "Wait here."

The housekeeper left him alone in the foyer as she walked through the house to find her boss.

Luca looked around for a few moments, soaking up the luxury all around him. The black and white marble floor he stood on was pristine, gleaming in the sunlight pouring in from the floor-to-ceiling windows on one side of the house. He noted a cozy living area with plush white couches that looked untouched — just for show, perhaps.

Large, imposing canvases of expensive-looking artwork adorned the walls, and in the middle of this high-ceilinged, museum-esque perfection hung a huge crystal chandelier.

Even though the central air conditioning system was broken,

the spacious house remained fairly cool. Whatever the issue was that caused the air to stop, it must have happened recently.

Along the left side of the house was a grand, white-carpeted staircase leading upstairs. Straight ahead of him was a long corridor through the house, but he couldn't make out much in the distance.

Luca heard the clacking of heels on the marble floor before he saw his new employer, accompanied by the housekeeper. Charlotte had her cell phone in one hand and was in the midst of a heated conversation with someone when she caught his gaze.

"I don't care WHAT you have to do, Melody. The benefit is this weekend. Figure it out. Isn't that what we're paying you for?" She hung up just as she reached the front doors, an annoyed expression on her face. "So, you're the repairman my husband called?" She glanced at him with snobbish distaste.

He imagined what she saw when she looked at him. He resembled a member of a 90s grunge band, with his longish, unkempt sandy hair, deep surfer tan, black jeans with paint marks on them, and a white T-shirt he was starting to sweat through in the heat. Probably not the kind of person she would have invited into her house.

Charlotte, on the other hand, looked like she was about thirty years removed from having been cheerleading captain for the football team, but still copped the bitchy attitude. She was blonde, fit, and had what appeared to be some surgically enhanced assets — probably personally crafted by her husband.

She was the exact replica of the entitled country club types he was beginning to grow accustomed to as he worked on their houses. Many of them seemed repelled by anyone who worked in the service sector of the economy, even though some of them started that way before rising to fame and fortune. But they seemed to forget all about that once they struck it rich.

"I'm Luca," he said, introducing himself to Charlotte, reaching out to shake her hand, although he doubted that she'd overcome her prissiness to touch the likes of him.

"Yeah, fine," she said, not even acknowledging his extended hand as she texted someone on her phone.

"Do you want me to take off my boots?" he asked politely.

"Whatever. Sophia will clean the floor." Charlotte pressed the phone to her ear again as she snapped her fingers impatiently and gestured for him to follow behind her.

Luca caught the housekeeper, presumably Sophia, rolling her eyes behind Charlotte's back before she set to work cleaning up the footprints he trailed behind him, muttering under her breath.

Charlotte guided Luca along the long corridor through the house while texting on her phone. Now that he was in the corridor, he was close enough to see some family photographs hanging along the walls.

He was walking too fast to stop and look at each picture properly, but he caught a glimpse of a gorgeous young woman in the photos, wearing sorority letters on her little white tank top, her blond mane cascading down her shoulders.

She was smiling and laughing with her friends on the front steps of their sorority house. He paused briefly and did a double take.

Right next to that picture frame was a family photo of the girl with Charlotte and Dr. Watson. The warmth of her smile radiated through the photo, but there was something mysterious glinting in her blue eyes that captivated him.

So, Charlotte had a daughter. And she was a total smoke show. Could she possibly be an ice queen like her mother?

His employer snapped her fingers again, startling him back to reality. His face flushed as he peeled himself away from the photos in the hall and joined Charlotte in the kitchen. The place was enormous, and he doubted Charlotte had ever cooked a single day in her life. It would probably threaten the integrity of her manicure.

Charlotte examined the diamond-encrusted watch around her wrist, nearly blinding Luca with the reflection of the light off of the piece. "Look, I'm going to be late. You can find your way around. The AC unit's out back," she added, gesturing to the sliding glass doors off the kitchen. "You can go out through there."

"Okay, sure. Thanks."

Charlotte was already walking away but glanced back at him. "If you need anything, ask Sophia." Then her heels clicked on the marble floor and out of the room, leaving only a whiff of her floral perfume behind her.

Well, it was time to get to work. Luca slid the glass door open and stepped out into the fresh air. He was immediately struck by the magnificent view of the private lake behind the house, and the expanse of freshly groomed lawn and hedges that lay between the house and the water. Even though Luca had recently seen many of his new clients' impressive homes, he was still awed by the grandiosity of this one.

He walked around the back of the house, searching for the AC unit, and found it tucked behind some hedges. The midday sun beat down on him unrelentingly and a bead of sweat dripped down his back between his shoulder blades.

Setting his toolbox down on the grass next to the unit, he knelt to examine the machinery. He grabbed a screwdriver and started to remove the front panel of the unit. After only a brief investigation, he discovered the issue. It wouldn't take long for him to fix, and he was thankful because he was melting out here.

Luca knelt in the grass and swapped out the screwdriver for a wrench to start working on the problem. He used the bottom of his shirt to wipe the sheen of sweat from his forehead, trying to ignore the beads that dripped down his chest and pooled in his navel. He felt as though he was swimming in his clothes and was dying to shed them.

Just as he began to toy with the idea of asking Sophia for a bottle of water, he heard loud moaning coming from somewhere. Wrench still in hand, he stood up and moved away from the house and into the backyard, looking around while trying to follow the sound. When he glanced up and discovered the source, his jaw dropped.

"Holy shit." Luca was almost positive that he was in the throes of heat stroke, or that his eyes were playing tricks on him, because he couldn't believe the view in front of him.

Through the open upstairs window, he saw a naked woman with luscious curves, her long, straight blond hair flowing between her ample breasts.

His cock sprang alive in his jeans. He couldn't take his eyes off her. She was completely naked, sitting on the window seat sideways with one knee up, her hand between her sun-kissed thighs.

Was she doing what he thought she was doing? Was she actually masturbating in front of the window in the middle of the day?

The woman's moans beckoned to him. The urge rose within him to approach and discover more about the source of this erotic soundtrack.

Luca wondered who else could see her but then realized there was a lake behind their house, blocking most — but not all — potential peepers.

Did she even know he was there?

He couldn't look away from the window as the erection grew painfully in his pants. He watched her play with herself, licking her manicured fingers and sliding them over her bare breasts and between her legs.

When her head dropped back and her face came into better view, he recognized her from the photos on the corridor wall as Charlotte's daughter.

She displayed her nakedness, kneeling on the window seat in front of the glass with her legs spread and her hand between them, revealing herself to him. Luca thirsted for the taste of her perfect skin under his tongue. He ached to replace her fingers with his own and feel the wet sex of this blond goddess, to spread her apart and breathe in the scent of her pussy. It was all he could do to prevent himself from scaling the balcony outside her window and consuming every inch of her body.

She pressed her breasts up against the window, her head falling back in pleasure. Was this young exhibitionist putting on a show just for him? Or was he just a lucky voyeur who'd stumbled into a fortuitous scenario?

Time stood still as he focused on her, separated only by glass. She was right there in the house, almost his for the taking. His dick strained against his pants zipper, impatient to be freed.

And then, suddenly, she looked directly at him.

Luca froze, not sure what to do as she caught him watching her. Would she call out for the housekeeper or scream for her mother that she'd let a pervert into their house?

But she looked unsurprised. Instead of shying away from the window, she turned to him, holding his gaze with unexpected intensity.

The wrench Luca held in his hand slipped out of his grasp and onto the grass. He was transfixed by the wanton look in her blue eyes, unable to move.

Still incredulous, Luca's impulses were screaming at him, instructing to embrace this once-in-a-lifetime, golden opportunity. But his rational mind told him to hightail it out of there as soon as possible. What if Charlotte or the housekeeper caught him sneaking upstairs?

He didn't dare approach her or risk doing anything she might not want. Maybe she just wanted to tease him and expose herself. How could he know for sure that she desired him the way he craved her? He didn't want to jeopardize getting a bad professional reputation.

His dick throbbed and made it harder for him to get a coherent thought process going. His conscience was slipping away the more he looked at her.

She slid her fingers from her pussy back up to her lips and sucked on them, staring at him. When she gestured to him with a come-hither motion, inviting him in, the last thread of Luca's restraint snapped.

He knelt in front of the AC unit again, quickly tightening the last bolt and replacing its cover, carelessly throwing his tools into his toolbox. He scribbled his fee on the receipt pad, ripping the sheet out of the book. His mind was focused only on hurrying up to get to the young exhibitionist upstairs. Luca slipped back through the glass doors, sliding them closed behind him.

In the kitchen, Luca left the receipt on the counter, noticing the trace of his dirty fingerprints on the paper. There was no way he was going to touch the her immaculate skin with dirt on his hands. He quickly washed them with soap in the kitchen sink and toweled them off, then quietly hurried to find his exhibitionist.

Even from the base of the staircase, he could hear her moaning, and ached to follow the sound. Luca looked at the white carpeting on the stairs and feared his boots would leave telltale footprints all over it. He hurriedly kicked them off and left them with his toolbox at the landing, almost racing upstairs to meet his goddess face to face.

As the upstairs hall came into view, he saw a dozen closed doors. He had no idea where he was going, but he followed the faint moans and discovered a partly opened door.

Suddenly nervous, he slowly pushed it open and saw her naked form. She was still splayed out on the window seat, except now there was absolutely nothing physically separating them. She was only a few steps away from him.

A burst of adrenaline shot through him and his heart raced, but he urged himself not to rush over to her.

"Close the door," she purred, not giving him a chance to

change his mind. He pushed the door shut and looked at her, ready to ravage her.

"Now come here." She beckoned him forward, her blue eyes never breaking his gaze.

* * *

Brooke focused on the strange man who she'd just invited up to her room. She didn't know him. He could be anyone. And the possibility of danger made her shiver with desire.

Up close, he was even taller, more rugged and muscular than what she'd seen when he'd been working in the backyard. She soaked up the view of his body and his rich brown skin, sleek with sweat and oozing virility. Her pussy twitched under her hand.

He was exactly what she needed to break the monotony of her restless pacing while being stuck at home all day. She was grounded as punishment for throwing a party at her parents' lake house without permission. At nineteen, she'd argued that was too old to be grounded, but then they threatened to take away her car.

Well, now it seemed that their discipline was actually a blessing in disguise. When she'd seen him outside the window earlier, all hot and sweaty, kneeling in the grass, her mind spun with images of him manhandling her with those hands and that *body*. He looked to be about a decade older than her and was likely more experienced than the clumsy college boys she was used to.

At first, she just hadn't been able to resist touching herself because he'd sparked that fire in her. But soon she wanted him to see her and find out if he'd be as intent on giving her the fix she needed as he was on repairing the AC. So, she'd opened the window to make damn sure he heard and saw her.

Brooke badly needed some kind of release, and a taste of rebellion from her uptight parents. This repairman seemed like the perfect cure for her boredom.

"Does your mother know you like to invite strangers into your bedroom?" he asked as he approached her. His voice was deep and throaty, exactly as she'd hoped it would be.

With her back to the window, she stretched open her legs completely and an inviting smile spread across her face.

"She doesn't know that the repairman could be so easily seduced by her only daughter, if that's what you're asking," she said.

"Who says I've been seduced?" he asked, approaching her with predatory slowness. The look in his eyes told her that he was ready to pounce on his prey. He walked past the full-length mirror in the corner and the four-poster bed in the middle of her bedroom, approaching her.

Her pulse raced wildly, a frisson of uncertainty kicking her adrenaline into action. "You came up here, didn't you?"

"I don't even know your name," he said.

"That's not a prerequisite," she countered. "I'm not asking for yours." She spread her pussy lips apart for him, showing him the glistening wetness between them. "Now shut up and take off your pants."

"No," he replied.

"*No?*" she echoed. She wasn't used to men saying no to her.

"You're used to getting what you want, aren't you? You're just a spoiled little rich girl," he said in a teasing tone.

Her blood boiled, mostly from her fierce attraction to him, and partly with her desire to get what she wanted. "So, what if I am?" Brooke retorted, not even bothering to argue with him.

"Well, I'm not going to take orders from you." He looked at her sternly.

Brooke struggled not to smile. She was enjoying the fact that he was resisting her. It was unexpected... and welcome.

"Are you saying you don't want to fuck me?" she inquired, standing up and taking a few steps towards him, her bare feet padding on the lush carpet.

Her heart fluttered as she closed the distance between them, displaying more confidence than she was actually feeling. Her knees faltered slightly with each step, but she didn't stop moving until she stood directly in front of him.

She could smell the sun and fresh outdoors on him, mixed with the sweet yet feral scent of his sweat. She wanted to taste his salty skin, to lick the bead that dripped down the side of his neck.

Brooke reached out and placed her hands on his broad chest, his T-shirt practically soaked through with perspiration. She longed to peel it off of him and expose his muscular form.

Sliding her hands down into the waistband of his pants, she discovered the bulge she'd helped create; it jumped under her palm. Her pussy clenched with need at his reaction to her, filling her with satisfaction that he wanted her the way she craved him.

But he didn't touch her and wasn't answering her. He was stoic, except for his dick moving in his pants. She needed his hands on her, and to hear his sharp tongue and that husky voice of his again.

"So you *don't* want to know how my pussy feels when you're inside me?" she taunted him, slipping her hand between her thighs again, then bringing her fingertips to her lips to taste herself. His lips twitched, as though holding back a smile, but he didn't reply.

She tried to kiss him, but instead gasped in surprise when he spun her around to face the full-length mirror, pinning her arms behind her back with one of his strong hands.

"Oh, I'm going to feel you," he growled, his other hand reaching up to wrap around her neck, showing her who was in charge. She stared at the reflection of his dark eyes in the mirror and shivered in a mix of fear and anticipation. "I'm going to fuck you. And there's nothing you can do about it. Do you understand?"

Brooke's pussy pounded with desire, and she nodded at him in the mirror. She loved his strength and the dominant way he grabbed her. So different than the inexperienced guys she'd been with. He was a real man. So much so that he seemed to intuitively understand exactly what she wanted. Or maybe this was just what he wanted, too...

"We'd better hurry before my mother gets home," she said softly before his hand covered her mouth to stop her from talking.

"Shh," he said, his hand sliding down from her neck to pinch one of her hard nipples before tracing a path down to the crest of her thighs. She gasped when his rough fingertips brushed against her clit and discovered the effect he'd had on her.

"You feel this?" he asked, taking her clit captive between his fingers, his brown eyes darkening. "As long as I'm here, you belong to me. You're under *my* control."

She sighed, elated at the idea of leaving herself vulnerable to him. She couldn't move as he crushed her against his body, her wrists still held tightly behind her back. Her hands were at the perfect level, and she could feel his hard cock through his pants, his heat against her open palm.

Brooke ached to unzip him, but at this angle she didn't have the dexterity. She squeezed him and he twitched under her touch, and he responded by applying more pressure to her swollen clit with his fingers. She groaned and leaned her head back against his strong chest, giving in to the pleasure, able only to watch him in the mirror.

"You wanted to get my attention, didn't you? Well, now you have it. Let's see if you can handle it."

Heat flooded her as his strong hand increased his tempo, and just as she was getting closer to her climax, he removed his fingers from her pussy. He brought his fingers to her lips and she took them into her mouth, sucking on them and tasting her juices. She watched him in the mirror and heard him sigh as her tongue slowly worked his forefingers as though they were an extension of his dick.

He moved his fingers from her mouth, releasing his hand on her wrists. He spun her around to face him with a look of severity and desire.

"Now get on your knees and take off my pants," he instructed in a deep voice.

Brooke's body vibrated, trying to contain her excitement at the prospect of getting to strip him and touch him. She looked up at him and knelt on the carpet in front of him, unbuckling his leather belt with trembling fingers.

At the same time, she watched him pull his soaked shirt up over his head and toss it on the floor, revealing his bare chest and stomach to her. She ached to reach up and touch him but kept herself in the zone and slowly unzipped his jeans, dying to see the bulge contained within.

With the excitement of someone unwrapping a gift, she tugged on his open jeans and brought them over his muscular legs. She looked up at him again and quickly dragged his boxers down over his bulge and down his thighs, his hard dick springing forward right in front of her face.

Hungry to taste him, she leaned forward to cover his dick with her mouth, but he pulled away from her. A twinge of disappointment ran through her. "Not yet, you dirty girl," he said, stepping out of his pants and boxers. He gripped her by the hair, firmly but not painfully, and pulled her to her feet.

He grabbed her round ass and spun her around, propelling her so that she faced one of the four bedposts with her back to him. The way he angled her body deprived her of seeing their reflection in the mirror. With her view only of her bed, she had no idea what he was going to do to her, and she was thrilled by the uncertainty.

"Don't move," he growled, and she didn't dare.

Brooke couldn't see him anymore, but she felt the heat of his hands on her, one at the back of her neck, the other between her thighs.

"Spread your legs," he said, his voice dark and serious. He lightly slapped her inner thighs and she widened her stance for him.

Her pussy throbbed painfully, not knowing what to expect. Whatever it was, she was ready and willing to feel him every which way he would let her.

She wasn't expecting him to get to his knees behind her and start to suck and lick on her pussy. She had never been tongued this way before — but then, she'd never been with someone so experienced, and with such an appetite.

Her head almost melted into the carved wooden bedpost as he devoured her. She didn't care how loudly she was moaning. Even if Sophia heard her, Brooke knew she wouldn't tell her mother.

Brooke's knees weakened as her pleasure built, and her grip on the bedpost tightened. The rhythm of his hot mouth on her clit sent fire shooting through her entire body.

He brought her to the brink of orgasm again, somehow knowing exactly when to stop. She ached for release. Her hips moved slightly just to connect with him again, and he slapped her ass. She gasped, the quick and welcome sting of his slap sending blood rushing to her ass cheek, adding to the intensity of sensations that flooded her.

"I told you not to move," he reminded her, and she struggled to stand up straight. He then slid two fingers into her pussy, rubbing up against her G-spot. She felt a pressure building inside her that she'd never felt before, and as he continued, speeding up his manipulations, she suddenly felt a release of fluids.

"What the hell," she exclaimed in surprise as liquid trickled down her legs, followed by his tongue licking up the mess.

"I made you squirt." She could hear the self-satisfied smile in his voice.

"That's never happened to me before," she said dazedly, touching her inner thighs to feel the wetness there. "I didn't even know I could squirt."

"Now let's see what else I can make you do," he said, giving her pussy a light slap, which she loved. Still behind her, he stood up, pressing Brooke's body between the bedpost and his chest and hard dick.

She jumped when he slid his hand up her back, stopping at the nape of her neck to grab her hair, making it clear he was in charge. A small moan escaped her lips, loving the way his fingertips felt against her scalp.

He brought her head back to his chest, and his dick pushed up against her ass cheeks, resting there. His breath was hot on her ear. "Do you deserve to feel my cock inside of you?"

"Yes," she managed in a low voice, gasping as his fingers suddenly pinched her nipples, sending shocks straight to her clit.

"Yes, *please*. Where are your manners?" He slapped her pussy again, a bit harder than before.

Brooke moaned, wanting more. She was starting to wonder if being a brat was actually more fun than doing whatever he said.

"Maybe I need discipline," she whispered, sighing as his cock twitched and he gave her pussy another slap, a bit harder this time. Her pussy lips tingled with pleasure and a trickle of her juices dripped down her inner thigh.

"You think you're a bad girl, don't you? Do you know what happens to bad girls?"

Another slap to her pussy lips. And another. She moaned with pleasure and her hips moved of their own volition to make contact with his hand. He built up the rhythm and intensity of his slaps, stopping occasionally to caress her pussy and soothe the sting of his rougher attentions. Heat built up rapidly between her thighs. She couldn't believe the way her body was responding to this — or maybe it was just because he was the one delivering it.

Then he slipped his hand between her legs to cup her in his palm, but not stroking her. Her pussy trembled against his hand, pleading for release.

His other hand moved from the back of her neck to her throat, squeezing her gently, just hard enough to make her feel helpless while still being able to breathe.

"If you want my cock, you're going to have to prove it to me." He removed his hands from her body, and the absence of his heat made her want him more. "Now come here and get on your knees."

She turned and saw him standing in front of the mirror, his hard dick waiting for her. She licked her lips unconsciously, craving the taste and feel of him on her tongue.

Brooke found herself getting to her hands and knees on the carpet, maintaining eye contact with him, and crawled over to him. She stopped when his cock was almost level with her face, and she rose up on her knees for a bit of extra height.

"Now be a good girl and convince me that you deserve my dick." Brooke's mind and body were ablaze with stimulation. Damn, she was really enjoying him speaking to her this way.

She smiled up at him, wrapping her hands around the base of his shaft, squeezing him. She felt his rapid pulse pounding between her fingers. Her lips closed over the head and slipped over a few inches of his dick before salivating all over the rest of him. He groaned as she found her rhythm quickly, slurping wetly at his dick while stroking him simultaneously. He was too big to fit into her mouth, but she made up for that with her enthusiastic hands.

She lost track of time as she worshiped his cock, watching her head bobbing up and down in the mirror. She licked and sucked his full balls, which were contracting under her tongue as though he was close to orgasm.

He groaned and pulled his dick out of her mouth, his eyes clouded with lust. "Get up."

He reached out a hand to help her and she rose unsteadily to her feet. He stabilized her with a strong arm, holding her close to his chest and looking down at her as though he was pleased with her. He was so solid, and she felt safe with him — even though she didn't know him at all.

For the first time, he leaned down and covered her mouth with his lips, kissing her deeply. She moaned against his lips, his tongue sliding in sync against hers. She wrapped her arms around his broad shoulders.

He came up for air, a small smirk on his lips. "You've proven yourself. Are you ready for me?"

"Yes, *please*," she said loudly, ready to beg him for his cock.

"Get up on the bed with your ass in the air. Face the mirror. I want to see what you look like when I fuck you."

She almost ran to obey him, sliding on top of her red bedspread, waiting to feel his presence behind her again. Anticipation built painfully in her pussy. She arched her back to present her ass to him.

In their reflection in the mirror, she saw him rise up on the bed, positioning himself on his knees behind her. Brooke sighed as he caressed her curves with rough hands. He reached one hand between her thighs, collecting her slick mess and rubbing it around her asshole, teasing her.

Brooke gasped as he poised her dick against her pussy and entered her, stretching her out to fit himself into her. She grabbed the comforter with her fists as he took his time, clearly accustomed to making women adapt to his imposing size. Her pussy clenched around him as he moved back and forth, nestling inside her.

She pressed her face to the cool comforter, muffling her moans into the fabric. Her slick juices coated his dick during his long, deep thrusts. His fingers traced the opening of her ass again, sliding his thumb into her slowly, using his spit to ease into her tight hole. She cried out with pleasure, feeling filled up and extremely tight with so much inside of her.

Her hips moved backward to meet his thrusts as they grew rougher, harder, faster, his thumb moving within her ass at the same tempo. With his free hand, he reached in front of Brooke and caressed her swollen clit as he fucked her, hitting all her hot spots at the same time.

Her pleasure heightened and a haze of bliss descended upon her. She began to quake around him, crying out a chain of obscene words. Her muscles spasmed, squeezing tightly around his dick and thumb inside of her. She went limp against the covers, the intensity and fullness of her orgasm exhausting her.

He pulled out of her and leaned down to kiss the back of her neck, stroking her head with a tenderness that surprised her. "Is that all you can take?" he teased. "Because we're not done yet."

Brooke whimpered into the covers, unable to speak. She was ready for more, impatient for him to touch and pleasure her, but she couldn't form the words to express herself.

He flipped her over onto her back, his strong arms supporting him as he hovered over her, spreading her legs with his dick between them.

She watched the fire burn in his eyes as he pushed himself inside her pussy again. His thrusts were slow and shallow, building her pleasure back up. As he slid his dick into her, he began lightly tapping her incredibly swollen clit with his fingers.

Pleasure shot through her, revving her up anew and shaking

her out of her post-orgasmic haze. His hands trailed up her body to cup her breasts, squeezing them and rubbing her nipples between his fingertips as he plowed into her more deeply.

She missed his finger in her ass and decided to resort to something more fulfilling. But she'd need to take control.

She looked him in the eye, slid her hand against his chest and pushed lightly. He stopped moving, still inside her. "Please let me ride you," she asked in a low voice, knowing she could get what she wanted if she was nice about it.

A grin curled the corners of his mouth and he pulled out of her.

She righted herself and crawled over the covers to her nightstand, grabbing a bottle of lube from the drawer. He watched her silently and lay back against the cushions, waiting for her.

Brooke moved to straddle his hips, but didn't take his dick inside her yet. She squeezed the lube onto her hand to warm it up first, then slicked her palm over his shaft, relishing the wet sound.

She reached behind her to slip his dick between her thighs, positioning the head of his slick cock at the opening of her ass, and started to sit down on him.

His eyes sparkled with mischief with the realization of what she was doing. "Mmm... so you think you can take all of me into your tight little ass? Be a good girl and try to fit me inside of you."

"Oh fuck," she cried out as her ass stretched out to accommodate the girth of his cockhead. She added even more lube on his dick. He groaned as he reentered her tightness, his eyes closing for a moment.

The slight pain she felt at first turned into pleasure as she eased him into herself slowly. She stretched herself out on his dick and took him in deeper and deeper until he was buried to the hilt inside her. This definitely wasn't the first dick she'd let into her ass, but it was by far the thickest she'd ever tried to handle. Luckily, she'd had a lot of practice.

Brooke supported herself with her hands on his strong chest as she worked her hips up and down, getting used to him in her tight ass. He reached behind her and spread her cheeks apart with his big hands. She moaned when she found the perfect angle for herself so that his dick rubbed her in the way she preferred.

Her pussy drooled all over his lower belly as she fucked herself on him, watching his eyes glaze over with ecstasy. Pleasure rose within her again, and she rolled her hips on his, fast and needy, moaning loudly.

Through her cries, Brooke thought she heard the bedroom door creak open, but when she looked over her shoulder, there was no one there.

She turned back to the sexy man underneath her and smiled, rolling her hips in circles with his dick still in her ass. "You see? I do deserve your cock."

He smiled, then pulled himself up to face her, kissing her deeply. "Then be a good slut and don't fucking stop."

*   *   *

From the hallway, Sophia peered into Brooke's room, staying out of sight in the doorway. She'd been watching for a while, soaking up the sight of her boss's daughter and the very enticing repairman consumed in passion for each other.

From this angle, Brooke's back was to her, and she doubted either of them could see her. She watched as Brooke's perfect body bounced on top of Luca's. He grabbed her ass with his big hands and fucked her from below. It took Sophia a second to realize Luca was in Brooke's ass. Holy hell.

Sophia had heard their moans all the way downstairs. And she'd noticed the repairman had gone missing, but his truck remained in the driveway. So, she'd just opened the door a bit to check that everything was good with Brooke. But she hadn't expected this.

Leaning quietly against the doorway, Sophia slipped her hand up her skirt and into her panties. She was already wet and had been since Luca had first stepped over the threshold and into the house. It wasn't every day that a man as sexy as him was allowed to enter this house unsupervised, although Brooke had snuck in her fair share of boys over the years.

Now, Sophia rubbed her throbbing clit as she watched them, imagining that she was the one on top of Luca instead. She was especially aroused at the fact that she was witnessing this stolen moment between Brooke and Luca, and they were completely unaware of her presence.

From the doorway, Sophia bit her lip to keep from moaning, watching as their perfectly shaped bodies glistened with sweat. Luca pumped upwards into Brooke, using his strong hands to elevate her hips. Brooke and Luca sped up their pace, their moans coming louder. Luca slapped Brooke's ample ass and the girl just moved faster on him. She groaned deeply and her head dropped back.

Sophia's pleasure mounted quickly, as though catching up with the naked duo on the bed in front of her. Her breathing came in shallow bursts as she moved her fingers faster on her clit.

Luca grabbed Brooke's ass and used his strength to put her flat on her back, all without pulling his dick out of her.

Sophia's heart skipped a beat as she thought Luca saw her lurking in the doorway, but he was too focused on Brooke to notice.

He threw Brooke's legs over his shoulders and seemed to bend the girl in two, lifting her hips up to meet his thrusts as he continued fucking her ass. Brooke grabbed his broad shoulders for balance, moaning loudly as Luca positively destroyed her.

Sophia's knees went weaker as her fingers sped up their pace on her pussy. She leaned more weight against the doorway to keep herself upright.

Brooke moaned loudly with pleasure, and Sophia watched a rush of fluids gushing from Brooke as she squirted all over Luca's chest and belly.

Luca groaned deeply and came too, fucking Brooke until he had fully released himself inside of her ass.

Prompted by their orgasms, ecstasy surged through Sophia too, and she trembled with her own climax. Her eyes rolled back and she grit her teeth together to keep from crying out.

When she caught her breath, Sophia fixed her dress and stood up straight, exhaling slowly, and realized she wasn't going to get caught in her voyeurism.

With one last look at Luca's muscular body, Sophia ducked back out into the hallway, quietly shutting the door to Brooke's bedroom behind her.

*　*　*

Covered in her juices, Luca looked down at the goddess lying below him. She was absolutely spent, and he was, too. He had cum inside her ass, and he knew if he pulled out of her, his juices would slide out of her and all over her comforter. Not that it wasn't already soaked with sweat and juices and lube.

"We need to rinse off," Luca remarked, although his energy was sapped.

"I don't think I can move," Brooke said with an exhausted smile. "And my shower's right over there." She pointed behind her.

"Ok, just grab onto my shoulders. I'll do the rest."

She wrapped her arms around his neck, her legs around his waist. Luca used whatever strength he had left to lift her up. His dick was still hard inside her, and he was careful not to slip out of her just yet. He maneuvered them off the bed and carried Brooke to her own private bathroom.

The sliding glass shower doors were already open, and he stepped into it, turning on the water. It was cold at first but warmed quickly. He helped Brooke move off of his dick and to her feet, watching his cum drip out of her and mingle with the water on the floor of the shower.

She grabbed the soap and washed herself off, mesmerizing him as she sudsed up her luscious body. Though he was drained, his dick didn't seem to agree. He was already coming back to life again, and Brooke noticed.

"You ready for more?" she asked with a laugh and started lathering up his body. She lingered on his dick, washing him off slowly. The slipperiness of the soap reminded him of the way she'd lubed him up before sliding his dick into her ass. His cock jumped in her hands and he groaned. Fuck, what was she doing to him? He felt like a teenager all over again.

Luca opened his mouth to respond to her, but a loud noise startled them both, his stomach knotting with panic.

"Brooke? Where the hell are you? Come down here this instant!" Charlotte's voice came over the loudspeaker.

"Fuck!" he exclaimed and jumped out of the shower. "What am I going to do? She can't see us like this!"

"Go out the window!" Brooke said hurriedly, grabbing a towel and pushing him out of the bathroom.

Naked, with water still dripping off him, Luca hurtled himself through the open window, crouching on the balcony on the other side so that Charlotte wouldn't be able to see him. Brooke threw his clothes out the window, nearly smacking him in the head with the cell phone that had fallen out of his pants pocket.

Luca's heart was pounding so violently he thought he would pass out. He struggled to pull his clothes onto his still-wet skin.

That was when he realized he was barefoot. His work boots and toolbox were still in the house. Fuck! He couldn't retrieve them looking like this and trying to be casual. How could he ever explain his disheveled appearance to Charlotte if she saw him?

Luca started to lower himself off the balcony, jumping the last few feet onto the grass only to fall backward into the hedges. He groaned in pain and tried to sit up, quickly taking stock of his injuries and realizing that nothing was broken, merely bruised.

He looked up to see the gardener, laughing and saluting him by taking off his cap. The smug bastard.

Luca recalled that his car keys were in his toolbox, too. He chastised himself for his lack of foresight and decided to go back into the house through the kitchen. He had no other choice.

Standing at the kitchen's sliding doors was Sophia, his work boots in one hand and his toolbox in the other. Like a fairy godmother sent to help him get himself out of this mess. An amused one, at that — she was smiling wickedly as he ran to her.

"Thank you," Luca whispered, assuming she must have seen him dangling from the balcony and deduced what he was doing there.

"I left you my phone number in your toolbox," she replied with a gleam in her eye. "In case you need anything at all. And I mean *anything*."

Luca was flattered by her interest — after all, she was a very attractive older woman and she was wearing a maid's uniform, to top that off — but he didn't have time to stay and flirt with her. "Oh... um... thanks. I might just do that."

Sophia handed him his belongings, brushing her hands against his as she did so.

"Bye!" Luca called out as he scurried away and around the side of the house with the cool bare grass under his feet.

When he was safely in his truck, he shut the door quickly and upended his toolbox on the passenger seat to get his keys. Revving the engine, he put his truck into drive, stepped his bare foot on the gas pedal and peeled out of there.

As Luca wound his way down the driveway and onto the suburban streets, he started laughing deliriously as his heart rate began to normalize. Wow, he'd been so close to getting busted by Charlotte, but had managed to elude her. He counted himself lucky that at least for now, his reputation would remain untarnished.

After his narrow escape, a thrill ran through him as he thought of the incredible blonde goddess whom he'd just fucked into submission. Brooke, as Charlotte had called her. She'd let him into all of her holes without knowing his name, and without telling him hers. Just pure, perfect animal sex.

And now, the housekeeper Sophia was also interested in him? Luca laughed again. He'd really hit the jackpot at that house. Maybe Sophia could connect him with Brooke, since he didn't have any way to reach her directly.

If that meant fucking Sophia for the information, well, that was definitely a job he knew he could handle.

MORGAN'S FIRST TASTE

I push around the crowds of shoppers in the grocery store, scrambling to get game-day snacks just like everyone else. I manage to squirm through the aisles of people decked out in head-to-toe New York Giants gear while gathering my groceries.

"Watch out, lady!" A man almost smashes into me with a stack of frozen pizzas in his arms. I step out of his way, sighing. It's playoff crunch time in the NFL, and I really regret not having picked up provisions yesterday to avoid this mayhem.

Watching football is a big part of my life, and I'm happy to share my love for the game with my roommate, Denise. We've had the same ritual every Sunday since we moved in together a year ago. One of us picks up beer and snacks at the store, while the other preps the apartment for whichever guests we invited to watch the games with us. I'm not sure who Denise called over today, but it doesn't matter, because even if no one shows up, at least I'll still get to spend time with her.

Denise is the only woman I've ever had a crush on, and she's made me rethink my sexuality. I've wanted to kiss her and touch her since the first day I met her. Although I've always identified as straight, over the last few months, I've become certain I'm bisexual. I've never been with another woman before, and I'm not sure if Denise is even attracted to me in that way — and I don't want to ask her in case she finds it too uncomfortable to continue living with me after. So, I haven't made any moves on her whatsoever — and honestly, I'm not even sure how I would go about doing that if I ever had the courage to tell her how I felt.

Back inside our apartment building, I balance the groceries in one hand and the beer on my shoulder as I push the button for the elevator. My belly flip-flops in anticipation of seeing Denise.

I can barely focus, and it takes three attempts before I can get my key in the lock on our door, stubbornly refusing to put anything down to free my hands. I press down on the doorknob and almost stumble over a pair of Denise's high-heeled shoes in the entrance. Hmm. It's unusual for my spic-and-span roommate to leave something out of place.

Clumsily kicking off my Chuck Taylors, I prepare to make my way down the long hallway to the kitchen so I can unload the groceries. But I stop in my tracks to figure out what that noise is and where it's coming from.

The living room is on my way to the kitchen, and it looks like Denise had been watching the football pre-game show on low volume. I press the mute button, but then there's that sound again. The TV can't be the source.

"Denise? I got our favorites! I even picked up extra Cheetos," I singsong, trying to draw her out from wherever she is.

The mysterious sound grows louder as I step closer to the kitchen. Was that a whimper? Where is it coming from? There it is again! It becomes clear — it's a moan, and it's coming from the kitchen.

Dying of curiosity, I quietly advance to the kitchen to peek around the wall... and lose my composure, going slack-jawed.

Denise sits with her back to me on top of our kitchen table, her radiant brown skin fully bare, her voluminous black hair more touchable than ever. Her knees are bent, with her feet propped up at the table's edge. That's all I see... until I realize that the shaved, dark brown head between her legs belongs to Carter, one of Denise's current lovers. He's kneeling on the floor in front of her with his mouth on her pussy, his erection sprung to life — and *what* a life.

Mesmerized by the scene, I can't bring myself to leave them to their own devices. My feet are rooted to the spot. I've barely watched porn before, and I've definitely never seen real people have sex right in front of me... let alone be this close to Denise's exquisite naked body.

The music of Denise's moans fills the kitchen. Jealousy twinges in my belly for a moment, wanting to be the one to make her experience so much ecstasy. But as I watch her companion's sizable dick stiffen more and more as he pleasures her with his mouth, the jealousy subsides as an overwhelming desire washes over me. I want to join both of them. I'm dying to play with Denise and Carter at the same time — a scenario I've never dared to entertain — until now.

My pussy aches at the sight of Denise throwing her head back in bliss. From this angle, I can see her face, eyes closed, pink lips parted, and the tops of her rich, dark brown breasts. I'm dying to touch her.

Denise bites her lip, her body tensing, and she opens her eyes and looks right at me. My stomach knots up, the tension between my legs heightening. I can't move, fully captivated by her inviting, sensuous gaze.

A small smile curves the corners of her lips, amusement dancing in her eyes. She's unsurprised to see me, almost as though she's been expecting me. Almost as though she'd planned this.

Carter looks up at Denise, noticing me over her shoulder, and pauses. He stands up slowly, watching me. He doesn't look surprised to see me, either. My body flushes with heat as a sly grin creeps over his face. Denise nods her head at him, like a secret code. What are they communicating to each other?

There's a brief silence, and I have no idea what to do. I can't even speak. All I can do is shakily put down the groceries I've somehow been holding this whole time.

"Come here, Morgan," Denise says, her voice husky with lust. I step towards them, almost shyly, immediately and unexpectedly feeling the warmth in the air.

Denise reaches out and takes my pale, trembling hand, pulling me closer to her on the table. Her hand is so warm, her touch inviting and friendly, with a sexy urgency.

I stare longingly at her beautiful body, her silky skin and irresistible hourglass shape. Her brown nether lips glisten between her toned thighs, her inner lips a dark pink. I've been fantasizing about this moment since I met her, but I never thought this could happen.

My roommate smiles, pulling her body closer to the edge of the table, her face approaching mine. She cradles the back of my head in her hand, covering my mouth with hers.

The smoothness of her lips startles me, and the softness of her mouth melts me. She tastes sweet and faintly of the bubblegum she loves to chew. Her tongue slips between my lips, rubbing gently against mine, teasing me. My hands find the back of her head and I hold her closer to me, my fingers entwined in her incredible hair.

Denise sighs against my moth as I kiss her back with the same pressure. This is so different than kissing a man. No one has ever touched me with such soft hands, with such a sensual touch. I revel in her stroking the sides of my face, down my arms, the sensitive sides of my breasts. My body hums as new sensations shoot through me, focusing on this moment, and on Denise.

From the corner of my eye, Carter watches us hungrily, staying a step back to allow us to connect with each other. His cock is still hard, and I watch him slowly stroke himself, patiently waiting for us.

She comes up for breath, pulling away from my mouth slightly. Looking me in the eyes with confidence, she folds my hands in hers and presses my palms to her bare breasts. Her firm nipples poke against my skin, inviting me to play with them.

"Do you want me?" she asks. Her breasts are so warm in my hands, her nipples so hard as I gently roll them between my fingers. I smooth my hands over the hot flesh of her soft belly and her luscious thighs. I can't believe how gorgeous she is. She's a goddess.

"I want you more than anything," I tell her honestly. Denise smiles and captures my lips with hers again, her hands traveling over my small breasts to feel my own hardened nipples. I moan against her mouth, my pussy twitching in anticipation of her touch.

She pulls away from my lips for a moment to ask, "Do you want him, too?" Her head nods in Carter's direction. We both look at him, and his cock stiffens even more at the sight of two women caressing each other.

I smile, my eyes roving over his athletic body. My fingers itch to feel Carter's smooth, velvety soft skin and every inch of his raging hard-on. I extend my fingers in a come-hither motion, gesturing for him to join us. Carter smiles mischievously as he comes up behind me.

His erection presses against my lower back, as Denise's soft body pushes into my front. I'm enveloped in the heat of their irresistibly sexy bodies, and I don't know who to touch first. I want it all, and all at the same time.

I sigh as Denise kisses me deeply, sliding her hands over my waist, edging her fingers under the hem of my shirt. Carter's strong hands explore the slope of my ass and back up to my neck, pushing aside the hair from my nape. Their touches feel so different on my body; my skin sizzles under Denise's soft caress and Carter's rougher grip on me. Both sensations course through me, the novelty of it all making my nerve endings fire crazily. I shudder and sigh with delight as Carter trails his full lips over my neck and collarbone on one side, while Denise's mouth takes the other side.

I've never been in a threesome before. I'm completely inexperienced, but my more practiced partners don't seem preoccupied by this fact in the least. So, I let myself go, delivering myself into their sensual hands.

Denise lifts the hem of my shirt, bringing it up slowly over my head and baring my small bra-less breasts. I lock eyes with her as her soft fingertips trace my hardened, pink nipples. She holds my gaze while lowering her mouth to my breasts, and I sigh softly at how incredible it feels. My hands caress her face, shoulders and back while she licks and sucks my nipples with a hypnotic rhythm.

Desire pools between my legs as I become enthralled by her. Each new thing she does to me is exciting. All of these are firsts for me. That I'm experiencing each of them with Denise is even more meaningful to me.

Carter unbuttons my jeans, unzipping them slowly. I shimmy my hips as his large hands bring my pants down over my legs, along with my white cotton panties. I step out of my clothes, and he kicks them aside on the floor. Leaving me standing bare and exposed... and slightly self-conscious.

The hot imprint of Carter's bare cock burns against the curve of my ass as he presses me against him, kissing and lightly biting the back of my neck. His hands touch both of us, but he seems to understand my need to connect with Denise before he gets more involved.

Her warm, playful eyes meet mine as her hands slowly slide up the insides of my thighs, slipping her fingers lightly between my legs. I shiver, my breath catching in my throat as her knowing fingertips glide against my swollen clit, testing me, teasing me.

Carter's strong hands grasp my waist and keep my knees from buckling, holding me in place so that Denise can explore my body. Pleasure twists in my solar plexus as her hot breath covers my nipples, and she slowly caresses my clit. Soft moans escape my lips as she works me up from the front, and my gaze drops down to Denise's pussy again.

Her legs are spread in front of me, her juices visible, her little lips entrancing me. I'm hungry to savor her pussy, eager and curious as to how she tastes and feels under my tongue. I'm too overwhelmed by her beauty and shy to touch her for some reason. I don't know yet how she likes to be touched, and I just want to give her the same pleasure she's giving me.

As though reading my mind, Denise's free hand grabs mine, placing my open palm on her thigh. She covers my hand with hers, staring me in the eyes as she slides my hand up from her knee, slowly, until I can feel the heat of her core over my skin.

I turn my fingertips towards her body, elated to finally touch her silky opening. Her slick wetness invites me in, and feels surprisingly natural to me. Denise purrs low in her throat in response to my movements, and I feel empowered to continue. My fingers follow her lead as she continues to play with my soaked clit and pussy, touching her the way she's touching me.

Carter reaches in front of me and covers Denise's hand with his so that they're both playing with me at the same time. His other hand reaches for my fingers so that we can both stroke Denise's pussy together. Denise and I groan with pleasure, and Carter's cock moves against the soft skin of my ass. I arch my back and turn my head slightly to look back at Carter. He takes my lips captive under his and starts to kiss me with the same rhythm that he and Denise are working me.

I look back at Denise, my desire building. "I want to taste you," she says in a lusty voice. She pulls away from me to do a smooth 180 on the table, lying on her back with her head hanging off the edge. Her face right is in front of my pussy. Carter pushes me closer to Denise's mouth, then spreads my legs further apart, getting on his knees behind me on the floor.

I groan loudly as Denise's mouth works my clit while Carter alternates between teasing me with his tongue and his fingers. I've never felt so many different sensations at once, from so many people at once. I sink into the exquisite feeling, turning my attention to Denise's pleasure.

I continue to play with her pussy, gliding over her wet lips, my free hand caressing her torso. My body trembles as I savor the way her curves feel under my fingertips. I lean forward in a sixty-nine position, my mouth perfectly aligned with her clit so that I can tongue her at the same time. And *fuck* , she tastes and smells so good. Her scent awakens a side of me I never knew existed.

All our mouths are busy feasting on each other, and my body becomes extra responsive as both of my lovers pay attention to my pleasure. I groan into Denise's pussy and she moans into mine.

They both speed up the tempo on me, working me faster and faster, until I can't take it. I cry out as I cum, my pussy clenching around Carter's fingers as Denise savors the liquid sex that slowly flows out of me.

I breathe deeply and try to recover from the spasms. I look down and see Denise and Carter sharing my taste between my legs, with Denise in her Spiderman-style move, hanging upside down from the side of the table. Thirsty for Denise's lips, I get down to my knees on the kitchen floor and share a delectable three-way kiss with them, my sex still hot on their tongues. I can smell my pussy on their breaths, invigorating me even more. As does the sight of Carter's obvious desire for us, which is also poking into my leg. Denise and I exchange knowing glances and I can tell she wants to devour him as much as I do.

We pull away from each other, Denise sliding her supple body off the table. She joins me on the floor on my knees, right in front of Carter's massive erection. I slide one hand up his thigh, encircling his girth with my hand and squeezing him, feeling his cock jump in my palm. Denise's hand grasps him with authority, rubbing up and down, squirting out a few drops of his precum. I'm drawn to taste him, and I cover the head of his dick with my mouth. He groans as I start to work him with my lips with Denise stroking and licking his balls.

I take his cock into my mouth, loving the way he throbs between my lips. Though I'm not used to pleasuring women, I'm more than experienced with men. I deep-throat every inch of Carter's dick, holding onto his ass as I engulf him with my mouth. My pussy squeezes as his dick slides in and out, wanting him to do the same with my other set of lips.

Luxuriating in his deep groans of pleasure, I want to make Denise feel just as blissful. My fingers rub her clit, and she parts her legs more to give me free rein of her body. I come up for air, and Denise rises to her knees to cover Carter's exposed head with her lips. Licking my way down his shaft to his balls, I take them into my mouth as Denise sucks on his cock.

Carter's thighs tense and he buries his hands in my and Denise's hair, holding our mouths closer to his body. Her pussy is quivering under my touch, and she moans on Carter's dick. He strokes the back of our heads as we take our time to devour him, until we feel him throbbing to the point that he's about to cum.

But it's not time for his release yet. Denise and I won't allow it. I crave his dick inside of me, and I know Denise must feel the same.

We pull away from Carter, and he takes our hands to help us up off the floor. Once we're on our feet, he sweeps us into his strong arms, gathering us close to his chest. Their bare skin smolders against mine, wrapping me in their desire. Carter lowers his head to our level and kisses me deeply. Denise joins in, and all three of our tongues are playing with each other again in a breathless kiss.

Denise pushes back and guides me to the table. "Lie down," she says, patting the tablecloth. I hoist my body up and lie on my back, welcoming the feel of Denise joining me on top. She straddles one of my thighs, lowering herself so that her wet sex burns and oozes deliciously over my skin.

Over her shoulder, Carter is stroking his cock and stepping closer to Denise's ass, which is upraised in midair — undoubtedly a stunning sight. Her tongue circles my nipples again, making me squirm with pleasure. I brush the hair back from her face so I can see her better, and she looks up at me and smiles. Her fingers gently slide into my pussy, caressing my clit with the pad of her thumb at the same time. The heat running through my body is all-consuming.

Carter runs his hands over her ass. "Come down a bit lower so I can fuck you," he tells Denise. Without removing her fingers from my pussy, Denise moves off of me, leaving only the trace of her wetness on my leg like her erotic signature.

Her feet now on the ground, she bends over at the waist with her head between my open thighs, her ass exposed for Carter to savor as he pleases. I sit up and shimmy to the edge of the table, closer to her face. She looks up at me, her thick black lashes framing the playful look in her eyes as she lowers her head down between my legs. My eyes flutter shut while her tongue slowly slides against my throbbing clit.

Carter and I have the best view. I can watch Denise move her tongue inside me, while Carter can see his dick disappearing into Denise's pussy. She moans between my thighs as he grips her hips tightly and fucks her from behind with his thick cock. I catch Carter's eye, sharing a long, lusty look, and I know I'm going to want to feel his cock inside me again before we finish. As he fucks her, his movements drive Denise closer to my pussy, so it's almost as though he's the one licking me.

The connection between us is electric, especially the one I'm sharing with Denise. I sink into bliss as she slips two fingers inside of me again and again, her lips taking my clit captive. I'm overloaded with pleasure, climax close to overtaking me.

I alternately run my fingers through her hair and pinch my own nipples, the sensation traveling from my breasts down to my pussy. Carter moves faster, plunging the length of himself deeper into Denise, his hips slamming against her ass. The vibrations on my wet slit from Denise's continuous moans rapidly mount my pleasure.

My breathing quickens, my heart thumping against my rib cage. Denise's speed increases, in sync with Carter's. His lips curl into a smile as he thrusts harder into her, making that nice, wet slapping sound I love.

Our mutual pleasure overcomes me. Fire spreads through my loins, and I don't suppress my loud moans. Denise cries out, too, then groans into my pussy as she loses control and explodes, seconds before I also dissolve into spasms. Did we just have an elusive, simultaneous orgasm?

Carter's pace slows. He gives Denise's ass a gentle slap, and she moans while he pulls his dick out of her, covered in her juices. I look at him and lick my lips, and he takes a few steps closer to me. Denise watches us as my mouth slides over the head of his engorged dick, my tongue teasing around him, tasting every sweet drop of her that I can.

Denise walks up beside Carter, her hand slipping over his balls, tugging and squeezing them. She kisses him and sucks on his lower lip as I move my mouth back and forth over his dick. Growling now, Carter's fingers delve into my hair, pulling it as my intensity increases. My need arises anew, aching to have Carter inside of me and thirsting for Denise's cream on my tongue.

Still sitting on the edge of the table, I grab Carter by his dick, pulling him closer to me as he spreads my thighs further apart.

"Sit on my face," I tell Denise, brazen now that I can see how much she's enjoying having me pleasure her. She approaches me, tracing my lips with her tongue, fondling my breasts lovingly as she gets up on the tabletop. Carter guides his dick into my tight pussy, the thickness of his head stretching me out. He feeds his length between my slick lips, filling me up with as much of his dick as I can take, and slowly starts to work himself deeper into me.

Denise silences my moans, kissing me while slowly easing herself onto the table, until her delicious snatch is hovering right over my mouth. Grabbing her firm ass, I spread apart her luscious cheeks to grant myself full access. Her scent is beautiful, clouding my thoughts and amplifying my excitement. I dip my tongue into her again, dragging it over her small lips, into her little pink hole, then sucking gently on her swollen clit. She gasps, leaning over me to rub my pussy while Carter rocks his hips and thoroughly pumps into me. All the friction on my hottest spots is driving me insane.

I push two fingers inside of Denise, thrusting lightly and using the softer underside of my tongue to stroke her clit. Her muscles relax as her hips start to rock against my mouth, and I know I've found the right moves. A thrill of triumph rises in my chest, knowing that I'm giving her pleasure. She keeps caressing my clit as Carter's cock rubs against my G-spot from my depths. I groan into Denise's dripping opening, making her moan, too.

The pressure between my thighs is building tremendously while I'm immersed in evoking the same intoxication from Denise as she elicited from me. Carter fucks me harder, splitting me apart with his size. I swirl my tongue around and over Denise's clit, my fingers working their magic inside of her. Thirsty for her, I slip my fingers out a few times to thrust my tongue inside of her and get the best, hottest taste.

Denise's body tenses up and I go just a bit faster, eager for my first chance to feel a woman quivering on my lips. Sensing her impending climax, Carter picks up his pace inside me, while Denise's nimble fingers manipulate my clit in rhythm with his thrusts. My body temperature flares up and my walls tighten around him, clenching, begging for release.

And then something magical happens — something else I've never experienced before. As the first droplets of her fluids stream all over my face and chest, I realize Denise is squirting, and it turns me on even more. Her squirt drips into my mouth as another orgasm shakes her body. I grip onto her ass with one hand to try to steady her. I tease out her shudders, relishing the blend of her juices on my tongue and her loud cries of bliss.

My face still covered in her squirt, I draw out all her pleasure and feel myself start to quake, tensing completely around Carter as he drives into me, deeper, harder, faster, his pulse throbbing inside me. As he pulls out of me, Denise moves off my face and we both start jerking Carter's dick, using my liquid sex as lubricant.

He groans profoundly as he explodes, copious amounts of cum splashing onto Denise's breasts and my belly at the same time. I'm soaked with everyone's juices, including my own, and I have never felt dirtier and more fulfilled in my life.

Denise looks down at me and bends over to lick her squirt and Carter's cum off my body. "Mmm, we taste so good together," she says, then leans down to kiss me so that I taste all three of us on her tongue.

Carter joins in our kiss, until I have to pull away because I'm laughing in disbelief, feeling completely high with the hedonistic haze settling over me.

"Our living situation just got a lot more interesting," I tell Denise as she holds me close to her, not caring that I'm still covered in all this stickiness.

"Maybe I should move in, too," Carter jokes as he tries to locate his clothes in the kitchen.

Denise turns to me, smiling, and kisses my mouth. "So, are you ready?" she asks, a mischievous gleam in her eyes.

"For another round? Yes, of course I'm ready," I reply, running my hands over her smooth skin, smiling at her seductively.

She laughs. "I meant — are you ready for a shower? We're both so filthy..." she pauses, glancing down at my naked body with a lusty look. "How about we clean ourselves up and get ready for some football?" I smile and nod enthusiastically.

Denise slides off the table, reaching out a hand to help me off. She pulls me close to her, pressing her soft lips against mine. "And as for that next round, you insatiable woman... there will be many, *many* more of those."

OBSCURE

Brandon and Gina spared no expense on their engagement party, and it's obvious. The fancy reception hall is decked out in dangling crystal chandeliers, pristine white tablecloths, expensive floral arrangements on every table, and a live band who is actually a famous rock group.

Since the event is in my small hometown, I'm surprised to see the droves of out-of-towners in attendance. A wave of nostalgia crashes over me like a sucker-punch to the gut when I see Damien again for the first time in years.

My mind spins, heart pounding at the onslaught of emotion when I meet his piercing blue eyes across the room. I can't help but stare at his kissable mouth, his soft, sandy brown hair, his confident posture. I remember what it was like to be close to him, to run my fingertips over his light skin, to have him look deeply into my green eyes, to touch him, to feel him inside me...

Damien. I can't believe he's here. It's been an eternity since we were in the same place at the same time. I hadn't braced myself for the possibility of seeing him again... ever.

Because the last time I saw him, the emotion was just as intense, and I made a decision that would change my life — and Damien's — forever.

* * *

Ten years ago

I lay naked next to Damien in bed, limbs intertwined, sharing a cigarette in post-coital bliss. Music streamed in through the walls of his university dorm. A party was going on outside his door.

The two of us were making up for lost time. The last few weeks had been exhausting, cramming for finals while trying to figure out what the hell I was going to do after next semester. Deadlines were fast approaching for applications to graduate school, but I wasn't even sure if I really wanted to attend.

Damien was going through similar challenges. After next semester, he was moving back home to Arizona, all the way on the other side of the country. I was nauseated thinking that he would be leaving soon and what that might mean for our relationship.

Not that we were official, but we spent a lot of time together, talking, drinking, going to parties, and of course, fucking. But we were also fucking other people. We were in our early twenties, horny and ready to explore. And I didn't like the idea of being tied down. When I first met Damien in my freshman year, he said he felt the same, and we never slapped a label on our connection.

131

Even if it was clear to both of us that what we had went beyond sex, neither of us ever used the forbidden L-word. I didn't want to be the one to say it first and scare him out of my life. Part of me was afraid to discover that maybe he didn't feel the same way. And I suspected he refrained from telling me that for the same reasons. I felt it, though. Try as I might to justify my feelings as being infatuation or a passing fling that I'd get over eventually, I was completely in love with him.

But I was in love with someone else, too: Nick. And though we were both fucking other people, at least Nick and I had talked about how we felt, and we'd said "I love you" on multiple occasions.

In the past, I'd always been a relationship monkey, jumping from one guy to the next. And now, I was done with that. I was mulling over the fact that I didn't want to have just one boyfriend. I wanted to be free to date anyone else I wanted.

But my desire to pursue an alternative lifestyle seemed to be way too avant-garde for the traditional guys in my life. They all asked me for monogamy and commitment. A choice had to be made if I wanted to be with them and I wasn't ready to choose.

I had five guys in my rotation, with Nick and Damien almost splitting time equally. The other three guys were thrown into the mix occasionally, when I wanted something fresh to shake things up a bit. But I only had an emotional investment in Nick and Damien. And both of them were quite jealous of the time I spent with the other, which manifested in different ways.

So, there I was, lying in bed with Damien, his fingers idly playing with my mane of kinky dark hair. My stomach grumbled loudly with hunger.

"I'm going to order a pizza from Mario's," I said, grabbing my cell phone from the nightstand. "You want the usual?"

"Good call," he replied, lighting up another cigarette as I dialed the pizzeria. We weren't supposed to be smoking in the dorm, but the RA didn't care.

I placed the order quickly, perching on the edge of the bed and stealing a few drags of Damien's cigarette. As I hung up, another call came in. It was Nick. *Fuck.* I'd accidentally double booked myself for the night and was due to meet him for dinner in an hour.

My pulse raced with panic. Should I answer the phone here with Damien, where he'd be able to hear my conversation with Nick? Did Nick know I'm with Damien right now? What was I even going to say?

With trembling fingers, I handed Damien back his cigarette.

"Who's calling you?" asked Damien, a question he'd never bothered asking before.

I didn't want to lie to him, and couldn't anyway, since Nick's name flashed on the screen of my phone. "It's Nick."

His face clouded over immediately. "Well, you'd better get it then." He stubbed out his cigarette aggressively and got out of bed to put on his boxers.

I grabbed the closest clothing I could find — Damien's rumpled T-shirt on the floor. Then I walked toward the desk in the opposite corner of the room. I wasn't sure why, but I didn't want to invade Damien's space with Nick, even though I already was by virtue of answering this call.

"Hey, Nick."

"Hey, Gorgeous. How's it going? Are we still meeting at 8 at that Portuguese restaurant you like?"

I didn't know what to do. I was in the zone here with Damien. We were waiting for our pizza and were presumably going to spend the rest of the night together. If I left Damien now, he'd be upset that I'd ditched him for Nick.

But I didn't want to cancel with Nick and risk upsetting him, even though we'd only scheduled this dinner date a few days ago, and I'd had plans with Damien tonight for weeks. My stomach churned as I realized there was no winning with both of them; I'd have to make a choice.

Damien glowered on the other side of the room, pretending to text someone on his phone while listening to my conversation.

"Nick, I'm really sorry. I accidentally double-booked myself tonight. I can't make it. Can you do tomorrow night instead? I can sleep over afterwards..." My attempts at flirtation didn't mask the guilt that churned in my gut.

"Oh. Well, that's okay." I could hear his disappointment on the other end of the line. "Tomorrow works too. That sounds good."

Relief flooded me, accompanied by a pang of sadness that I'd disappointed Nick. I would just have to make up my scheduling confusion to him tomorrow. "Thank you for understanding, Nick."

"It happens. No worries. I'll just go over to Brandon's for the game." Nick paused, then added casually, "So, what are you up to tonight?"

My stomach knotted again. I didn't want to lie. And it would be weird to lie with Damien sitting right there.

"Oh, I'm with..."

"Hey, Nick," Damien called out loudly from the other side of the room, making sure Nick could hear him.

My heart stopped beating for a second. "Was that Damien?" Nick asked, jealousy creeping into his voice.

"Um, yes." Why did Damien have to do that? I was going to tell Nick anyway, but the way Damien outed me on his own terms felt so territorial and invasive of my space.

"Oh. I see. Well, enjoy your night. I'll see you tomorrow, okay?" Nick sounded upset, like he was rushing me off the phone. "I love you, Jade."

"I love you too, Nick," I replied, the way I always do, so naturally that it took me a moment to realize I'd said the L-word to Nick. And I'd never, ever said it to Damien.

Damien's face fell as I hung up the phone. His expression went from victorious at having made Nick feel like second best, to dejected and looking like he'd lost a battle.

I left my phone on the desk and walked over to Damien, who was lying back against the pillows, deep in thought.

"The pizza should be here soon," I said, trying to break the silence. I was dying to know what he was thinking but had no idea what to say in this twisted situation.

"So, you love him?" he asked, turning his head to look at me. It was impossible to read the look in his eyes. There was hurt and jealousy and something else I couldn't identify.

I sat next to him on the bed, wanting to reach out and touch him but deterred by his cold countenance.

"Yes, I do."

Damien turned his head away from me.

I wanted to tell him I was in love with him, too. If not now, then how much longer would I wait to tell him? But he spoke first.

"I don't like that you're seeing Nick," he said.

I bristled, frustration rising inside me. "Yeah, you've made that perfectly clear. But you and I have discussed seeing other people many times before. And you're fucking other women, too," I pointed out.

"Yeah, seeing them, fucking them, but not telling them you

love them. That's different." He paused and took a deep breath. "I want you to stop seeing Nick."

My blood boiled. I couldn't stand when anyone thought they could tell me what to do. Nick had never, ever tried to get me to stop seeing anyone, even if he'd made it clear he did enjoy having me to himself. He respected my choices and he didn't let his jealousy, or any other emotions, get in the way of that.

And up until now, I thought Damien was the same way.

I rose from the bed, too angry to sit. "You can't actually be asking me that. You want me to stop seeing someone I love because *you* don't like it? Do you know how crazy that sounds?"

Now he stood from the bed, his cheeks flushing. "Why is it crazy? I don't like having to time-share you with anyone else."

"And what about how *I* feel? Are my feelings not even a consideration to you?"

"Of *course* they are."

"But yours are more important."

"No, that's not what I'm saying —"

"You know I've been seeing Nick for months. Why are you just telling me this now?"

"Because I... because. I didn't know you *loved* him. I thought it was just... you know... casual."

"Like the way you and I are just *casual*?"

137

His countenance darkened. "What you and I have is different, and you know it."

I did know, but I needed him to say it. "Really? Different how?"

He went quiet, pacing the small dorm room a few times before approaching me.

I trembled with anger. I didn't know how I would react if he touched me, but he didn't dare. He'd never seen me like this before.

"Damien, what are we even doing here? What do you really want with me?" Everything spilled out at once, all of the doubts and fears I'd been having. "You're leaving in a few months. You'll be on the other side of the country. And I'm staying here. What did you think was going to happen?"

He shook his head, dejected. "I didn't have that all figured out yet. I thought..." He sighed, running a hand through his hair and looking at the ground. "I don't know what I thought. That we'd still be together. That we'd figure it out together."

The blood pounded in my ears, my frustration escalating. Anger overruled my love for him.

He stepped closer to me and reached out to take my hand, but I shook him off. He sighed deeply again. "We're good together, Jade. Like, *really* good. I don't want that to end."

Damien was saying some of the right things. But I couldn't get past him having the balls to ask me to stop seeing Nick. And even now, he still couldn't say what I most needed to hear.

"Then tell me how you actually feel about me, right now, or I'm out of here."

His eyes widened with surprise and uncertainty at my ultimatum. His mouth opened and closed several times as though he was about to say something but couldn't find the words.

I waited what seemed like forever, too stubborn and immature to tell him I loved him first. It occurred to me that I couldn't be vulnerable with him. I didn't know why I felt that way. He was trying to conjure the words to say, but he couldn't do it, either.

Tears sprang to my eyes, and I turned my back to him and blindly collected my discarded clothes. "I can't do this anymore," I said, shoving my clothes in my tote bag.

"Jade, please… don't leave. Let's talk this out."

Wearing only Damien's T-shirt, my bag about to burst, I opened the door to his room. The vibrant party outside was still going strong.

I couldn't look back at him. I didn't want him to see I was crying.

"Jade, wait —"

My stomach clenched in agony as I slammed the door behind me. Tears streamed down my face as I tripped over some of the partygoers, crashed into the pizza delivery guy, and ran down the staircase into the night to my apartment.

* * *

Here at the engagement party, the same despair I felt then seeps in. The time that Damien and I spent apart doesn't seem to make any difference in the intensity of my feelings. The wound is as fresh as it was the last time we saw each other.

After that argument in Damien's dorm room, he didn't call and I didn't call him. For months, I avoided social events he might attend because I didn't want to risk the emotional upheaval that would come with seeing him.

During that time, Nick and I became closer and more serious. He never asked about Damien. I told Nick about my need to be in an open relationship, and though he was a bit reluctant at first, he was interested in exploring what being open could be like for us. I felt heard and understood, seen and loved.

One night, many months later, I received an unexpected message from Damien. *Hey you, it's been awhile. Just wanted to say hi. How are you?* My anger had subsided, but not entirely. Our conversations revealed a different side of him I'd never known. We got personal with each other while joking around. We never talked about what happened. Both of us knew something was still there between us, but I think we both felt that we'd blown it, and that our time was over.

In the meantime, my relationship with Nick progressed and we moved in together. I was incredibly happy and felt so lucky to be with a man who respected my choices and wanted me to be my own woman. I've never regretted choosing him over Damien, but I can't help but wonder what life would have been like if I'd wound up with Damien instead. Somehow, a part of me was still with Damien, and it never left.

Had Damien moved on, too?

As Damien and I continue to stare at each other across the hall, a cute brunette in a royal blue minidress sidles up to him, sliding her hand up his arm. He finally tears his gaze from mine as he realizes someone's there.

Jealousy unfurls in the pit of my belly as he wraps his arms around her and leans down to kiss her. I feel dizzy and have to look away. I turn back to the bar, but I can't avoid their reflection in the bar mirror. I catch a glimpse of myself, looking a paler white than usual in my emerald dress.

Curiosity overtakes me as I watch Damien and his girlfriend, seeing how he interacts with her. I can't stop comparing her to me and the way he is with her. Their body language speaks volumes — there seems to be something missing between them.

A few of our friends approach Damien and his girlfriend, greeting him with warmth and introducing themselves to her. She's smiling but fidgeting with the strap of her dress and her hair, clearly nervous and insecure. I catch myself smirking in the mirror, watching how out of place she seems in my group. A petty wave of self-satisfaction spreads through me to my fingertips when I notice that Damien keeps looking in my direction.

"Are you waiting for a drink, babe?" Nick's voice startles me, and I try to hide how conflicted I am as I turn to face him. He kisses me, tasting faintly of Scotch. He grabs my ass playfully and I secretly hope Damien's watching us right now.

"I'm just hanging out here for a bit." I lift my glass of gin and 7 Up to demonstrate my point. Nick understands that I sometimes need space away from people because big crowds can overwhelm me, and I occasionally need a breather.

"Ok, well, I'm going to go have a smoke outside with the boys. Are you good here?"

I nod, and Nick smiles and gives me a long, deep kiss on the lips, squeezing my ass again and winking at me.

In the bar mirror, Damien's face darkens with envy as he watches me laugh and kiss Nick. Then my boyfriend leaves me standing alone, leaning against the bar and sipping on my drink. And I'm burning up with the heat of Damien's eyes boring into my back.

Damien approaches me with purpose from across the room, leaving his date to socialize with the gaggle of girlfriends and wives who are all too eager to gossip with her.

My hand trembles slightly as I down the last of the fizzy liquid in the glass tumbler in my hand, tossing it back quickly. Liquid courage. I set the empty glass down on the bar and look up to see Damien looking at me in the mirror. He's right behind me.

My heart pounds, and I'm fluttering with anxiety. Damien stands in front of me and leans against the bar with that same determined look in his eyes as the last time we saw each other. I know that he's also thinking about our past together. How could he not be?

Somehow, I manage to hear him over the din.

"Jade."

His voice is seductive, husky and deep, softly saying my name as though telling me a secret.

It's been a decade and still I'm a trembling wet mess when he hasn't even touched me yet. Has *nothing* changed the way I feel about him?

He steps closer to embrace me, and I inhale his cologne — it's the same one he always wore. I want to bathe myself in it. I want every inch of my body to wear his scent.

I'm dying to kiss him, to taste his lips and have my body melt when his mouth explores mine. And if he had the audacity to try and kiss me here, in front of everyone, I know my lips would yield easily under his.

But there are too many people around, including our respective partners, and we have too much to lose. Nick and I are open, but that openness does not extend to past flames — especially any we'd had an emotional connection with in the past. *Especially* Damien. And his girlfriend is here. Given what I know about his monogamous mindset, they're exclusive. We'd both be hurting people we care about, and in a very public way.

Settle down, Jade. Don't draw attention to yourselves.

My breath catches in my throat as he leans down to kiss my cheek. His soft lips plant a kiss near my ear, his hot breath whispering so only I can hear him.

"I missed you."

My pulse intensifies as he wraps his arms around my back in a hug, still looking friendly from an outsider's perspective, while deeply intimate to both of us. I kiss his freshly shaven cheek and long to bury my face in the side of his neck, to enfold myself around him completely.

I know what he's doing. He's gingerly testing the invisible boundaries of my restraint for fault lines. He wants to confirm that the spark between us is still there, waiting for any sign. Whatever his relationship with that woman across the room, the way he feels about her does not seem to quell the connection between us. Just as my love for Nick doesn't dissipate my feelings for Damien.

His touch on the bare skin of my arm creates an involuntary spasm between my thighs. I soak my panties in anticipation, expectation, powerless in my desire. I try not to let the memories crash over me. Even though I don't want him to let go of me, I need to regain some control.

I summon the willpower to fight the haze of nostalgia and step back from him, hoping the physical distance will subdue the heat between us. Now an arm's length away from me, I still feel his imprint on my body.

Despair creeps back into my stomach and I try to fight it. I catch the bartender's eye and glance down at my empty glass, and he nods and starts preparing me a fresh drink.

"Make that two," says Damien, noting the silent communication between us. The bartender nods again, and Damien turns to me. "So… how have you been?"

"Great… really great." My voice is squeaky and uncertain, revealing my nervousness. I have the urge to flee and avoid him for the rest of the night, because all I truly want is to be alone with him. And I can't — shouldn't — be alone with him. "How about you, and…" I point toward Damien's girlfriend.

"Stacey," he replied. "It's good. We've been together for about a year."

Jealousy stabs through my gut. "Oh, wow, that sounds serious."

"I guess we'll see." He shrugs noncommittally.

The bartender interrupts the intimacy when he places our glasses on the bar and pushes them towards us.

"Thanks," Damien replies, and moves to clink glasses. I raise my gin and look him in the eye as our glasses touch. His fingers inadvertently brush against mine, sending an electric shock through my body.

In the bar mirror, I notice Nick and a few of our friends coming towards the bar, laughing and giddy from the party and the booze. Nick sees Damien next to me and his smile fades slightly. Nick sidles up next to me and slides his arm around my waist possessively, kissing my neck.

"How's it going, Nick?" Damien nods towards Nick, being polite for my sake. I notice that neither man is extending their hand to shake.

Nick's demeanor seems frostier. "Good, thanks. You?"

The awkwardness is making me uncomfortable, but luckily the tension snaps when the MC's voice comes over the speakers, telling all of us to join everyone at the buffet where dinner is being served. Meanwhile, the only appetite I have is for Damien, and he's not on tonight's menu.

I need to escape Damien or be suffocated by my desire for him. I turn to Nick. "Let's go check it out." I kiss him on the mouth, making Damien glower with envy. Nick and I weave our way through the partygoers to the buffet, leaving Damien at the bar. I fight my desire to look back at him and stay focused on being present with Nick.

* * *

A few hours later, all of us are well fed, emboldened by alcohol, and laughing obnoxiously. I've tried desperately to ignore Damien and Stacey, preventing myself from looking his way too often. He's kept his distance and remained at the table next to us. Yet he's been stealing glances towards me.

I'm sweating under my dress, hyperaware of his presence and the smolder of his gaze. My legs are crossed under the table, my thighs pressed together to prevent myself from dripping through my panties and dress onto the chair. But when I feel a slow trickle down my inner thigh, I need to stop the leak.

Standing from my chair, I excuse myself to go to the ladies' room. By some miracle, the other girls don't volunteer to come with me. I wink at Nick, then head out of the party hall and into the main corridor.

My high heels click on the marble floor as I head to the restroom at the end of the hall, waving at a few friends walking back towards the festivities. Behind me, the music gets louder and then lowers again as they shut the door to the party room.

"Jade."

A shiver runs down my spine and I stop in my tracks. That's unmistakably Damien's voice behind me.

Spinning around on my heel, I turn and see him walking towards me, a determined look on his face. We're alone in the hall. Nobody to see that Damien and I are together.

My heart speeds up as he approaches me. He grabs my hand and grips it firmly. My gut clenches in excited trepidation.

"Come with me." His blue eyes are dark with mystery.

He starts to pull me behind him, and I follow him.

"Where are we going?" I ask, but he doesn't reply, leading me to the end of the corridor. I have no desire to let go of his hand and turn back to the party.

We stop at a door marked STAFF ONLY. I glance around nervously, making sure there's no one else around. He pulls the handle and the door opens invitingly.

Damien tugs at my hand and leads me into the near-dark room. The pounding of my heart in my chest echoes between my thighs.

In the light of the red EXIT signs and the dim spotlighting along the walls of the room, I can make out the outlines of stacked extra chairs and tables and other props for the hall.

And I can see the hungry look in Damien's eyes.

He pulls me towards him, enfolding me in his arms. All I can smell is his scent and my pussy quivers. Guilt gnaws at my belly as I think of Nick… but every fiber of my being is aching for Damien.

His mouth hovers right above mine, the perfect height difference with me in my high heels. My breath quickens as he tilts my face up to his.

"I missed you so much," he says, the torment in his voice audible. A twinge of pain stabs through my belly, reeling at the enormity of his words.

I clench his shirt in my fists, pulling him down to kiss me. My lips melt easily under the pressure of his mouth. I slide my hands over his shoulders and behind his neck, pressing my body completely against his. My pussy throbs with unrelenting yearning to reconnect with him, stirred by his hard cock pushing into my belly.

His fingers bury in my messy curls as he kisses me more deeply. Our tongues dance together, exchanging breath for breath. I'm about to jump out of my skin with the intensity of my need to feel him inside me again.

I claw at his clothes, nearly ripping the buttons off his shirt, content only when my fingertips touch the hot, soft skin of his strong chest. The same chest I'd touched and kissed and laid against so many times. He helps me undress him, his blazer and shirt falling to the floor.

Still kissing me, his hands run over the top of my dress to cup my otherwise naked breasts, seizing each hard nipple between his fingers. A surge travels from my chest to my clit as he pinches them through the silky fabric. I gasp at the pleasure of it, pushing my body even closer to him. God, I'd missed his rough touch, his scent, the urgency of our animalistic need for each other.

His hand drifts under my dress and between my bare thighs, down to my hottest spot. I squirm with pleasure as his fingers slip into my silky panties and graze my swollen pussy. A seductive, smug smile crosses his face when he discovers how wet he's made me. I groan as his fingertips discover my aching clit and spread my legs further to give him more access.

My pulse races, my pussy tightening as he slowly slides two of his fingers between my soaked lips. He kisses me as he works his hand inside me, his tongue and fingers finding the same hypnotic rhythm. I moan against his mouth as the pressure builds between my thighs. I need more. I need to feel his mouth on my clit. And I absolutely need his cock to fill me, to physically connect with him again.

I pull away from his kiss and grab his wrist, sliding his fingers out of me. Bringing his glistening digits to my lips, I stare him in the eyes and lick and suck off my juices. He grabs me and kisses me again, tasting me on my tongue.

"Mmm... I need to drink you from the source," he says, his seductive tone giving me goosebumps. He hoists me up by the ass, lifting me in the air and propping me up on the tablecloth-covered edge of a nearby table. His hands move up my thighs to gather my dress around my waist, then back down to pull my panties off my legs.

He balls up the skimpy fabric and looks at me. "Open your mouth."

I smile slyly and comply, parting my lips for him. He'd done this to me many years ago and I'd loved it. He slowly feeds my panties between my lips, filling my mouth with the taste of my pussy and the soft feel of the fabric. The eroticism of this move stirs me again, making me even more impatient for him.

My hands reach out for his dick, longing to expose his hard flesh. But he moves his hips away the moment my fingers graze his bulge. "Not yet. I want to rediscover you first."

Damien ignores my whimpers and lowers the thin straps of my dress, pulling them down on either side to uncover my breasts. His lips descend on my neck, tracing the soft curve of it. I shiver as his hot breath caresses my ear.

"God, Jade, you're so beautiful."

I can't reply as I have panties stuffed into my mouth, but I moan and grip his shoulders appreciatively. His hot tongue travels over the slope of my shoulder, tickling me in a pleasurable way, and moves further down.

He cups my heavy breasts in each hand, marveling at them while pinching my nipples again. My groans are mostly muffled against the silk panties in my mouth as he rouses me even more by licking and biting each of my nipples.

His hand explores my uncovered sex, sliding between the wet folds as he gets to his knees on the floor in front of my pussy. His hot breath toys with my clit, but then pulls away. My swollen cunt is nearly bursting to finally feel him inside me. But he moves his hand away, grasping my legs and pushing them further apart.

Damien's tongue travels from my inner thigh down to my knee, my calf, then back up again. He alternates with his lips and fingers, getting closer to my smoldering core, grazing purposely, purposefully, against my clit. My nails bite into his shoulder to mark my building frustration.

Just as I'm about to scream, his mouth closes over my dripping sex, licking back up to my clit. My hips move towards him as he starts to suck my pussy lips into his mouth, torturing me.

The friction of his tongue over my clit is maddening. My fingers twine in his hair, trying to communicate my urgency. I need him to fill me, to break me in half, to deliver me from this infernal, excruciating need.

He gives my clit a final kiss and slowly pulls away from me. His eyes are wild, drunk with desire.

"Open your mouth."

I do, and he pulls my wet panties from between my lips.

"These are mine now." He stuffs the skimpy fabric into his pants pocket, and I don't object. I love the idea of him wanting to keep a piece of me with him.

"You fucking pervert," I tease, but he interrupts me by dipping his head to kiss me, sharing the sweetness of my pussy with me.

Groaning, I grab onto his belt buckle and run my hands over his cock, which is straining against his pants zipper. My fingers unfasten him as quickly as possible, sliding his pants and boxers down his thighs and setting his cock free. I soak up the sight of his hard body, every inch of skin ready for my touch.

Damien kicks off his shoes, wearing only his socks now. Reaching out to wrap my hands around the familiar thickness of his dick, I gaze at him with widened eyes.

I lick my lips, hungering for his flesh on my tongue. My pussy twitches at the same time, aching to be split apart by him. My body can't decide which of my holes I want him to fill first.

He decides for me. As I try to bend my head to his cock, he pulls me back up by my hair and looks at me intently with his deep blue eyes.

"I need to be inside you, Jade. I can't wait anymore." His impatience reflects my own. My hands still around his dick, I pull him closer to me, positioning his head against my slippery entrance.

Damien watches my eyes roll back in pleasure as he slides himself into me in one stroke, my pussy fitting over him like a satin glove. My legs wind around his hips to pull him closer to me. I feel complete with him buried inside me. Fuck, I'd missed him.

He covers my thighs with his big hands and starts pumping into me with long, deep, torturous strokes. His mouth seizes mine, kissing me as I moan against his lips. I indulge in the pressure of his cock inside me, the familiar way that he's possessing my pussy.

My nails imprint the flesh of his shoulders, his back and his ass, gripping onto him. He groans and fucks me faster and harder, squeezing my thighs, my ass, my breasts. Covering me in his touch, marking his territory. Fucking me like he's making up for lost time... like this might be our last time.

The pounding in my chest echoes the one between my thighs, overloading me with sensation and heightened emotion.

Damien hoists my petite body off the table easily, continuing to fuck me in midair with my high heels flailing around helplessly. Exhilarated by his spontaneity, my legs and arms wrap around his powerful body for leverage. My breasts bounce erratically against his chest as he pumps his cock into my pussy, my hard nipples rubbing against his flesh. I'm on the brink of spilling over with pleasure.

Before I can climax, Damien slows down and sets me onto the table again, sliding himself out of me. My pussy twinges as though whining at the absence of his cock inside me.

"Get back inside me," I complain, watching him look around at our surroundings. He grabs a tablecloth off a nearby table and lays it down on the ground.

"Come and lie down."

Giddy to touch him again, I hop off the table, finally stripping off my dress and leaving it on the tabletop. Fully naked but for my heels, I walk towards him, joining him on the white cover.

Sinking to my knees next to him, Damien grabs me and lies me down, positioning his body between my thighs. My exposed sex aches for him, and I reach out and grab his dick to try to guide him inside me. But he captures my wrists in one of his big hands and pulls them back up over my head, pinning them down on the satiny fabric of the tablecloth, rendering me almost helpless.

Then he pauses, his mouth hovering above mine, looking into my eyes with seriousness.

"I love you, Jade."

Just like that. The words I'd been longing to hear for a decade.

His confession is like a shockwave. My heart flutters and explodes in my chest, sending vibrations through my entire body.

Before I can respond or wrap my brain around what his words could mean for us, he leans down and kisses me again, pressing the front of his body against me. Heat spreads throughout my core as his tongue moves against mine with intensity.

Damien slips inside me again. I cry out in pleasure as his cock fills up my pussy, connecting us. This time, with the certainty that he feels the same way I do.

My hips arch up to meet him as he picks up his rhythm, driving his dick into me. He has to release my arms to lean back, kneeling between my thighs and grabbing my hips to lift my pussy closer to his dick.

He maintains his gaze while he unleashes everything on me, holding me by the ass and driving into me with deep, hard strokes. My hands now free, I finger my swollen clit at the same rhythm. My orgasm builds faster the harder he fucks me, my clit throbbing in sync with my pulse. A wave of heat sweeps over me, spreading outward until I'm tingling all over.

I give myself over to him completely, closing my eyes as my walls tighten around his cock. Erupting with near-violent spasms, my otherworldly cries echo throughout the room. He continues to thrust into me slowly, teasing out my last involuntary shudders.

My pussy squeezes as I try to catch my breath. My juices are spread all over our thighs, covering us in the feral scent of our sex, and filling the room with our musk. The haze in my mind starts to clear, and I remember he'd just told me he loves me.

"Damien..." I raise my body off the tablecloth and he sits back on his ass and takes me into his lap. I'm face to face with him with his cock still inside me, throbbing in tune with his heartbeat.

My fingers tenderly caress the back of his head and his neck, his hands softly exploring my back. I gaze into his eyes the same way he looked at me before admitting his feelings.

"I love you, too."

Damien smiles at my confession, grabbing me and bringing my mouth down to his to kiss me again. This time, with extra intensity, knowing we both love each other.

My pussy grips his cock inside me, urging me to keep fucking him. I grind my hips into Damien's as we kiss, rocking my body into his. He holds me close to his chest, crushing my breasts against him as I move on him.

Even though I just came, the heat escalates between my legs. My hips quicken their pace, gliding my pussy over his cock at blinding speed. Damien grabs hold of my long hair with one hand, twisting my mane around his wrist. He smacks my ass with his free hand, his mouth capturing my neck and indenting his teeth over my pale throat. His cock starts to thrust into me from below at the same rhythm as my hips.

Damien groans my name into my ear, and I lose control again, erupting with a vengeance. My pussy squeezes tightly over his dick, my body shuddering against his. He holds me close to him, his cock still moving inside me.

My climax subsides, and I can tell by the ecstasy on his face that he's close, too. I quickly slip off of him and kneel in front of him, bending over to cover his cock with my mouth and my hands.

He cries out and grabs the back of my head as I tongue and suck and stroke his swollen flesh, his cum spilling down my throat in powerful spurts. I swallow every drop of his cum, then use my tongue to clean him of our juices.

I smile at Damien, fulfilled and pleased beyond imagining at everything we'd just done together, and everything we'd just said to each other. He grins back at me, standing up slowly and reaching his hand out to help pull me to my feet.

Suddenly, his eyes cloud over, reality sinking in. Now that we're less drunk with sex and our minds have cleared, the realization dawns on us that we still have to return to the party. Return to our respective partners and some semblance of normalcy.

Because being with Damien here, now, after all this time, and connecting with him like this, admitting our love for each other, fucking him like we're in a bubble of our own creation where time and rules don't exist... it's surreal. And we know this can't last forever.

"We should get back," I say, unable to diminish the misery in my voice.

Blinking back the hot tears that threaten to spill from my eyes, I turn around to locate my dress. I breathe deeply, trying to control the onslaught of emotion.

I hear him fumble around for his clothes and turn back to take a last glance at his naked body, memorizing his form.

Everything about this night will be burned into my mind forever. Bittersweet though it is, I'm elated to have found some kind of closure with him.

My dress slips on easily over my head, and I try to fix the mess that is my hair, not knowing how I'll be able to explain my tousled appearance to Nick. When I turn back around, Damien's fully dressed, tucking his shirt back into his pants and fixing his blazer.

I come up to him, smoothing my hands over his now-covered chest and back. Taking his face in my hands, I kiss him one last time. I savor the way his hot tongue feels in my mouth, the strength of his body pressed up against me. I kiss him deeply until we have to resurface for air.

When we pull our lips apart, he brushes a wild curl from my eyes, tucking it behind my ear. "Jade... you need to know... it's not too late for us."

I shake my head. "But it is," I say, caressing his cheek affectionately, trying to memorize the exact feel of his rough stubble under my soft fingertips. His glacier-blue eyes cloud with the truth of our situation, ripping me to shreds on the inside as he mirrors my pain.

"You'll go back home with your girlfriend, miles and miles away from here, and it'll be years until we see each other again. And you'll forget about me and move on with your life." As I say this, I wonder which of us I'm trying to convince.

My lower lip trembles as he kisses me intently, and my desire sparks anew as he presses against me.

"I'm thinking of moving back here," he says. "There's a new work opportunity that might be available."

My mind burns, trying to process what he'd just said. This isn't the closure I thought we would have. Even if his proximity could make being together physically possible, what of all the other reasons besides distance that have kept us apart? Damien's jealousy, his reluctance to embrace my polyamorous needs, our inability to communicate, our stubbornness... even after all this time, I wasn't sure much had changed.

And what about my life with Nick, our open relationship, and how happy we are with each other and our respective partners? Does Damien imagine he could be a part of that, too? Do I?

My mouth opens and closes a few times, but no words come out. I don't even know what to say first.

The door to the room flies open, breaking the spell between us. A few staff members walk in, stopping when they see us. "You can't be in here," one of them says as the others chuckle. It's clear by our disheveled appearances that they know exactly what we were doing. Plus, the entire room is redolent with the smell of our sex.

"We were just leaving," Damien says, his hand behind my back to steer me out of the room.

Outside, the hallway is thankfully unpopulated, and I start stealing away to the ladies' room to clean myself up and try to process everything. But I can't gather the strength to move away from him.

"This isn't over," he says, the hope in his voice as overt as the distress.

I shake my head, trying to get my thoughts clear. Were we really doing this here and now? "Damien... I'm not going to leave Nick. We're happy together. I love him."

"But you fucked me. And you said you love me, too."

He's right. I did fuck him, knowing that Nick wouldn't be thrilled if he knew I was intimate with Damien. A pang of guilt shoots through my belly. It's only a matter of time before I come clean to Nick and tell him about what I've done. And I do love Damien. But right now, I need to be true to myself, and honest with Damien, once and for all.

"Damien... I'm polyamorous. You're not. Moving back here won't change that." He sighs deeply as I continue my argument. "And even if you were, Nick would never be comfortable with me having a relationship with you. There's too much history. I won't put him through that. I can't."

My heart sinks as I realize this really is the end. I have to let Damien go forever. I'm stunned to be in this position, to have such clarity on who I am and what I want. I've grown quite a bit since I first met Damien, and I owe a lot of that to Nick.

Damien seems too devastated to speak, and I'm struggling not to cry.

I press my face against his neck, breathing in his scent one last time. "I love you, Damien. And I'll never forget you, or this night. But this is where it ends for us."

Looking up at him, I see in his eyes that he understands that it's over. Any misplaced hopes and fantasies either of us had are now dashed.

"This can't be over." His voice cracks as he caresses my cheek. "I can't lose you again. I love you." He crushes my body close to his chest and starts kissing me.

A tear rolls down my cheek as I press my lips against his, not wanting to let go of him. But I finally do, releasing my grasp on his body and stepping back. His arms fall away from me, and I immediately miss his heat, his touch. Yearning boils in my chest but I try to push it down and collect myself.

Damien gives me one last, long look and then steps away from me, walking towards the exit in the back of the building. He obviously needs some time to process all of this — I know I've just broken his heart, and my own, in one fell swoop.

My body trembling, I turn back around and see Nick standing by himself in the hallway, watching me. By the look on his face, he saw me with Damien. Fuck. Time to face the music.

I walk towards him, still uncertain as to what to say. God, I never wanted to hurt Nick. Self-loathing roils in my belly as I approach my boyfriend.

"Nick..."

He puts up a hand to silence me. "I saw him kiss you..." He pauses, looking at my disheveled hair. "What else happened?"

I almost crumple into tears, all of the guilt and heartbreak crashing over me. "Nick, I'm so sorry..."

Nick shakes his head, coming up to me and putting his arms around me. "Jade, look at me. Stop talking. Just listen." I nod in assent, sliding my arms around him. Loving the feel of his solid body, his familiar shape, against me. He feels right. He feels like home.

"Brandon told me a few days ago that Damien would be here tonight. And I knew you'd feel weird coming if Damien was here, so I didn't say anything. And I also knew what you might do if you saw him again. So, I mentally prepared myself for any possibility. And I mean, *any* possibility."

I look up at Nick in amazement. Was he serious? "You mean... you know that we just had sex? And you're not angry at me?"

Nick sighs. "Well, I'm definitely not happy about it. I'm feeling a lot of things that we'll talk about later. But I love you. And I know you wouldn't have risked upsetting me if Damien wasn't important to you."

I'm astounded by how understanding he is. How much thought he put into this, the mental preparation he must have done. How much he loves me to have done that. And how well he knows me and accepts me. All of me.

"Just tell me one thing, Jade. Is it over with him?" His eyes are serious, and I see a flicker of fear there.

My heart wrings in my chest. "Yes, it's over."

Nick nods, exhaling slowly. "Okay. Okay. I can live with that."

Tears of relief and sadness stream down my cheeks, pouring out of me all at once. I feel like curling up into a ball and just letting all of these emotions out of me.

"I love you, Nick," I choke out through my tears, reaffirming to myself that I'd made the right choice by choosing Nick from the very beginning.

He takes the car keys out of his pocket with one hand, wrapping his other arm around my shoulders. "I'll text Kara and ask her to bring your purse over tomorrow, so we don't have to go back." I'm weak with gratitude and emotional exhaustion. Blinded by the tears that continue to flow down my face, I lean against him for balance as we start to walk to the parking lot in front of the hall.

"Come on, baby," Nick says in a soothing voice. "Let's go home."

SUBMISSION

Leather whips kiss the bare flesh of my thighs; I welcome the stinging pain that follows.

Pleasure courses through my body so even the tips of my fingers tingle.

I kneel before him with my ass arched upwards, face pressed into the immaculate white sheets on his bed. His clean scent invades my body with every inhale, stealing its way deep inside me, clouding my senses. My wrists are bound together in front of me with silky black ropes and I strain against the bonds, wanting to move, wanting more.

The whip cracks against my ass again. And again. And *again...*

All the muscles in my body relax as I completely give up control to him. Fully trusting him. Leaving my mind and body totally vulnerable. Pleased whimpers escape my throat as he whips me, slaps me, makes me his.

Fluids trickle from my sex and drip down my inner thigh. There's no way I can hide my desire for him.

Even as he beats me, I feel safe and protected.

My mind slips away. There's nothing I can do but surrender. My Dominant won't allow me to make any decisions. I'm permitted only to feel, and to obey his every command.

"Harder?" he asks — rhetorically. He asks for show, a part of our game. I have no say, but he wants me to beg.

He loves it when I beg.

"Yes, Sir, if it pleases you. Harder, Sir. Please, Sir. More. More. *More…*" The words spill out of me on their own. I'm not speaking — I'm obeying. There are no thoughts, only mindless obedience as I sink into subspace.

The sound of his voice is my only tether to reality. I slip out of my body, out of my consciousness, out of myself, settling into the comfort of my pain and the absence of thought.

He flogs me harder as I slip deeper.

This flogger is my favorite, and he knows it. It gently caresses my skin before the leather whips sting my ass. He lets the tails drag between my legs as he slaps my pussy, completely in control of me and the whip. Leather trails slowly over my clit and enflamed lips, before rediscovering the tender flesh on the underside of my ass again.

Each stroke resonates throughout my entire body, wracking me with spasms of pleasure.

Every now and then, the whipping stops and he covers my ass cheeks with his hands. Warm, knowing fingers massage my skin, soothing the sting as he whispers sweet words of encouragement in my ear.

Cool air washes over my ass as he lifts his hands, and I brace for the whip. It's coming — it's just a matter of time. I hold my breath, caught in that lingering, torturous moment between punishment and pain.

The anticipation is almost more potent than the slap itself. Every nerve ending lights up while I wait, my entire body vibrating.

Which tool he will use on me next? Where will he hit me? My ass? My thighs? My back? Will he flip me over and lay whip marks across my breasts? There's no way to know, and the uncertainty is intoxicating.

He didn't blindfold me this time, but he still won't permit me to look at him. And I won't disobey.

To disobey would invite punishments that don't leave me tingling... including possibly depriving me of his touch.

My toes curl into the mattress as I wait, a bead of fluid dripping out of my sex and rolling down my thigh.

I hear him walking around, feel the power of his presence behind me, and shiver involuntarily.

His presence looms over me, and I try to brace myself, tensing my muscles right before the paddle comes down on my ass. Cold, smooth leather smacks against my already-sensitive skin, soothing my soul with the delectable pain of it.

I groan into the coverlet, the pleasure weakening me so I can barely hold myself up.

These are the moments when I feel the most alive.

"Who do you belong to, my little slut?" His words comfort me as much as his touch.

"I'm yours, Sir," I say, my voice barely a whisper. "I'm yours." I whimper into the mattress helplessly.

Smack, smack, smack. Each stroke is a resonant reminder of who I belong to.

The headiest part of all is knowing that I can stop this whenever I want. Knowing that one word from me will freeze him in his tracks, have him rushing to untie me, to hold me. To stop the tremors and soothe my abused rear.

But I don't want it to stop. Not ever. I choose to give myself to him.

"Mine," His voice is deep and loaded with affection as he brings the paddle down hard on my ass again. And again. And *again.*

We're both entranced by the rhythm, moving perfectly in sync with one another. Entwined in a delicate balance of power, the inexplicable, inextricable connection between us fueling our need for each other.

"Mine," he groans deeply, possessively. Each stroke of his paddle on my reddening ass is closer to branding me with his mark. He knows I love seeing traces of his punishment on me, long after we've been together, reminding me constantly of my submission to him. Of his ownership over me.

He knows my limits almost better than I know them myself.

He stops again, setting the paddle to the side. Rough fingers gently massage my flesh, tender despite the callouses.

"That's my good little submissive," he says. "You were so good for me."

My eyes well up as bliss rises inside of me. His praise, and the pleasure of hearing him claim me, is as satisfying as the stinging of the lashes on my skin.

He helps me up from my knees, finally looking at me, looking into me. Eyes gentle and full of affection as his arms envelop me with the intensity of our connection.

"Thank you, Sir." He kisses me in reply, a passionate and loving kiss that demands nothing in return. His fingers discover the scorching space between my thighs that still aches and I gasp, writhing with pleasure in his strong arms.

He pulls away with a smile, a devious gleam in his eyes as he says words that thrill me to the core: "I'm not done with you yet."

OBEDIENCE

I crave his sensual discipline.

My body aches for the blissful pain only he can give me.

I need him to free me, to liberate me from the mundane thoughts that constantly invade my mind. I need to let go of it all.

I am his. All his.

Only he can transform me into a blank slate and make me into whomever he wants.

He stirred up something primal inside me, his impact so profound that, whenever I cum with one of my other lovers, I have to cover my mouth so I don't accidentally scream out his name in pleasure.

When I shake and quiver with orgasm, it's for him.

I long to inhale his woodsy scent, taste the salt of his sweat, feel his cum drip down the back of my throat or the curve of my ass… wherever he chooses to make his mark on me.

The way he feels pressed up against me, around me, buried deeply inside me haunts my skin.

From the first time we met, he knew I was his. And I knew I belonged to him.

Whenever we're apart, I think of our first time together. The true beginning of my masochistic self-discovery.

*   *   *

It all started when I heard the unmistakable sound of a woman's pleasured cries, followed by smacking noises.

I moved down the corridor with the hurried flow of other eventgoers, eager to find the room at the other end of the hotel in time for my next seminar about polyamory.

I was loving every minute of this sex education conference. This was intended to be part of my research for a book I was writing about alternative relationships, and I was overwhelmed with all the erotic ideas that emerged from each workshop I attended. I'd have to write a series to cover them all.

The moaning grew louder as I neared the center of the hotel's conference area. Even in my haste, I was curious to stop by and discover the source of the erotic sound. I couldn't see much, because a bunch of onlookers populated the open space and blocked my view of the action.

Following my ears, I fought through the group, trying to get a better peek of the demonstration.

The man's red blazer caught my attention first, as did the black and red twists in the flogger he held in his large hand.

Then my eyes focused upon a willing female volunteer bent over a chair, her beautifully curvaceous ass and her light brown skin exposed for him. And this sharp-dressed man behind her was somehow stealing the show.

What struck me most wasn't just his skilled hands or that he was adept with his tools, but rather the way he interacted with the woman and was so attentive to her.

He'd smack her ass, choke her, pinch her nipples, all while soothing her, relaxing her and murmuring comforting things to her in his deep, sexy voice.

I was more accustomed to flogging my submissives than bending over and taking the blows from a dominant. I'd only ever allowed one man to dominate me, but I never felt with him the intensity and affection I'd just witnessed with this man and his volunteer. Goosebumps rose on my skin, a shiver running down my spine. I wanted to know to how it would feel to be on the receiving end of his sensual discipline.

The demo ended with one last hard smack to the submissive's ass. She cried out loudly and the crowd grew quiet.

My clit thrummed as a pang of envy shot through me. I wanted what she was having. Who was this mysterious man?

He massaged her ass, taking away the sting of his blows. Running his hands up her back and behind her head, he came around to the front of her as his fingers buried in her black hair.

He spoke soothingly to her, pulling her head up to look her in the eyes until she nodded and smiled. Then he took her by the hand and helped her to her wobbly feet from her kneeling position on the chair.

As they took a bow, the onlookers clapped, as did I. They both smiled, their white teeth glinting in the light. He affectionately kissed his submissive on the forehead and held her close to his body, letting her soak up the comfort of his aftercare.

I stood off to the side, admiring his confidence in the way he held himself as he spoke to people. When she was fully comforted by him, the submissive slipped away from him his grasp and went to pull on some clothes. The crowd had dissipated somewhat when he looked up and caught my gaze.

His deep, dark eyes trailed down to my mouth and over my body, soaking up the sight of me. I wondered if he could see my hard nipples under my fitted purple top. Did he know just how wet my pussy was beneath my ivory skirt? Could he see how I was trembling slightly in my high heels? A sly smile curled his lips, as he met my eyes again.

I found myself walking towards him, as though he was pulling my body by an invisible string. My heart raced, my clit still throbbing from before. Our chemistry was instantaneous.

"Well hello there," he said, gracing me with a smooth, deep voice. My pussy trembled at the tone of his words, as though they held a more profound meaning. Now, only inches away from his body, probably too close to be standing to a stranger, I realized how easily I could lose myself in his eyes. And how much I wanted him to lose himself inside of me.

Heat emanated from his body, beckoning me even closer. My fingers ached to run along the velvety fabric of his blazer, then up the deep brown skin of his bare neck, to his salt-and-pepper beard that looked deceptively soft to the touch.

"Hi," I replied, my voice more seductive than I'd planned.

He licked his lips, drawing my gaze there for a moment before returning to his eyes again. When he smiled, there was a small gap between his front teeth, which made him even more charming, somehow. My belly knotted in desire, my pussy leaking out liquid sex. I more than wanted him. I wanted to belong to him. I needed him to take control of me.

I'd always craved this kind of heated connection. I'd lacked it with my previous dominant, but I never expected it would be so instantaneous — and with a perfect stranger. I didn't even know this man's name but my entire being recognized its counterpart in him. And the way he looked back at me reflected my own yearning.

"I'm Landon," he introduced himself. His name was as sophisticated as he looked.

"Mila," I said. Usually I'd shake his hand, as I normally do when I introduce myself, but that somehow didn't seem good enough, given how badly I wanted to touch him.

"May I hug you, Mila?" he asked, a request that would have sounded innocent coming from anyone else.

"Yes, please," I said, surprising myself with my reply. Something had snapped inside me — his very presence made me want to serve him. Inspiring me to kneel and beg and let him have his way with me.

He smiled and wrapped his long arms around me, pressing me to the front of his body while still looking down at me. His lips were only inches away from my upturned mouth, tantalizingly close. I melted against his body, running my hands over his back, the nape of his bare neck and smooth, shaved head. The soft fabric of his blazer tingled beneath my fingertips, the sensation shooting up my arms and directly down to my pussy.

His hands roamed over my back and up my arms, his bulge pushing against my belly. A flush crept over my cheeks as I imagined his naked flesh sliding against mine.

With a lustful look in his eyes, his hand slowly traveled from the back of my neck to my throat. His fingertips trailed along the sensitive skin, examining the tender, vulnerable area. I straightened my back, extending my neck further, silently communicating my request. He smiled seductively as his hand found its way around my throat. It was a perfect fit, as though my neck had been created with his hand in mind.

I moaned as his grip tightened slightly, reveling in the power of his fingers around my neck. My panties flooded with desire, my heart racing. His fingertips were on my pulse, so he felt the effects of my arousal. His smile widened, watching my enjoyment of his control of me.

And then he released me, leaving me breathless. He slid his hand back to my shoulder, still holding me.

"Wow," I said, amazed by the intensity of our connection. It felt so natural to have his hand wrapped around my neck, even though no one had ever touched me like that before. I'd never let anyone do that to me, and I didn't realize how much I'd like it.

"It's my intention to dominate you before this weekend is over." His tone was serious, with a playful note.

A shiver ran up and down my spine at the self-assuredness in his tone. Here was a man who could fully overtake me... to whom I would willingly, willfully, completely submit.

I smiled. "And it's my intention to let you."

We stared at each other with a thick haze of lust between us, smiling and running our hands over each other's backs and shoulders. My hips pressed up against the bulge at the front of his pants. The air crackled with the fire we'd sparked. I wanted him to kiss me, to feel those succulent lips against mine.

Someone jostled me from behind, breaking the spell. I turned and saw a conference-goer passing by on their way to the adjacent rom.

"Sorry," they apologized, then ducked into the nearby conference room. It occurred to me that I was supposed to be at another workshop, too. How long had I just been standing here with Landon?

I turned back to look at him again. "I have to go —"

"As do I, my Queen." A thrill ran through me. *My Queen.* Simultaneously revering me and claiming me as his. "How can I reach you later?" he asked.

I dug into my purse and found one of my business cards, handing it to him. He looked down at my name and media credentials, seeming impressed, then tucked it into the breast pocket of his blazer.

"I'll be in touch," he said, his voice full of promise. My body trembled with yearning in all the places I wanted him to touch me.

I smiled, stepping back from him with hesitation, already missing the warmth of his body against mine.

Nearly stumbling over my heels, I entered the conference room, looking back to see him smiling at me, right before the doors closed.

I took my seat, crossing my legs and feeling the incredible wetness between my thighs. Had that really just happened?

My mind was in a haze during the class, unable to focus. Halfway through, when my phone vibrated against my leg, I saw a message from an unfamiliar number.

"I can't stop thinking of you, my beautiful Queen," it said.

I smiled in pleasure and squirmed, flashing back to the way his hand had felt against my throat. I uncrossed and re-crossed my legs, afraid my pussy would drip all over my chair.

"I can't wait to feel your hands on me again, my King," I typed back, putting the phone away just as the instructor shot me an annoyed glare.

My phone vibrated again, but I painstakingly ignored it until the end of the workshop, trying desperately to focus on the subject matter instead.

When the session ended and I could finally check my phone, his last message read, "Let me know when you're ready for me. Because I'm ready for you."

My knees weakened. I couldn't wait a moment longer, but I did have to put in some work at this conference before I was free to play. I leaned back against the doorway to steady myself, and typed, "Tonight."

*   *   *

We met up that night at the bar in my hotel.

I arrived early, dressed for easy access in a short black dress that fit me like a second skin, wearing no bra or panties underneath. My nipples hardened and my clit throbbed incessantly as I waited for him in anticipation with a chilled glass of chardonnay in hand. My seat was at a table a few feet from the bar itself, front and center at the restaurant. I was looking and feeling good, and in the mood to be seen.

When he showed up, our eyes met and a mischievous smile spread across his face. He looked so refined in a different dark red suit and black shirt, a black pocket square tucked inside his right breast pocket. My pussy was so wet that I was sure I was soaking my barstool.

I stood up to greet him, and he swept me up in a full body hug, running his hands down the curve of my ass. We were both aware of all the eyes on us, but reckless in our exhibitionism. He hoisted the hem of my dress up over my ass, revealing me in all my bareness to anyone who was looking. I made no attempt to pull the fabric down to cover myself. I wonder if he realized how much exposing myself turned me on.

His fingers slid between my thighs from behind, feeling the slickness of my pussy. His eyes widened, an even bigger smile spreading across his face.

"Is this for me?" he asked, slipping his fingers into his mouth to sample my juices. "Mmm *mmm*, you taste good."

"It's all for you," I replied, my eagerness evident in my seductive tone. I was so incredibly stimulated by him that he could have bent me over the bar and fucked me with everyone watching, and I would never have stopped him.

But he made me wait. He released me, pulling my dress back down over my hips. "Sit down, my Queen," he instructed, sitting on the barstool next to mine and signaling to the man at the bar to bring him the same thing I was having.

As we waited for his drink, I hoisted myself up on the barstool, turned towards him, my legs crossed. He placed one large hand on my knee, looked down at my thighs, and then up at me.

"Spread your legs for me. Let me see that pussy."

My heart raced. Fuck, he was wicked. We were in public, and there were dozens of eyes on us. My exhibitionistic side was elated. And I loved that he seemed to know that he could tell me to display my pussy to anyone watching and I would comply.

I uncrossed my legs, inching them apart slowly as he sat back and watched.

"More," he instructed, demanding yet affectionate. With trembling fingers, I pulled my tight dress up further so I could spread my legs wider. The cool kiss of the air on my bare slit told me I had spread them wide enough.

"Stay just like that," he said. "Mmm, that is one beautiful pussy. Don't you dare move."

My pussy quivered at his instructions, and my thighs remained parted for his viewing pleasure. And they stayed that way even as the waiter came by with the second glass of wine.

The waiter raised an eyebrow at me. I knew he could clearly see my wet slit, and the thought of him seeing how exposed I was in public made me throb even more.

"Your chardonnay, Sir. Let me know if you need anything else." The waiter smiled at us, then disappeared back to the bar, leaving me alone with my sexy, dominant companion, who didn't touch his glass.

"You did very well, my Mila. You obeyed me." Landon brought my barstool closer to his, brushing his hands over my thighs again and burning me with the heat of his touch. He took one of my hands in his, raising it to his lips and kissing it with great affection. Just as I was thinking how gentlemanly he was, his other hand slid between my thighs and dipped into the wetness of my pussy. I moaned as he slid two of his fingers knuckle-deep inside me. "Does it feel good to obey me, young lady?"

"Yes, my King," I breathed, focused on the fingers rubbing against my G-spot and over my clit.

Knowing that people were watching us, without understanding anything about our connection and how far we were prepared to go, made me moan even more deeply.

"Tell me about you, Mila. Have you ever been dominated before?"

"You're only the second person I've ever wanted to be submissive to. I'm usually dominant," I confessed, struggling to think as his fingers continued to move inside my pussy.

"I'm honored that you chose me to deliver your sensual discipline," he said, his free hand burying in my hair and pulling me closer to him. "And what are your limits tonight? Anything specific you want to do? Anything I should know?" I loved that he was asking me these questions. Even though, up to now, we were on the same page, he was making extra sure of it. It was so sexy.

"You can call me whatever names you want. You can do anything you want to my body. Just don't break my skin, and don't slap me in the face — anywhere else is fine." I blushed with sudden shyness. "I... I haven't played like this in a long time..."

He nodded, listening intently. "I understand. I'll be careful with you. I like to use green-yellow-red for you to tell me how you're feeling throughout until I understand your boundaries. Is that okay for you?" I nodded. That was the same system I used with my own submissives. "Do you have a safe word?"

"Red." We both smiled.

With his fingers still inside me, he pulled me closer to him. I shimmied my hips to the edge of the chair, but I wasn't close enough, so I stood up between his open legs instead. My dress was up over my hips, and anyone looking would have been treated to a clear view of my bare ass and pussy. We could have gotten ourselves kicked out of the bar, but I was too turned on to care.

His thighs touched mine, his heat transferring through his pants and onto me. My hips were at the same level as his cock, and I reached out to grab the bulge that beckoned me, rubbing him with the palm of my hand. He stiffened under my fingers as I examined the generous size of him, wanting more.

"Not yet, you greedy little slut." My pussy twitched at the sound of the word slut — I absolutely loved being called a slut. He seized my wrists easily in his free hand and held them captive behind my back. "Hold them there and don't move unless I say otherwise. Understand?"

I couldn't hold back my smile. "Yes, Sir."

He released the hand that was holding my wrists, slowly wrapping his fingers around my throat. "Breathe deeply. Don't speed up your breathing," he told me in a calm voice as his fingers tightened around my neck with a gentle roughness.

All my vulnerability, my life, my pleasure, were in his hands. The immediacy of my trust was as obvious as my physical need.

I was ready to explode with all the physical and psychological stimulation — his experienced touch, his deep voice, the novelty and mystery of him, being so exposed in public, my complete submission to him... the eroticism overwhelmed me.

With his hand still gripping my throat, I tried to breathe normally while slowly growing more lightheaded. His fingers still moved inside me, pleasuring me while he controlled my breathing with his other hand. He was in total possession of me. It was the ultimate surrender.

My pussy began to shudder, so close to orgasm, and I moaned into his neck. My body relaxed completely as my pulse slowed. His hot mouth caressed my ear, his teeth sinking into my shoulder.

"Keep breathing normally," he said, then released his grip.

Blood pumped hard through my body, and the sensation of his fingers touching my pussy was more vivid than ever.

"I'm going to cum," I whispered, unable to speak as he choked me.

"Beg me for permission to cum." The hand on my throat loosened just a bit, air rushing back to my lungs.

"May I please cum for you, Sir?" I was whimpering now, on the precipice of exploding.

"Not yet. Don't you dare cum yet." The gruffness of his voice made me even wilder. His hand clenched around my neck again.

He kept fingering me, and I struggled as much as I could to hold it back, my hands balling into fists behind my back, my toes curling in my shoes. Just when he knew I was physically unable to restrain my orgasm and obey him anymore, his hand released my throat. A rush of oxygen flooded me, blood pounding in my head and between my legs.

"I order you to cum for me. Right now," he said.

I let my powerlessness take me over, erupting with pleasure. Heat shot through my pussy and out to every part of my body, dizzying me. I buried my face in his fragrant neck, muffling my uncontrollable moans. He held me up with a strong arm, supporting me as my legs weakened and my pussy squeezed his fingers.

When the waves of pleasure had subsided within me, he slid his fingers out of my slit and directly into my mouth. Our eyes met as I worshiped his fingers, cleaning up my mess.

He withdrew my hand from his mouth, placing it behind my ass to pull me closer.

"Mmm, good girl," he praised me, his words making my clit swell with renewed need for him.

His mouth covered mine, capturing my lips under his. He kissed me deeply, tongue sliding against mine. I kissed him back, pressing my body against him, eager and grateful to be closer to him. I forgot for a moment about obeying him and impulsively moved my hands from behind my back. I slid them over his chest, reaching down again to try and grab his cock through his pants.

He stopped me, moving my hands behind my back again. "I said not yet. Do you need behavior correction?"

I ached all over for his discipline, for his control of me.

"Yes, Sir. I've been so bad... I deserve to be punished."

"I'll be the one to decide if you're bad and what you deserve."

Boldness surged through me. "Would it please you for me to get on my knees right here, in front of all these people, and worship your cock to show you my devotion to you, Sir?"

His bottom lip twitched with amusement. "Not here," he said sternly. He pulled the hem of my dress back down to my mid-thighs, covering me again. Disappointment began to wash over me, but then he said, "My tools are waiting for you upstairs."

My heart raced at the sensual foreboding in his voice, the promise of more to come. He signaled the waiter, who came rushing over, likely wondering what naughty things he might intrude upon this time.

"We'll take the bill, please," Landon said, grabbing my hand and getting ready to lead me out of the hotel bar.

"Forget the bill. Just charge it to my room — number 936," I told the waiter. "Give yourself a nice tip," I added over my shoulder as my sexy dominant was already walking us towards the elevator. My body buzzed in anticipation of the surprises he had in store for me.

In the elevator, he chose his floor, then pinned me up against the glass wall, kissing me with intensity. He stole my breath with his mouth, so fiercely passionate. He didn't stop until the elevator dinged to tell us that we'd arrived.

I didn't care where we went — I would have followed him anywhere. I just wanted to feel him inside me.

As he led me by the hand down the hall to his room, my pussy throbbed, even though I'd just had a powerful orgasm. I couldn't believe how much I wanted him, how easily I trusted him already, even though we barely knew each other. A thrill ran up my spine, excitement mixed with a sense of danger at the uncertainty of all of this.

He slid his key into the door, granting us access to his temporary space. My legs wobbled as I walked over the threshold and into his territory. The door closed behind me, locking me in with him. In this space, the intensity of his presence and his dominance over me became more real, and so did my desire to submit to him.

The lights were out, but the blinds were open. The city lights cast an erotic glow in the room. I was drawn to the bed, where he'd carefully laid out a few tools and toys. I noticed the gorgeous red and black flogger he'd used to demonstrate on that girl before, my skin burning to feel those leathery tails on me. I didn't know if he'd use them or just tease me with the sight of them.

He crossed the room to where I was standing by the bed, and he sat down on the covers, patting his leg. "Come here."

I stepped closer to him, sitting on his lap, and he immediately started kissing me again, his hands roving over my body like he owned it. My pulse raced as his lips possessed me, making sure I was fully aware of who was in charge. As though I could forget.

"Turn around so I can unzip your dress."

Still sitting on his lap, I turned my back to him and moved my hair out of the way. I gasped when his fingers brushed the sensitive skin of my bare back, bringing the zipper down as far as it would go.

"Now take it off for me, like a good girl. And look at me while you do it."

I stood up in front of him, locking eyes with him as I brought the straps of my dress down over my shoulders and arms. His eyes darkened with each new inch of my bare flesh revealed to him, until my dress fell to a small heap on the floor. I shivered at the feel of the air conditioning on my skin, stepping out of my dress. Somehow, even with my high heels still on, I felt more naked than I'd ever been — my body stripped bare, my mind open to him.

"Keep those on," he said, indicating my heels. "Now, be a good girl and kneel at the edge of the bed, your ass in the air."

He stood from the bed and waited for me to obey.

My heart thudded in my chest as I did as he'd instructed, exposing my ass and pussy to him, completely vulnerable. I couldn't see him and had no idea what he would do. And that was such a freeing thought.

My wet pussy started dripping down my thigh. I heard him shift behind me, coming closer to me. My breath caught in my throat, as though bracing myself for pain.

His big hands caressed my bare ass, covering me in his touch. "You're a goddess," he told me, draping me in his adoration. His fingers smoothed the skin of my back, my thighs, avoiding my pussy, which craved his touch the most.

"Have you ever been properly spanked, Mila?" he asked.

My whole body ignited at the thought of his hands all over me, delivering the blissful spanks I so craved.

"Not properly, Sir," I replied, trying to contain my excitement.

He removed one hand from my ass, and I braced myself, tensing my muscles. The first slap of his hand on my rear was infused with affection, even in its toughness. I cried out, hot pain searing through my ass. His hand immediately covered where he'd spanked, massaging my flesh and minimizing the pain. But he'd known not to hit me too hard, so he'd delivered the perfect spank on the first try. My body relaxed, and my face pressed against the bedcovers, a small smile curling on my lips.

"How did that feel?" he asked.

"Mmm... Green," I moaned, ready for more. I was putty for him, malleable and ready to be played with and shaped however he desired.

"Good." Then came the next blow, this time to my other ass cheek. I gasped, the sting of it surging through my ass. His fingers massaged away the pain. "Are you ready for more?"

"Yes please, Sir," I groaned into the covers.

He moved away for a moment, reaching to grab a pillow from the head of the bed. He gently lifted my face, sliding the pillow underneath it. I immediately felt more comfortable and grateful to him for his thoughtful gesture.

"Thank you, Sir," I mumbled.

"Don't thank me yet." He got back behind me, his hands again prepping my reddened flesh, which was stinging in the best way.

He began spanking my ass, moving from one side to the other to even out the sensations. I cried out in pleasure each time, gripping on to the pillow and pressing my face in it to muffle my reactions. The room resounded with the sound of his slaps as the force of them intensified very gradually, moving down to the backs of my thighs, building me up to be able to take each new spank pleasurably.

Adrenaline coursed through my body, canceling out any pain I might have felt in the moment. Each time he paused to stroke my sensitive skin, I had a brief moment to breathe and melt deeper into the bed before he started again.

Time slipped away as he spanked me. I started to lose myself in the ecstasy of his sensual discipline. My flesh called out to be invaded by him completely.

And then he stopped, grabbing me by the hair. He lifted my back up, snaking his other arm around the front of me to grasp my small waist. Pressing my body against his, I could feel that he was still wearing clothes, and I itched to rip them off of him in defiance.

He pulled my head back, kissing me with tenderness. His other hand caressed my breasts, lightly pinching my hard nipples. Dizzy with pleasure, I softened in his arms, soaking up his affection. The flesh of my ass throbbed, reminding me of how hard he'd spanked me and how incredible it felt.

His fingertips traveled down my belly to the apex of my thighs, finally sliding over my dripping pussy. I quivered under his touch, moaning against his lips.

"Please fuck me," I begged him.

He grabbed my hair roughly, his fingers pinching my clit. I gasped at his unexpected gruffness. "Please fuck me, *Sir*," he repeated, emphasizing the Sir I'd carelessly left out.

"I'm sorry, Sir. Please, please fuck me, Sir."

He chuckled deep in his throat. "So, you think deserve my cock, you little slut?" he teased. He pushed me back down on my knees with my face in the pillow. "Don't move."

Sliding his big hands down my body, he grabbed my hips and positioned himself behind me. His hot breath tickled my exposed pussy and the backs of my legs, and I shivered with expectation. He kissed his way up my inner thighs, placing his face between them. My pussy pounded as each breath on my skin made me insane.

He buried his mouth in my pussy, his hands on my ass as his silken tongue slid between my folds. I cried out in pleasure, burying my face into the pillow, my back arching further to give him even more access.

"Mmm, what a delicious pussy." Goosebumps raised on my body, delighted at his adoration of my most sensitive parts. His hands clamped down on my ass, slapping my cheeks while he continued savoring my cunt.

I groaned, overwhelmed with the blissful combination of his hard smacks and the wet heat of his tongue on my clit. My skin was on fire from his attentions, my body trembling as he worshiped me. Reaching forward with his tongue, he tickled my clit, then slid his tongue between my lips and licked up the juices that dripped from me.

"Whose pussy is this?" he asked when he briefly came up for air.

"Your pussy, my King," I replied, moaning louder as his tongue resumed its teasing. Then without warning, his arms slipped away from me. The absence of heat behind and around my body made me shudder and only increased my desire to feel him against me again.

I whimpered while I waited, my muscles tensed, my clit throbbing as the anticipation filled me even with more lust. I heard the rustling of clothes behind me, the metallic clink of him unfastening his belt, the sound of him removing any obstruction between us.

And then I felt the heat of his bare flesh behind me, the silkiness of him as he lifted me by the hair again and pressed my back to him. He wrapped his fingers around my neck, squeezing slightly. "If you want my cock so badly, come and suck it. Then let's see if you deserve to be penetrated, my filthy slut."

His words taunted me, challenging me. I was starving for his dick and had no doubt I could convince him that I deserved to be fucked.

Letting go of my throat, he backed away from me, and I turned around to face his exquisite nakedness. Meeting his eyes, I slid off the bed and crawled over to him until I was kneeling on the floor in front of him.

I looked up at him with a smile, then gazed back at the beauty of his mouth-watering dick, with its slight upward curve that promised a future of G-spot pleasure. When my hands wrapped around his shaft, end to end, the head of his cock poked out, beckoning to be sucked. I stroked him, loving the smoothness of his hard flesh under my fingertips. He groaned when I squeezed him, his fingers tangling in my hair to urge me forward.

Guiding his dick to my mouth, I accumulated saliva on my tongue and spit it onto his shaft. My hands spread my saliva around his dick, lubing him up before I slid him between lips and over my tongue. I devoured him, relishing every inch of his cock and balls. I sucked him deeply into my mouth and the entrance of my throat, massaging him with my tongue.

When I looked up at him, his eyes were closed in pleasure, a lusty smile on his lips. His reaction spurred me to intensify my rhythm, my hands moving at the same pace as my mouth. His hands caressed my head at first, but as I moved faster on him, his grip tightened. I knelt still before him and fully took him into my mouth and throat, and his hips began to thrust forward until he was roughly face-fucking me.

The sensuous way his cock slid against my lips added to the aching between my thighs. I needed all of him inside me. Anywhere he could fit, I wanted him to fill me, to use me, to possess me. I choked on his cock gratefully, and he gave me breaks to let me breathe before pushing his dick back into my mouth.

His groans deepened, and he moved his dick away from me, not wanting to cum. "Get back on the bed, the way you were before, my Queen."

Giddy with pleasure, I almost jumped back onto the bed, positioning myself on my knees and spreading my thighs for him. Waiting for him again, this time with the knowledge that I was about to receive the pleasure of his cock.

"Good girl," he said, and I heard the crinkle of what sounded like a condom packet opening. He approached me from behind again, his body pressed up against mine. He pushed down on my ass to lower my hips to the perfect level, and then I could feel the head of his cock positioned at the opening of my pussy.

He reached in front of me and covered my mouth with his hand, muffling my moans of relief as he slipped easily into my wetness. I nearly blacked out with pleasure, and he'd only just penetrated me.

He worked me slowly, his thrusts deep and purposeful. The curve of his cock rubbed perfectly against my hot spots, massaging my walls with every inch of himself. I was so close to climax again, but I didn't want to beg and risk him depriving me of his cock, so I didn't dare speak a word.

His hand released my mouth and roamed every inch of my body, delivering sharp and authoritative smacks to my ass and thighs. Every time he slapped me, all of the muscles in my body stiffened, and my pussy gripped his cock more firmly. He groaned and started moving a bit faster and harder within me, driving me even closer to bursting.

Smack, thrust, smack, thrust... I got lost in the rhythm, giving myself over to him and his control, letting him fuck me however he wanted. Knowing he was using my body for his pleasure, that he'd claimed my pussy as his, fulfilled me in ways that his cock alone couldn't.

He lowered his head to my ear so I could hear his deep voice as he possessed me. "You belong to me, you little slut. I own you. And I'm going to take whatever I want from you." His words caressed my thoughts while his dick rubbed my G-spot and his hands soothed the reddened cheeks of my abused rear. "All of your little holes belong to me. Your mouth. Your juicy cunt. That *ass*..."

I arched my hips up to him teasingly, and he rewarded me with more smacks to my cheeks, fucking me deeper, faster, harder. My thighs shook under the force of it, trying to withstand the pleasure that threatened to consume us both.

Before I could cum without permission, he withdrew his cock from me. That empty, disappointed feeling crept over me. My pussy swelled with painful need, my skin thirsting for his touch again.

He lowered his mouth to my pussy and licked up the mess of juices that flowed down my inner thighs. Delivering tough smacks to my ass, he consumed me tirelessly, sucking on my clit and dipping his tongue into my cunt. He spit my juices back over my little asshole, and it tickled as the fluids seeped between my thighs. His tongue dipped into my ass, stretching my tight hole apart, as though trying to prepare me for further abuse. I moaned, balling my fists in the comforter, almost unconscious with bliss as his hot tongue danced over my sensitive, puckered opening.

"Get up." His voice was a growl, preparing me for the gruffness that was sure to follow. His fingers entwined in my long mane, secured at the root, and dragged me up by the hair until my high-heeled feet were back on the carpet. His touch was rough as I would expect from a dominant, but also affectionate and loving.

He brought us over to the wall of windows, the city lights streaming in. I hoped people could see us in our rapture. I wanted everyone to see what a real slut looked like, what a real dominant looked like.

Landon spun me around to face him, pressing my bare back up against the cool window with my breasts crushed against his chest. He leaned down and kissed me again, tasting of my pussy.

I moaned against his lips, his hands grabbing my ass and lifting me up in midair, an easy feat with my petite frame. My thighs spread and my legs wrapped around his waist, his cock pushing into me again. I gripped onto his strong shoulders for balance.

As he filled me, his hand found its way back around my neck. He pulled his mouth from mine, holding my gaze as his fingers began to squeeze my sensitive throat, making me lightheaded.

"Don't you dare cum yet. You don't have my permission," he warned me in a gruff voice, but his tone only made me juice more for him.

He fucked me like that, filling me while dizzying me with his sensual asphyxiation. My pussy pounded at first, and then my racing heartbeat began to slow. My muscles relaxed, my fingers releasing their grip on his back — giving myself over to him. I bit my lip to prevent myself from exploding with ecstasy.

Lightheaded, it was impossible to tell where his sensual punishment ended and my reward began. They were one and the same. I struggled to control myself for him as I nearly drowned in the pleasure he gave me.

And then he released my throat, pulling his cock out of me. I gasped as a rush of oxygen flooded my lungs, coursing through my body and pounding through me with each heartbeat. He carried me over to the bed and lay me down on my back. When I looked down between us, my inner thighs and his package shone with my juices. I'd drenched us both.

He kissed me tenderly, his hands traveling over my breasts and tweaking my nipples. I groaned at his touch, melting into the mattress.

"Flip over, my little slut. Show me that ass."

"Mmm... yes, Sir!" I rolled over onto my belly, my breasts pressed against the mattress, my face in the same pillow as before.

He spread my thighs apart, spitting on my asshole. As his saliva dripped down to my pussy, his tongue dipped into my quivering cunt again. He spread my juices back to my ass with his tongue, and his experienced finger teased my asshole. I wanted him to invade me and stretch me apart.

Straddling my legs, he ran his hands over my back and my ass. His experienced thumb teased my asshole while slapping his cock against my ass cheeks and my pussy lips, tormenting me. His finger slid into my ass, using his saliva and my juices as lubricant to ease his way in. My tight ass gripped him, then released slowly as I began to relax around his finger.

I wasn't expecting him to slide his cock into my pussy again, but he glided into my cunt in one wet stroke. His finger pumped into my ass, spitting whenever needed, until he'd worked himself as deeply as he could. My moans were drowned out by the pillow I screamed into as he filled up both of my little holes.

He thrust his cock deep into my pussy, fucking me roughly until I thought I would cry with the pleasure of it. Slowly withdrawing his finger from my ass, he spit into my gaping hole, lubing it up more. His saliva tickled as he drooled into my ass.

"Are you ready for me?" His cock slid out of my pussy, then pressed up against my even tighter orifice, getting ready to penetrate my slicked-up hole.

"Yes, Sir," I moaned, about to burst with anticipation.

"Your ass is mine." He pushed his dick inside me to claim my body.

I moaned as he entered me, gradually fitting the entirety himself into me. The thickness of his cock made me feel like I was being split open, but I knew that I could handle him. Even in his aggression with me, he was gentle. My muscles relaxed and I opened myself for him as much as I could.

As he stretched me out, his hand reached in front of me, slipping his fingertips over my sensitive clit. I squirmed, heat flooding my core, so ready to spill over with pleasure.

"Your pussy belongs to me," he said, sliding two of his fingers into my pussy. I groaned, grateful at the unexpected fullness inside of me. His cock and hand moved at the same rhythm within their respective holes, working me up even more.

My pussy and ass squeezed around him, ready to explode. I was about to beg him for permission when he commanded, "Cum for me, my little slut."

I erupted, abandoning myself to him and the pleasure he allowed me to feel. My body quaked and my knees buckled, but he held me up so he could keep fucking me at the same angle. He anchored my hips to him as I clenched his dick and his fingers within me.

When my trembling subsided, he softened and became tender with me. He eased his grasp on me, not moving inside of me. His hot breath caressed the nape of my neck, my ear. "Good girl," he said, stroking my hair and wrapping his strong arms around me as I nearly dissolved into tears at the intensity of it all. *Good girl.*

His fingers slid out of my pussy, and he brought them to his mouth to taste me, purring with delight. I could feel his cock twitching inside of my ass, but he remained patient and focused on my body.

"Are you ready for more?" he murmured in my ear. "Or do you want to take a break?"

"More, please, Sir," I groaned into the pillow. I didn't want this to end. I wanted him to use me for his pleasure.

He glided into me with excruciating slowness, sliding his hands over the curves of my ass and hips. His arm slipped around my midsection, holding me tight, while his other hand found my clit again. My juices drooled out of my swollen pussy, all over his hand, my thighs and his balls as he fucked me. In my heightened state, every movement of his cock in my ass and his fingertips over my clit was blissful. Another orgasm lurked in wait, threatening to crash over me soon.

My muscles began to tense, my ass tightening around his dick. This spurred him to pump harder and faster into me, bringing me even closer to the brink. His fingers slid back into my soaked pussy, working on my G-spot. As he built up the pressure between my thighs, loud moans filled the room, and I barely recognized them coming from me.

"You're mine." His free hand curled around my throat possessively, but not squeezing this time. "You ready to cum for me again?"

"Yes, Sir," I whimpered, my eyes rolling to the back of my head as I began squirting all over the place. Fluids released from within me, relieving me of the pressure in my core. As my breathing slowed, I realized that my thighs and the comforter below me were drenched. And he hadn't stopped fucking me.

"Good girl," he said with affection, his own breathing coming faster now. His cock was throbbing within my ass, and I knew he was about to cum. "Are you ready for your reward, my Queen?"

"Yes, please, Sir," I begged him, wanting to be covered in his cum.

"Turn over," he commanded, pulling his cock out of my ass as I flipped onto my back. He slipped off the condom, stroking his bare cock, his face beautifully ecstatic. Hot cum spurted out of his dick and dripped all over my breasts and belly, onto my thighs.

I rubbed my hands over the mess, smoothing his cum over my body, covering myself in his warm, slick juices. I leaned up to catch the last drops of cum still at the tip of his cock, sucking his still-swollen dick into my mouth to clean him. He tasted so good to me. My tongue lapped up my juices from his balls until he gently pushed me away, too sensitive to continue.

When I was done, I looked up at him, lying back with my legs spread, body covered in his cum. "Thank you, Sir," I said, licking my lips with a smile.

"Thank *you*, my Queen." He leaned down and kissed me on the mouth with great reverence, then took me by the hand, mischief still in his eyes.

"Let's get cleaned up," he said, leading me to the shower. "And then I'm going to introduce you to my tools."

RELEASE

There I was, in the middle of Le Jardin d'Eden, a naturist resort, bent over with my ass and pussy exposed, wearing only my high heels.

My Dominant stood behind me with a whip in his hand. Each crack of the whip drew even more voyeurs around us. In this French haven of Eden in Cap d'Agde, we fetishists were in excellent company. Our wildest kinks could be fulfilled.

He was clothed, his deeply tanned skin covered up... for now. Authoritative in his black suit and ivory shirt, he made me feel even more like a toy he was showing off to the crowd. And I loved it.

Being put on display like this satisfied my exhibitionism, fulfilling my desire to perform, my need to be debased.

Eden's hedonistic playground allowed me to explore the depth of my perversions while indulging my darkest fantasies. My idea of paradise.

This impromptu public humiliation session had been my idea. I'd explicitly asked — no, begged — my Dom to play with me this way. He'd only agreed because I'd been so good for him lately and I deserved a reward.

As I gripped the white painted cement partition between the pool and the bar area, the setting sun cast a soft pink glow on us. The perfect spotlight for this slutty, spontaneous sex show.

Sir's blows to my ass started coming a bit faster now and I looked up at the crowd forming around me. I could see a mixture of emotion on people's faces: excitement, curiosity, desire. It was fairly obvious that my domination session had just begun, because my pale ass bore marks that were only a light shade of pink instead of an angry red.

Some of them were used to witnessing carnal spectacles such as this or had been on the receiving end of someone else's sadistic attentions. They understood the pleasure I was experiencing, and their eyes burned with envy, watching me bask in the freedom of my submissiveness.

Other voyeurs were new to the naturist village and were watching a woman get blissfully degraded for the first time. They cringed each time the leather implement came down hard on my ass. One woman said, "I could never do that. It looks so painful." I wanted to tell her it was some of the most exquisite, erotic pain I'd ever experienced, but the next blow to my ass made my cry out instead.

I didn't dare look behind me at my Dom. He had forbidden that. I only had the view of people approaching me from the front to get a closer glimpse at the action. And among these curious voyeurs was a sexy, fully naked couple. I'd seen them around these last dew days, remarking at their beauty, but I hadn't yet introduced myself.

Well, I was sure making one hell of a first impression.

These dark-haired strangers strode towards us confidently with firm, sun-kissed flesh and a provocative look in their eyes. The woman was stunning and curvaceous. Her full lips had a devilish smile on them. Her smooth skin called out to be touched and tasted, all the way from her graceful neck to the neat triangle of hair between her thighs.

Her partner's attractiveness nearly equaled hers. His tall, toned physique made me want to wrap my entire body around him. His cock was impressively large, hard and ready, his balls shaved and tight against his body. But even his beauty could not rival his female partner's raw, goddess-like presence.

My pussy throbbed as these sexy strangers ravaged me with their eyes. As I withstood blows to my ass, I gave them a smile, nodding my head slightly towards them. An invitation for them to approach.

I craved their hands all over me, exploring every inch of my bare flesh. But my Dom was in charge of me and my body... of what would or would not be done to it. He knew my rules and my limits. He also hadn't let me cum since yesterday and I was impatient for release.

The gorgeous duo stepped closer to me, looking behind me

towards my Dom. He stopped whipping me for a moment, pulling me up by my hair so that I was standing up straight. His arm wrapped around my midsection, pinning me closer to him, extremely territorial and protective.

"I'm Dahlia, and this is Marc," the woman told my Dom, pointing to her male companion. The couple smiled down at me.

"I'm Javier. Her name is Zoe, but you can call her slut," said Sir, slapping my ass for emphasis. I gasped and my muscles tensed before settling back into my submissive position.

"May we play with her?" Dahlia asked Sir.

"Yes, you may. She likes being public property. Don't you, my little whore?" His voice was loud enough so everyone in the crowd could hear. He reached in front of me and slipped his hand between my thighs, burying his fingers in my wet pussy. Reminding me that I belonged to him.

I gasped, my pussy clenching around his fingers. "Yes, Sir," I moaned, faltering slightly in my high heels.

Dahlia smiled, licking her lips as she saw Sir's fingers slide out of me, glistening with my juices. He brought them to my mouth, and I thirstily cleaned them from his hand. Marc's cock jumped as he watched my tongue snake out of my mouth to lick my lips.

Suddenly, Sir smacked my ass with his hand, just once, but firmly. My ass cheeks stung slightly where he'd hit me, and my clit trembled even more.

"Bend over and spread your legs for me. Show Dahlia and Marc what they get to play with." He turned to the naked couple, talking about me as though I wasn't there. "You can do anything you want to her. She loves being used." My heart raced, my body tingling to be touched and pleasured.

Sir slapped my ass, making me cry out. "I told you to bend over. If you don't listen to me, I'm going to punish you for it."

I complied, getting back into my submissive position with haste. "I'm sorry, Sir," I apologized. He slapped my ass in reply, then grabbed and massaged the stinging cheek. I knew from experience that this was his way of saying he'd forgiven me, but that I'd better watch myself — he wouldn't be so nice the next time I defied him.

As Sir resumed his flogging, I held on to the wall for balance. He was working me faster so there was less time between his blows. He knew I could take it — and that I could take much more. He was just warming me up.

Dahlia and Marc stood in front of me, smiling as they watched. She glanced up at her tall partner, and he pulled her close to him, his hard cock pinned against her lower belly. They shared a long, deep kiss, connecting with each other before they started playing with me. I longed to share their intense chemistry with them. My cunt contracted, impatient for them to touch me.

Whimpers escaped my lips as Sir took a break from flogging me, massaging my ass and running his warm hands over my tender flesh. My eyes fluttered shut for a moment, savoring the affection in his touch. When I opened them again, Dahlia and Marc had pulled themselves apart. She came up to me in front while Marc approached from the other side. A shiver ran up my spine. I didn't know what to expect and I was powerless to stop it. My pussy drooled down my thigh, the pressure inside me building without having been touched yet.

Dahlia reached out with her long fingers and played with my hair, watching Sir soothe my flesh. Her succulent mouth was so close to mine that her breath tickled my lips. Her rich caramel eyes stared into me, invading me in a way no physical touch could. From her vantage point, she could see whatever my Dom was preparing to do to me and would surely witness all of my facial expressions as I endured his rough attentions.

Dahlia's voluptuous body was in full view in front of me, with her luscious, heaving breasts, and her flawless, evenly tanned skin. I fought against reaching forward and touching her, wanting to run my fingers over her sensitive light-brown nipples and capture her lips with mine.

But I didn't dare disobey Sir again, or he might decide to stop playing with me and deny me pleasure.

I tried to relax my muscles, giving control to the three of them. But I was too excited to be at the center of all this attention, and both my mind and body thrummed.

Smack. The familiar sting of Sir's favorite leather flogger wasn't as loud as my cry when his tool came down on my ass again.

Marc ran his hands over my back, bending slightly so he could reach my breasts. As he pinched my nipples, his voice deep and seductive in my ear. "I love seeing you on display. I want to fuck your throat while you're helpless like this in front of everyone." My pussy twitched at the thought of being used like a sex toy by this decadent man. "Would you like that, slut?"

"Yes," I managed to reply through my moans of pleasure and pain as Sir flogged me again and again. All while Dahlia stood in front of me, running her fingers over my neck and down to my chest, rolling my hard nipples between her fingertips. She buried her fingers in my hair, her light floral scent intoxicating me as her warm lips pressed against mine. I moaned against her lips, tasting the sweetness of her mouth. My pussy ached to feel her tongue move that way over my slick little folds.

Marc squeezed my breasts in his hands, biting my ear. He snuck behind me to talk to Sir, who set his whip down on the small of my back. The leather tails trailed freely between the crack of my ass and my swollen lips, teasing and tickling me.

I was too heady with Dahlia's deep kisses to listen to Marc talk to Sir about what he wanted to do with me, but I did hear Sir reply, "Go right ahead."

Someone's hand slipped between my thighs, cupping my wet sex in their palm, then slapped my pussy. I moaned, reveling in not knowing which man was being rough with me.

"Dahlia," Marc said from behind me, "sit up on the wall. I want to watch this little slut pleasure you." He slapped my pussy lips, the sting of it making me inhale sharply. More blood rushed to my clit, my desire heightening.

Dahlia gave me one last kiss, biting my bottom lip playfully before positioning herself in front of me. She sat up on the partition, spreading her legs and exposing her glistening pink sex to me without an ounce of shyness. My mouth watered, dying to taste this voluptuous goddess. More smacks came down on my pussy, making me squirm to make more contact with the hand delivering my pleasure.

"Devour her pussy, slut," Sir commanded me, "but don't use your hands." He pinned my arms behind my back with one hand, so I didn't have the luxury of even trying to defy him.

His other hand guided my head between Dahlia's thighs. I inhaled her fragrant pussy, looking up at her and smiling, preparing myself to taste her. She gazed down at me reverently, brushing my hair from my eyes.

Marc came up to Dahlia, kissing her neck and smoothing his hands over her thighs and the back of my head. Behind me, Sir retrieved his flogger from the small of my back and placed it on the wall next to Dahlia.

I looked up at the vixen above me while my tongue slid over her clit. She tasted as good as she smelled, and I buried my tongue inside her hole to better savor her. Dahlia's eyes rolled back in pleasure and her hand tangled in my hair, pulling me even closer to her cunt.

Still holding my wrists behind my back with one hand, Sir

slipped his free fingers between my legs, pinching my clit before penetrating my pussy again. He slid inside my tightness, my body tensing and struggling not to explode. He spread my juices from my dripping hole and around my clit, working me into a feverish state.

I moaned against Dahlia's pussy, sucking her clit into my mouth and rolling the tip of my tongue around the swollen nub. Her hips pushed towards my face, and if my hands had been free, I would have grabbed her and pulled her even closer to me.

Marc's hands slid over my back and down to my ass cheeks, which were still stinging a bit, pinching and releasing my bare flesh. Sir's fingers penetrated me roughly, mercilessly playing with my G-spot. The pressure built between my legs, reminding me how much he was depriving me of my much-needed release.

"I want to watch you suck Marc's cock," Sir said, and I gave a few final licks to Dahlia's pussy, kissing her clit before lifting my head to smile at her.

She grabbed my face and pulled me up to kiss her, tasting herself on my tongue. She moaned against my mouth. When she released me, Marc had settled into position next to her, his big cock in my face. I licked my lips, ready to swallow him whole.

"Suck it like the cock-hungry slut you are, slave," Sir told me, my belly twisting in desire. His hand, now totally wet with my pussy juices, rubbed my sensitive asshole. I longed to feel him in my ass and frustration twisted between my legs.

Marc's cock taunted me with his size and thickness. I couldn't reach out and grasp his shaft in my hands because my arms were still restricted. I opened my mouth to slide him inside, rolling my tongue over his hard head. He groaned deeply as he pushed himself into my mouth, surprised to discover I could fit the entirety of him into my throat. His hips moved back and forth, his hand gripping onto the back of my head as he started face-fucking me.

I lost myself in the roughness of his cock sliding in and out of my lips, the hypnotic rhythm of his thrusts to the back of my throat. I glanced up at Dahlia, who was playing with her pussy as she watched us. Behind me, there was a rustling of what sounded like Sir removing the belt of his pants with his free hand, his other hand still grasping my wrists behind me. My ass and pussy shuddered in delightful uncertainty.

As I sucked Marc, he took Dahlia's perfect nipples into his mouth, groaning and burying his face in her ample chest. He fucked my throat faster, and this time he went so fast and deep that I began to choke on his cock. He withdrew his dick from my lips once I started to cough and gag, giving me the chance to spit on his thickness and get him even wetter and sloppier before taking him into my mouth again.

Just as I was missing Sir's touch, his hands smoothed over my ass, dipping his fingers between my pussy lips and spreading my juices over my asshole again. My holes seethed with heat, inviting my partners to invade them with their hands, tongues and cocks. Desperately trying to penetrate myself on Master's fingers, my hips began to move backwards.

He slapped my ass hard, exerting his dominance over me. "Don't you move, you little slut." He held my hips in place and spit down the crack of my ass, massaging my asshole with his saliva until he could easily slip his thumb inside.

I gasped as Sir filled my ass with his finger, teasing me inside, and making me even more conscious of how empty my pussy was. My entire core throbbed with restlessness, but I knew Master enjoyed prolonging my torment, making me wait until I'd been used to his satisfaction.

Marc stroked his cock in front of me, and I ached to feel him inside my cunt, spreading me open. "Switch between us," he told me, pulling my head back down to Dahlia's pussy. My tongue slid into her, tasting her honey again. I moaned appreciatively as I slurped up her juices, licking them as they ran down from her pussy to her ass.

Dahlia's hand joined Marc's on his shaft as they jerked him together, lubricated with my saliva. I kept licking her until Marc grabbed my hair and pulled my head back to his cock. His hand played with Dahlia's pussy when my mouth was busy sucking his dick.

My hunger for them intensified, insatiable as I switched back and forth between them. Meanwhile, Sir's finger was deep in my tight ass, and my pussy was drooling down my inner thighs. I was so close to my peak that I was certain a single touch to my swollen clit would make me explode.

The four of us remained connected through touching me, like a human chain of ecstasy. My nerve endings were extra responsive, pleasure coming from all directions — the sensuous sliding of my mouth and tongue on their sexes, Sir's finger in my ass, Dahlia and Marc's hands pinching my nipples and squeezing my breasts. Having their touch all over my body made me extra conscious of how empty my pussy still was.

My Dom pushed his body up against the back of me, and the twitching of his hard cock against my ass awakened me. He slid his finger out of me, spitting into my hole and down the crack of my ass, getting me ready. Was I finally going to get penetrated? My legs trembled slightly in anticipation, my thighs parting to give him even more access to me.

With his thumb still in my ass, he used his other hand to slap my pussy. His voice was loud and deep as he tortured me with his words. "You don't deserve an orgasm yet. You have to make Dahlia and Marc cum first."

Then I suddenly felt the familiar and welcome invasion of Sir's cock in my ass, and I cried out. He glided into me gradually until he was so deep I could feel his balls against my slick pussy. I was completely helpless as he filled me, moaning between Dahlia's legs as he thrust himself into me. She and Marc were holding my head closer to her, her hips moving on their own. Right as she seemed about to cum, Marc moved my head and made me switch, thrusting his cock into my mouth again.

Marc's long arms allowed him to reach over and slap my ass while Master fucked it. They used my holes as roughly as they desired, fucking me at each end. Dahlia watched us and played with herself as her man slid his cock down my throat, groaning with pleasure. I suppressed the urge to erupt, struggling not to disobey my my Dom. Marc removed himself from my mouth, pushing my face into Dahlia's soaking pussy again.

I was so close to dissolving into spasms of pleasure but I tried to focus on making her cum. My tongue worked faster until I heard her screams and her thighs smothered me. As she shook under my lips, I lapped up her juices and delighted in her sweet taste, which only made my pussy throb harder for release.

Sir fucked my ass faster, deeper. I switched back to Marc, who grabbed my hair and fucked my throat again as he sought his own release. And as he was ready to climax, Sir warned me, "You'd better swallow and not spill a single drop of his cum, or you'll be licking it off the ground."

But he made it even more challenging for me to obey by fucking me so hard that I was moving and shaking under his power, my moans muffled by Marc's dick in my mouth and the choking sounds coming from my throat.

When Marc burst, I sucked him into my throat, making sure to clean him up completely with my tongue so as not to waste his sweet fluids. I knew to do otherwise would mean disappointing Sir.

I slipped Marc's cock out of my mouth, which was still slightly hard and glistening with my saliva. I licked my lips, looking up at him gratefully. "You really are a slut, aren't you?" Marc asked rhetorically, his eyes still glazed over after his orgasm. Sir moved inside my ass a bit slower, giving me a moment to breathe.

Dahlia hopped off the wall, leaning down to kiss me and taste her man's juices on my tongue. "Delicious," she told me, sucking on my bottom lip. I smiled at her, my entire body shuddering with the need to climax. "Such a satisfied smile," she noted.

"Oh really? She's smiling?" Sir sounded disappointed. He grabbed my hair, pulling my head back to him so that I was standing up straight. He pushed his cock as deeply inside my ass as possible, starting to thrust into me again. My pussy quivered, so ready to cum. "Do I need to remind you again that this was all for my pleasure, not yours?" I felt his cock harden inside my ass even more as he said this.

He pushed me down so that I was bending over again, my hands now free to grab onto Marc's strong legs as he stood in front of me. Sir seized my ass in his hands as he fucked me faster, harder, deeper. Marc pressed my face into his hard chest, holding me for balance while Master used my ass for his pleasure.

Incredibly, I felt Sir explode inside me, rewarding me with his own orgasm. He'd never cum inside me before. The tickle of his juices inside my ass remained even after he pulled out of me, filling me with satisfaction as drops of his cum trickled out of my ass and down to my pussy and thighs. He might not have realized it, but his release gave me more pleasure than my own orgasm ever could.

As applause began, I looked up and realized there was still a crowd of people around us. Everyone had seemed to disappear when I was in my erotic trance, but now dozens of naked guests were applauding our performance. A deep feeling of gratification filled me, so many of my needs sated, even while my pussy was breathing fire and threatening to consume all in her path.

Dahlia moved behind me, getting onto her knees to lick the liquids trickling down my trembling legs, a combination of Sir's cum and my juices. She briefly licked my clit, sending pleasure shooting through my body as I pushed my hips closer to her face.

Knowing I was close to orgasm, Sir pulled me away from her, not wanting me to cum yet. He held me back against his chest as he helped Dahlia to her feet.

"Thank you," she said, kissing me on the lips again. I tasted Sir's and my own sweetness in her mouth. His hot cum continued to drip out of my ass and down my thighs as Marc kissed me next, smiling at me.

"Are you and Marc here for a few more days?" Sir asked, and she nodded in reply. "Then we'll all have the chance to play together again." I could hear him grin, even though I couldn't see him.

"We can't wait," Dahlia replied, waiting there with Marc as the rest of the crowd continued watching. Sir grabbed my hair again and turned me towards him. He saw right away that I couldn't stop myself from smirking.

"Well, look who's smug," he said, an amused smile on his lips. "I'm going to have to teach you a lesson, you little slut. Not only am I going to deprive you of your orgasm, but I'm going to make you walk all around the resort to our room — the long way — all while my cum leaks out of your ass."

My heart raced. This was exactly the kind of degradation I wanted, and he knew it. My clit throbbed even harder than before.

"Clearly, I need to remind you and everyone here that you're my filthy slut." He grabbed his flogger from where he'd set it down on the wall earlier and twirled the tails between his fingers.

He smacked my thigh with the leather. "Now start walking."

I obeyed, weaving my way through the crowd of shocked onlookers as Sir followed behind me, flogging my sore ass every few steps I took.

I tried to keep my smile reserved and hidden, inwardly victorious that he'd chosen to release himself in me. I took pride in having fulfilled my purpose as his submissive, at least for the time being...

SUCCUBUS

The stranger sleeps soundly in his bed as I enter the dark room with predatory slowness. The window is slightly open and the sheer curtains rustle with the warm night's breeze. I wait, standing by his bedside, watching this vulnerable man dream.

A few strands of dark hair cover his eyes, his powerful chest rising and falling as he breathes steadily. The mortal's erection is barely concealed by the thin sheet that covers his bottom half. His muscular form reveals he's in excellent physical shape, which is why he's been chosen; the strength of his seed is more valuable to Lucifer. And I've been sent here to procure this mortal's energy, to fulfill my task as a succubus.

My demon body can shapeshift into any form I choose. I can invade humans' dreams and manipulate them any way I want, priming them for seduction. Whatever appearance they crave the most, whatever body parts they want to be pleasured with — I can satisfy their filthy desires and do things they lust for but would never dare confess wanting to anyone else.

Perching myself at the edge of my prey's bed, I use my abilities to suspend his experience of time; he thinks he's still in a dream. His human eyes cannot discern my demon wings. I've shifted into my succubus form, appearing to him as a confident, seductive, and voluptuous female. An embodiment of what I know this man craves the most.

Many of the myths and stories about demons are false; humans visited by a succubus or an incubus are not helpless victims. Humans want us. They *need* us. They seek us out in their dreams, beckoning to be taken, desiring to be ravaged. And we demons oblige them. All we ask for in return is their powerful sperm or a temporary space within their womb. Small prices to pay for the fulfillment of their deepest fantasies.

Watching this human sleep fills me with physical desire, the heat of my demonic need rising from within the depths of my belly and spreading throughout my body. I wait patiently. I have no need to touch him before he touches me. His seed will be infinitely more valuable if he willingly lets me take it from him. If he were to struggle, it would weaken him. And I need every ounce of his energy.

The breeze from the window brushes the ends of my long red hair against this mortal's naked flesh. He stirs gently. As his eyes slowly open, he sees me sitting next to him. His eyes widen, but he's not afraid.

I don't usually connect with my prey before ravaging them, but I'm drawn to this man, to his sculpted body and immaculate milky skin. I've been working tirelessly for Lucifer. Haven't I earned the chance to indulge my desires and experience pleasure of my own, even if just for a few moments?

I won't have time to linger here once I acquire this man's sperm. I'll have to quickly move on to my next human, albeit one with a womb this time. I'll transform into an irresistible incubus to impregnate them with this mortal's fresh seed, which I've infused with my demonic power. Helping Lucifer create an army of human-demon hybrids is challenging but crucial, especially since we're on the cusp of the Apocalypse.

And I'm a very necessary evil.

The man gazes up at me with wonder, propping himself up on one strong arm to get a better look at me. The room is bathed in darkness, save for a sliver of white moonlight poking through the curtains. He looks into my black eyes, the infinite depths inviting him in. His yielding to me is imminent. Desire floods between my thighs, aroused by my own power over him.

After I drain him of his vitality, I'll leave him temporarily weakened. Though it would be easy to kill him, doing so would just be a waste of a perfectly strong human source. When he regains his former strength in a few days or weeks, I'll return as a succubus to capture more of his potent life source.

Reaching for me, my prey pulls the silky locks of my crimson hair back from my body to expose my large, bare breasts. He gazes at me with yearning as he runs his hand from my hair to my cheek, his fingertips brushing against my full lips. Need builds and aches throughout my core. Is it so wrong to take pleasure in my hellish work?

We don't speak. Words are unnecessary. This man believes this is all in his imagination, a vivid dream. And I allow him to think this. My psychological spell over him thrills me even more, my skin tingling as I gain more control over him, increasing his desire to yield to me.

I lean down and cover his waiting lips with mine, breathing in his essence as he sighs into my mouth. His breath invigorates me, my body humming with his energy. His large hands spread over my back as I slowly move to straddle him. He brushes his rough palms against my delicate human flesh, increasing my hunger.

His dick throbs between my thighs, the thin sheet still between our bodies. As his tongue slides over mine and his body presses up against me, skin on skin, I'm empowered by his physical strength. I allow him to show me just how masterful he can be.

Our kisses intensify as he twists my hair back with one hand to expose my collarbone, sucking and biting my neck, trailing his mouth down to capture my hard nipple between his lips. I moan as the incredible sensation makes my sex liquefy, soaking through the sheet between us.

He sits up, sliding his strong arms around me and pulling me down to the mattress. I let him roughly push my back on the bed, his hands pinning my wrists above my head. This position would make anyone else feel helpless. Anyone but a demon.

The man covers my neck with his warm mouth and tongue, ravenous in his appetite for me. His breath tickles my sensitive skin, and I close my eyes as his mouth trails down my breasts and my soft belly. He dips his tongue into my navel briefly before sliding between my nether lips. My scent intoxicates him — just another one of my succubus tricks — and draws him in, his mouth closing over the fragrant wetness of my pussy.

He groans into my most tender flesh as he devours me, and I lay back and luxuriate in his skilled attentions. Most humans are not this adept at the sexual arts, so I'm delighted to let him pleasure me.

The more he tastes me, the more my fluids enter his system, making him drunker with lust. My dark red demon likeness is reflected in his eyes, surrounded by fire. The surest sign that I've invaded him, permeating him with the same inferno that burns me from within. Priming him to be drained. He's completely mine for the taking. I lick my lips in anticipation, craving his potent fluids.

That's when I notice a dark shadow behind this man. The one of Lucifer, my one and only overlord. My human can't see him — Lucifer has chosen not to reveal himself to this man. I alone can feast my eyes on the Devil.

Red-fleshed, horned, and monstrously large, but with human body parts… that's how Lucifer presents himself to me tonight. He's a cross between his devilish self and the human form he prefers to take when he visits Earth. The body of a man in peak condition, he's naked and fully erect in his regal magnificence. Every inch of his glory is encased in crimson skin, still slightly steaming from his recent ascent from Hell. I long to feel the heat of home on Lucifer's flesh.

I shiver with fear as he stares at us, my belly twisting with uncertainty. He's never joined me on any of my quests. Lucifer doesn't waste his time — he is quite busy ruling The Underworld. His being here with me now must be important to him. Confusion and excitement rise within me at Lucifer's proximity. Has he come to witness me harvesting this man's life source for him, like a devilish voyeur?

An evil smile haunts Lucifer's lips, his eyes glowing a hotter red as he watches the man worshiping me. He doesn't just see me — he sees *through* me to my demonic core. For the first time ever on one of these exploits, I feel nearly defenseless in the presence of a being greater than I.

Lucifer watching this human savoring my body awakens the animal within me. Only he can see the flames that rise within my human and I the more our ecstasy mounts. The man's tongue slides over my swollen clit, licking and sucking on the sensitive pink nub. I tighten my legs around his shoulders as a quivering climax overtakes me. I growl as energy explodes throughout my body.

When my eyes open again, Lucifer is staring at me with fire in his eyes, still across the room. I try to ignore him, pushing the man from my thighs and onto his back. His mortal body is a temple, a true masterpiece, above and beyond any other human form I've conquered so far. My hands run all over his sculpted torso as I hover over him, tasting myself on his lips, sucking my juices off his tongue. I want Lucifer to watch me and see the evil things I'm capable of.

Repositioning my body, I straddle the man's face backwards, facing his manhood, with Lucifer in my line of sight. My prey groans with pleasure into my wet sex, his tongue finding my most sensitive spots again.

Lucifer's eyes burn into me as I lower my mouth to the human's thick, throbbing cock. His life source begins to flow through me as I suck some of his pre-cum from him. His juice combines with my saliva, burning a welcoming fire as it travels down my throat and into my belly, where it surges within me. Fortifying me.

I look up at Lucifer with the man's flesh between my lips, sliding my mouth down to fully encase him in my throat. Lucifer approaches us with a sinful grin, seating himself on the bed next to my human. I'm drowning the man in the immortal juices between my legs. My core swells with need, and Lucifer's eyes burn brighter as he watches us. A flash of rivalry reveals itself in his stare. Is he jealous of my human?

Lucifer lowers himself to my level, his face a few inches from mine. My eyes don't waver from his as my lips slide around this human's sizable flesh. The man can't see anything that's happening, not just because I'm practically suffocating him with my thighs, but because Lucifer does not allow himself to appear to this human.

I'm privileged to be in Lucifer's presence here on Earth — an honor few demons have ever enjoyed. His strong hand holds my hair back and roughly control the movements of my head as I take this man's cock into my throat. I have no need to breathe; I could go on sucking this man forever without coming up for air.

Lucifer's diabolical gaze stirs my pussy as I consume this man, focusing on each stroke of my tongue as his ultimate release nears.

Some of the human's carnal energy passes through the roots of my hair down to the ends, the flames spreading up and through Lucifer's hands and body. His crimson flesh begins to shine, the dark horns on his head growing upward to give him a more threatening presence. Fear flickers through me while my immortal blood boils with unprecedented need. In all my years, I have never been so tempted to ravage any being this much.

Lucifer can read my thoughts and knows that he's evoked something greedy in me. And he's pleased by that knowledge. His desire is evident in the size of his erection, growing a deeper red the harder he becomes.

Yet my hunger defeats my discomfort at being so exposed in front of the Devil himself. This human is not enough for me. My power is close to its peak, and I still want more.

With my back to the human, I drag my hips down his body until his cock is nestled between my thighs. Lucifer's fiery eyes burn brighter as he watches me grab the human's dick in my hand, sliding it over my pussy lips, teasing all of us. Lucifer's enormous hand moves from my hair to my neck, the searing imprint of his fingers branding my flesh as his property. I welcome the heat.

Impaling myself upon this man's shaft, I enclose him within my scorching tightness. We both moan as I fill myself with his dick, his pulse beating within my body, heightening my pleasure. Lucifer's hand clenches around my throat, using my body as the medium for which the power flows through himself. His massive appetite fuels me even more. I groan gruffly as I fuck my human, my hips grinding into his to get him as deeply inside me as possible.

Without releasing his grip on my neck, Lucifer rises from the bed and stands in front of me. His enormous red dick is in my face, more imposing than when I first saw him watching my tryst. Every part of him seems to have grown since he began to touch me. He smiles evilly, looking down at me as I ride the man. I'm compelled to take Lucifer's immense cock into my hands, the intensity of his energy vibrating through his entire body to my fingertips. I look up into Lucifer's red eyes and he watches me take him into my mouth.

The instant my lips wrap around Lucifer's dick, red light bursts in my mind. A thousand hells rage within me, more ferociously than I've ever experienced before. My body and all of my orifices are tools for stealing a human's energy. The thought that Lucifer is also sharing some of his own energy with me infuses me with even more power.

I feast on Lucifer's enormous cock, worshiping him voraciously with my mouth. My victim suffers with pleasure beneath me as I move my body faster on him. The man grabs my hips and pushes himself into me from below. His hands are cool against my flaming skin, in contrast with Lucifer's smoldering fingers as he pinches my nipples. Wherever Lucifer touches me, energy passes from his fingertips through my body, and then the vitality flows back through him and into my mouth. His dick trembles on my tongue with the force of it, saturating me with more strength.

Drunk with power, my pussy clenches down hard on the mortal, making him gasp. I savor Lucifer's thickness in my mouth while the man's dick moves inside the fiery pit of my belly. I'm a wet mess at each end, luxuriating in the ecstasy mounting at dizzying speed. The mortal's physical human strength and Lucifer's immortal force consume me as my body seethes in the inferno.

Flames rage through me as I explode with orgasm, groaning on Lucifer's dick as my pussy contracts around my human tool. The ferocity of my climax shoots through my body and into Lucifer. His cock grows bigger in my mouth, feeding off of my growing power.

The tight grasp of Lucifer's fingers around my neck loosens as he spins me on the man's shaft while I'm still on top of him. I'm now facing my prey, whose face bears a blissful expression. He leans up to kiss me, not knowing that the Devil has just been inside my mouth. The secrets between Lucifer and I inflame me as a small amount of my energy passes into the man's mouth. His eyes open wide as the heat invades him, then flows back into my core through his dick.

The man thrusts upwards into me to meet the feverish movements of my hips. He slides into my soaked cunt over and over, reaching up to grab my bouncing breasts. Lucifer is behind me, his enormous hands pulling apart my ass cheeks, exposing all of me to him.

My pussy twitches in anticipation, knowing what ungodly things Lucifer could do to me. His spit drips down into my puckered orifice like a trail of molten lava. He slides in his large thumb, now grown to several times the size of a human's. The tightness of Lucifer's finger and the human's dick fill me, their existences separated only by the thin wall inside me. A burst of fire passes through his fingertip and into my ass. The mortal's dick twitches within me, and he groans and fucks me even harder, the friction of both cocks driving me insane.

But I crave more. Always more. Ever the insatiable beast.

I'm Lucifer's monster. I belong to him. He owns my soul, every fiber of my being. Whether in my natural immortal form or in this transient human embodiment, I exist for him.

He reminds that I'm his possession by removing his thumb and sliding his dick into my waiting hole.

I cry out blissfully as he fills my ass, his impossibly large cock able to fit because my demon form can mold itself to handle anything. Heat shoots through my pussy and diffuses into my human. Grunting, the man thrusts faster, approaching the brink of release. I'm so close to relieving him of his life source.

Lucifer pulls me towards him so that my back is pressed against his hard chest, his hand squeezing one of my breasts as he fucks my tight ass. The size of him makes me feel split apart, but his power surges through me and gives me the strength to endure it. Knowing that I'm using this human for pleasure while being used for Lucifer's satisfaction ignites me even more.

Moaning loudly, I yield to the quickening rhythm of Lucifer's dick in my ass as he meets the tempo of the human fucking me from below. The man rubs my clit with his thumb, flames in his eyes as he plunges into me deeply.

I'm so tight, so filled with cocks, my pussy juices spilling over as this circle of energy spirals out of control. I almost lose consciousness in the tempo of both man and beast within me.

I cum more intensely than before, my nerve endings combusting as I momentarily see Hell. I'm ablaze within the bowels of The Underworld. I'm home. And then my mind returns to this room, with both of these beings still inside me.

Fighting through the aftershock of my ecstasy, I remind myself that I still have a job to do. Lucifer releases his grip on me but doesn't slide himself out of my ass yet, keeping me filled with his massive dick.

I carefully move off my prey and lower my mouth to his cock, licking up my juices that are glistening all over him. My tongue drags over every inch of his throbbing flesh as I suck him into my mouth again. A few drops of his hot precum drip onto my tongue and blaze a trail down my throat, a mere appetizer of what I'm about to gain from him.

I lick and stroke him faster, until the taste of my cunt mixes with that of his seed as it pours onto my tongue and down my throat. I suck every drop of his life source out of him, depleting him.

My body fills with power as I swallow his juices, my ultimate fuel. Extreme heat bubbles up from within me, spreading out to my fingers and toes, almost too much to contain in one vessel.

With Lucifer's cock still buried in my ass, some of the energy floods into his body, and his dick grows bigger inside me.

The human goes limp on the bed, drained, groaning in exhaustion. Such a rare, perfect physical specimen rendered temporarily useless. I lean down to press my mouth to his, breathing a bit of life back into him to speed up his healing. Given the level of intensity I'd experienced from this man, he'll be a valuable source I'll return to drink from again and again.

I turn back to look at Lucifer, gratified by the satisfied look on his face. He wraps a strong arm around my waist, pushing me back down on my knees on the edge of the bed next to my sleeping mortal, and thrusts into me with a viciousness he knows I can take.

Lucifer growls as he erupts inside of me, his liquid fire filling my body, almost melting me from within. Power surges within my body like never before, my thoughts blurring as I see only red. His muscles clench behind me and around me, growing in size. Flames sizzle between us, my human form burning away, rendering my flesh red again as I begin to take on my natural demon form.

When he's filled me with his juices, he pulls back, withdrawing his cock from me. I look at Lucifer with surprise when no fluids trickle out of me — every drop of his juices somehow remains contained within my demon body. A new strength hums inside of me, trembling in my fingertips. The fire has never burned hotter in my core.

Now that the haze of my desire is beginning to dissipate, I understand why Lucifer came here. He needs me to help him fulfill The Prophecy. He wants me to shift into the form of an incubus and use the human's sperm as a conduit for his own seed — to impregnate my next human with the child of Satan.

And he'd chosen *me* — above all his other demons — for the honor of this vital, historic task. *Me.*

A wicked smile curls on his lips as he reads my mind and witnesses my face change with the realization.

Then Lucifer steps back into the shadows and disappears back to the Underworld, leaving me alone to do his evil bidding on Earth.

THE SECRET PASSAGE

The enormous black dildo in the window of the sex shop was what caught my attention.

It wasn't the dildo itself, really. I was more intrigued as to what other surprises a sex shop like this might be selling. After all, I was in the heart of Amsterdam's Red Light District.

I'd always dreamed of traveling to Amsterdam, and now that I'd finished my last year of university undergrad in Journalism, I wanted to assess my future options while going on an adventure. My goal during this European trip was to explore the world and all its possibilities.

To that end, my friend Tristan was the ideal globetrotting companion. We were really good friends and, as a major bonus, the sex between us was absolutely electric. This was the perfect chance for both of us to try new things and test the boundaries of our comfort zones.

So, lured in by the erotic wonders and possibilities that lay within this sex shop, Tristan and I entered.

I was dizzied by the smell of latex and leather immediately after I'd stepped into the shop, but it didn't seem to bother Tristan. A smile spread across his face.

"If you find anything you want to try with me, surprise me." He grabbed my ass and pulled me closer, kissing me deeply. My pulse beat between my thighs, but as quickly as his tongue had entered my mouth, it was gone. When my eyes opened, I saw him gravitating to one side of the shop, looking at the leather whips and chains.

The shopkeeper, who had witnessed this exchange, looked back down at his magazine with a bored look on his face, leaving me to pursue my lewd shopping excursion.

The shop was a labyrinth of dildos, dongs, sex dolls, and pleasure gadgets in every possible shape and size. I eyed each toy, smiling and imagining what Tristan and I could do with it once we brought it back to our hotel room.

My attraction to Tristan hadn't waned since we first met at Aural Fixation, the bar he worked at back home. Our school and work schedules were out of sync, so our trysts were at random times of day and night. We were also casually seeing other people and enjoying our sexual freedom. Since we were both bisexual, we had quite a range of fuck friends… although Tristan was currently my favorite and most open-minded. And my erotic exploration with him had only just begun.

Behind the shop's section with realistic sex dolls, a red neon sign flashed the words "Live Sex Show" with a glowing red arrow leading to a red-curtained area. Deep, sensual music played invitingly, beckoning me closer.

My pulse began to race. I'd heard rumors about these live shows but still wasn't sure what to expect.

With trembling fingers, I pulled back the red velvet curtain. Behind a pane of glass in the middle of the section of private booths, a gorgeous naked woman was pleasuring herself. Arousal ran through me as my eyes roved over her curvaceous body. Hot pink metal nipple clamps adorned her naturally heavy breasts. Her legs were spread wide, and she was thrusting a bright pink dildo into herself, her head thrown back in ecstasy.

Awestruck, I leaned closer until the tip of my nose touched the cool glass of the window. Could she see people through her side of the glass?

The performer answered my unasked question when she turned in my direction, watching me watch her. She winked slyly at me, setting aside her pink dildo on the towel next to her, among several other sex toys and a giant bottle of lube. She selected a big purple dildo with a suction cup at the end and planted it on the floor of the booth. Lubing up the toy, she started lowering herself onto it, sliding it into her ass.

That's when Tristan found me, mouth open in amazement, cheeks flushed with lust.

"You've got to check out this sex swing..." His voice trailed off when he saw the girl penetrating her ass with the dildo. His jaw dropped, eyes widening, a flush creeping over his otherwise pale cheeks. I was sure my face looked just as pink.

I glanced down and saw the bulge at the front of Tristan's pants grow. Impulsively, I reached out and grabbed his dick. He looked at me in surprise, then smiled. "Come here," I said, tugging him by his belt towards the private viewing stalls off to the side. We looked for one that was unoccupied and found one with the curtain open.

Tristan and I squeezed side-by-side into the black leathery seats of the stall, just in time to watch the woman on the other side squirt all over the glass partition that separated us. I was amazed. I never knew a woman could squirt like that. Was it natural? Her squirt dripped down the window, a carnal reminder of what we'd just witnessed — as though she hadn't already left a lasting impression. We could barely see the performer as she waved goodbye, and a blurry figure entered the stage area to quickly clean up the mess. The young man barely looked at us as he sprayed and wiped down the glass in front of us.

As he hurried out of sight, two other people entered the stage area.

This couple was slightly older than us and very attractive. I squirmed in my seat, my panties flooding with my sex as the duo started to touch and play with each other. As she knelt and took his erection into her mouth, I caught myself salivating.

Adrenaline surged through my body, inspiring me. I grabbed Tristan's dick through his pants, stroking his bulge. He groaned and unzipped his jeans to free his erection, tantalizing me with his bare flesh. I leaned over and wrapped my lips around him, watching the couple performing out of the corner of my eye. My mouth moved with the same tempo as the female sucking on her partner.

Pressure built at the apex of my thighs as Tristan's moans intensified. I took his cock as far as it would go down my throat, building up that really thick, sticky saliva. I spit onto his shaft, replacing my mouth with my hand, and sat back down next to him. He reached over to unzip my pants, slipping his hand inside. His fingers teased my wetness as the man lay the woman down on a blanket, sliding into her.

Tristan rubbed my clit with his fingertips while his dick throbbed in my hand. The pressure inside me was mounting quickly, all of my senses on fire. Neither of us could take our eyes off the explicit scene in front of us.

The woman took out a big purple strap-on dildo and slipped the black straps of her harness over her legs. Her male partner got down on all fours and presented his ass to her. She lubed up the dildo and started to slowly enter him. He moaned and arched his back as she reached in front of him, stroking his cock. My clit throbbed painfully, wanting to be played with too, aching for release.

Tristan strummed my clit faster, and my hand sped up its pace on his dick. We moaned, our pleasure in sync with each other. My eyes fluttered shut as I focused only on the rising heat of my pussy and my hand's tightening grip on his dick. My pussy clenched hard as I came, shuddering and dripping my juices all over his fingers.

When I regained my senses and opened my eyes again, Tristan's dick twitched in my hand — he was on the brink of climax. I spit on his cock to get him wetter, and the sound of slick sloppiness filled our small booth.

I looked up to watch the expression on his face turn blissful, glancing briefly at the couple fucking in front of us. Leaning over, I covered him with my mouth again, my tongue on his flesh making him groan deeply. A powerful jet of cum spurted out of his cock to the back of my throat as his hips raised up off the seat with the intensity of it.

Now drained, he slumped back into the seat and leaned his head back against the wall behind us. He looked over at me, laughing, and I started giggling. I couldn't believe what we'd just done and how liberated I felt.

The couple still performing looked towards us with a smile, as the woman continued fucking her partner. Had they heard our outburst?

Tristan gave them the thumbs up, which made me laugh harder. Caught in a hysterical fit, we zipped up our pants quickly, then I grabbed my bag and exited the voyeur booth and the viewing area.

On the other side of the curtain, I leaned against the wall and tried to control myself. Giddiness danced in my stomach and gave me a natural high. I felt indestructible.

Smiling, Tristan pinned me up against the wall, kissing me. I stopped giggling immediately and my lips melted beneath his.

A heady haze crept over my thoughts and stirred my clit again, surprised by the intimacy of this kiss.

When he finally came up for air, I had to lean back against the wall for balance. He smiled down at me. "Before we continue our adventures, I'm starving. Let's go find someplace to grab a bite."

Grinning, I followed him back through the front entrance of the store. "What is it with men needing to eat right after they cum?"

"We have to keep our energy up so we can have more sex."

"Hmmm... well when you say it like that... let's make sure you're always well-fed."

*   *   *

After our orgasmic experience in the sex shop, Tristan and I walked around De Wallen to search for a place to have supper.

The area was busy, mostly with gawking tourists. I couldn't judge, given that I was just like them. And who could blame us for gawking? This place was a feast for the eyes.

Sex workers posed and danced in front of their windows, encased in the glow of the red lights, displaying a live museum of all shapes, genders and sizes. Some of them wore extraordinary lingerie and sexy outfits, enticing potential customers. It was a veritable all-you-can-fuck buffet.

My pussy throbbed nonstop despite my orgasm just minutes ago. I was overwhelmed by the eroticism of my surroundings… and my freedom of choice. Here, in this permissive environment, I could do anything I ever dreamed of sexually, and in total anonymity. If only I could figure out what I wanted to try the most…

Having never lived anywhere other than Denver, a nomadic thirst had been building in me for years, along with an appetite to experiment more sexually. And, looking at Tristan's curious eyes drifting over the unique sights as we walked the streets together, I knew I'd chosen the perfect wingman for this journey.

The air sizzled with endless possibilities. Now, fresh out of that sex shop experience, I felt lighter — as though I'd shed my inhibitions and stripped off any shame or fear.

De Wallen seemed to have this same effect on other tourists, too. Every so often, someone would linger at a window, trying to talk with one of the prostitutes. The sex worker would pop out of their small room, naming their price. When a negotiation was reached, the customer disappeared inside.

What would it be like to enjoy the luxury of anonymous sex here, with an expert in the carnal arts?

My stomach growled, reminding me how hungry I was, briefly pulling my thoughts away from sex. We passed by an alehouse that looked pretty decent and had a unique charm. The exterior was made of rustic stone and wood, and we could see through the window that the décor matched the outside. The menu outside the door, written in both English and Dutch, showcased a list of sausage dishes bearing clever, sexual names.

I giggled and turned to Tristan. "How about this place?" I asked. He nodded and opened the door for me.

Once we stepped inside, the host greeted us at the door. "Welkom! My name is Maarten. Would you prefer to sit at the bar or at a table?"

"Table, please," said Tristan. Maarten nodded, turning to lead us through the alehouse.

The tables by the front window and the bar area were packed with many tourists, and it seemed there was no free space. But Maarten guided us past everyone and down a corridor.

The place was much bigger than it appeared on the outside. We entered a back room with a man and woman sitting at one of the tables. I couldn't see more because Maarten stopped us at the door.

"Please wait here a moment," he told us. "I must ask permission."

He entered the room and Tristan and I peeked in to see what was going on. Maarten leaned down to talk to a man in a suit. The well-dressed man sat with his back to us, but I could see him nod, making a hand gesture to allow us access to the area.

Wow. Who were these people that the host had to ask permission to seat us in this private room? Did they own this establishment? Were they famous or something?

Maarten returned to us. "You may eat here. A waiter will be with you soon." He led us to the corner seats. From my chair, I faced the woman at the other table. Now that we were closer, I was struck by how stunning she was.

My stomach twisted as she caught me staring at her, heat pooling between my thighs. Her clear blue eyes were anything but cold, warmed up by the playful look in them. My heart raced, not sure what to do, but I couldn't look away. I'd never been so instantly drawn in by someone before. There was something unique and mysterious about her and her male companion.

The duo's clothes were quite sophisticated and seemed expensive, the kind of luxury that I knew I'd be able to feel if I brushed my fingers against the fabric. I longed to touch the silkiness of her jade green dress and know if it was softer even than her milky skin. Her décolletage was visible, just the right amount of skin to entice without being over-the-top. The faint outline of her hard nipples under her dress made me wonder if she was wearing a bra underneath.

I suddenly felt totally underdressed by comparison in my simple black T-shirt and jeans and wished I'd put on something sexier before leaving the hotel earlier.

After a few moments, she broke the spell between us, looking back at her dining companion. But it was nearly impossible for me to tear my eyes away from her, even when the waiter returned to hand us each a menu.

"So, what do you want to eat?" Tristan asked, flipping through the pages of the menu. I opened mine, looking at the list of sausage, but the words blurred on the page. My eyes flitted back to the entrancing woman at the table near us.

I became so distracted that I struggled to pay attention to Tristan, hearing his occasional jokes about the dirty names of the sausages on the menu. My gaze fixated on the woman's legs under the table, long, lean and bare, crossed elegantly at the ankle above her spotless white stiletto sandals. What was someone so classy doing in an establishment like this? She couldn't have been walking around a neighborhood like this and be able to keep those high-heels so pristine.

I shifted my eyes towards her dinner date, who I could only see from the side. His thick, dark hair, the five o'clock shadow on his strong, tanned jaw, and his perfectly tailored dark gray suit made him look like a GQ model. He smiled seductively at my mystery woman, and I ached to inspire that same lusty look in him. The two of them were an exceptionally sexy pair.

The waiter stopped by to take our order, and I was able to focus long enough to blindly point to an item on the menu. "That's an excellent choice," he said, then he turned to Tristan.

"I'll have the same, please, and beer for both of us," Tristan told the waiter. The man nodded, taking back our menus and heading towards the kitchen.

Tristan smiled at me, and I grinned back while watching the woman in my peripheral vision. Her long, manicured fingers swept her straight blond hair away from her face, revealing the curve of her neck and her collarbone. I had the urge to put my mouth to her bare skin and feel her under my lips, to breathe in her fragrance.

She must have felt me staring at her because she looked up from the wine she was drinking and held my gaze again, smiling at me before looking back at her man.

I mentally slapped myself and returned my focus to Tristan. There he was, beaming with satisfaction, his eyes bright and ready for whatever was coming next. I'd never seen him this way, but then again, neither of us had ever done anything like what we'd just done in the back of that sex shop.

"That was so hot before in the sex shop." Tristan said, leaning closer to me. "Amsterdam is unlike anything I ever imagined. I feel different here. I feel like myself." He paused. "Do you know what I mean, or am I just delirious now?"

I laughed, shaking my head. "I feel the same way," I confessed. "I feel... free."

"Yes! That's exactly what it is. Freedom. Like we can do anything." He leaned over the table and kissed me full on the mouth, his hand holding the back of my head. I moaned against his lips, sliding my tongue sensuously against his. My clit ached, ready for action again.

When he pulled away, my eyes fluttered back open, and Tristan was sitting back in his seat, grinning from ear to ear. At the corner of my eye, the woman at the next table was watching us, dabbing her mouth with her napkin. She smiled, amused by the show we'd inadvertently put on for her, before turning back to the attractive man across from her.

"I'm so hard for you," Tristan confided in a low, deep voice. How was he already hard after he'd just exploded in my throat a few moments ago?

"My panties are drenched," I confessed, leaving out the fact that the beautiful mystery woman nearby was mostly responsible for my throbbing clit.

The waiter came by with our food, and the peppery aroma of the sausage reminded me how famished I was. He set down our plates and our big mugs of beer. "Let me know if you need anything else," he said, giving a respectful nod to the well-dressed couple near us as he passed by them.

Tristan and I took a bite of our respective meals. "Mmm," we said at the same time, laughing before digging into our food. As we ate in silence, too busy chewing and swallowing, I looked over at the couple beside us. They were lingering over their wine and laughing. She looked back at me, and a blush rose to my cheeks. Suddenly shy, my eyes returned to my plate, wondering how unsexy I must have looked with my mouth stuffed full of sausage.

When Tristan and I had practically cleaned our plates, I dabbed my mouth with my napkin, thinking I should go to the bathroom and check to see if I had anything stuck in my teeth.

"So tonight... I want to do filthy things with you," Tristan said, sipping on his beer. "We can go back to the hotel, change, and then get ourselves into trouble." His dark eyes gleamed impishly. "What do you think, my partner in crime?"

A thrill of excitement ran up my spine. "I'm in. Get the bill... I'm just going to go wash my hands." I took a sip of beer and stood up, catching the attention of the couple near us. The woman looked up at me as I walked by her and headed out of the back room.

The ladies' room was just down the hall and easy to find with the signage. I entered the ornate area, spotting my reflection in one of the numerous mirrors on the wall. A flashback of Tristan and I in the sex shop ran through my mind, and I smiled mischievously. I checked myself in the mirror, seeing that my face and teeth were clean, even if my mind was dirty.

Turning on the taps, I washed my hands, then rinsed out my mouth with water. As I wiped the excess droplets from my lips, the bathroom door opened behind me and startled me.

The mirror caught the reflection of my mystery woman, now approaching the bathroom counter. She met my gaze in the mirror, a grin on her lips. Heat flooded my body, a flush rising to my cheeks. Here I was, alone with this glamorous creature. Close enough to smell her vanilla perfume, near enough to reach out and touch her. But I didn't dare.

Entranced by her, I leaned against the marble countertop, slowly drying my hands with a small towel, and watched her.

It surprised me how much my pussy ached for her. I'd never responded this way to anyone else before.

She set her small red pocketbook onto the counter. She removed a tube of expensive-looking lipstick and looking at herself in the mirror. Did she even realize how gorgeous she was? I was so intimidated and awed by her beauty and the confident way she moved.

"You don't need makeup," I blurted, immediately regretting my clumsy first words to her.

She turned to me with a smile, her ravenous gaze roving from my eyes and down to my curves, reflecting the admiration I'd shown for her beauty. "You flatter me," she said with a slight Dutch accent, setting her lipstick down on the counter before she even had a chance to apply it. She leaned forward to look at me, taking a step closer.

My body vibrated with excitement at her closeness, my fingers trembling with the urge to touch her. But she reached out first, brushing a loose strand of my wavy dark hair behind one ear, her fingertips brushing my sensitive neck. Her touch jolted me, my nipples hardening instantly.

She leaned against the counter right next to me, one of her hips pressed up against mine. The soft silk of her green dress grazed my arm, raising goosebumps on my flesh.

"I am Anke," she introduced herself. *Anke.* Now I knew the name of the most seductive woman I'd ever seen. "What is your name?"

My name sounded far less exotic than hers. "Ivy."

Anke smiled, her face close enough to mine that I could kiss her. "A fitting name for such a beautiful young woman," she said, lightly brushing her fingertips over my lips, making me sigh at the softness of her touch on me. "And such a perfect mouth," she added, lightly pinching my bottom lip between her thumb and forefinger.

My pussy throbbed harder, desperate to connect with her, and my knees weakened with desire. I wanted to kiss her. I wanted to taste her. I raised my hand to touch her lips, my fingers traveling over their soft lushness. I wondered what her mouth would feel like on my body, her hot breath on my skin.

Anke's hand moved down my neck to one of my breasts, grazing my hard nipple. Unexpected pleasure shot through my body, making me gasp.

"Mmm, you are very sensitive," she said approvingly, pinching the other nipple. A small moan escaped my lips, aching to feel her soft, warm touch on my skin.

Her silky dress caressed my fingertips as my hands roamed over her back. I wrapped my arms around her slim waist, and she pushed her body closer to me until my back was up against the mirror-covered wall. My pulse sped up in anticipation of sharing an erotic moment with this mysterious woman, and in a restaurant bathroom, no less.

We were almost the same height with her in heels, and her

breasts crushed into mine. With one hand on the delicate nape of my neck, she leaned forward with deliberate slowness. My clit swelled and almost exploded with my need for her.

Anke's luscious lips grazed mine, teasing me. She kissed me lightly at first, her tongue gently exploring my mouth. Her lips were so soft and pliable, her tongue moving sensuously over mine. I kissed her back eagerly, going at her pace and savoring her.

She deepened her kissing as our hands roamed each other's bodies, impatiently exploring the curves of the other's breasts, our backs, our hips. Her hand slid between us, flat to my body, and slipped between my thighs, pressing up against my pussy. I groaned, my mound pushing against her fingers, making me wish I wasn't wearing my jeans.

The door to the ladies' room opened and someone entered, intruding on the erotic moment between Anke and I. The woman ambled to the sink, smiling at us politely, seemingly unaware that she'd intruded upon us.

My pulse beat in my ears in rhythm with my clit. My body was so ready for Anke. This couldn't be over.

Anke seemed undisturbed by the woman washing her hands near us, focusing instead on applying her lipstick in the mirror. The light pink tone accentuated her perfect mouth, drawing attention to the lips that had just been pressed against mine. God, I wanted her so badly.

Anke slid her makeup back in her bag, withdrawing a black business card from the inside pocket. She leaned forward, her lips near my ear, brushing her lips against my neck.

"Come meet me and Stefan tomorrow night. Ten o'clock," Anke said, "and bring the beautiful man you are with." She slipped the card into my back jeans pocket, discreetly squeezing my ass. "Call the phone number on the card when you are ready to get picked up."

And just like that, she turned and walked straight out of the bathroom. The swinging door gave me a final view of her swaying hips as she headed back to her table.

I tried to collect my thoughts, leaning against the counter. Had that really just happened to me? In the mirror, I noticed the faintest trace of her lipstick on my neck. I smiled, loving that she'd left her imprint on me... proof that she *was* real.

Looking down at the card, I noticed there was just a phone number on one side, engraved in metallic gold, which just added to the intrigue of Anke's mystique.

When I came out of the bathroom and headed back to the table, Anke and her male companion were gone.

"What happened? That took a while," Tristan joked with me as I approached him. He rose from his seat, having already paid for our meal.

"I have a story for you," I gushed while collecting my handbag, hurrying to head back to our hotel.

* * *

The next night, I tried on every single piece of clothing in my suitcase. I had no idea how to dress to meet Anke, or even where we were supposed to be going. Tristan loved the mystery of it all and was excited to be going along for the ride.

Nothing I'd brought with me to Amsterdam seemed sophisticated enough for Anke. I was getting nervous, like when I was in high school and about to go on a date. The hotel room was covered in my discarded clothes. Meanwhile, Tristan paired some nice black pants with a deep blue button-down shirt and was ready in minutes.

I settled on a black leather skirt that came to my mid-thigh, with no underwear. I added a matching zip-up tank top that made my small breasts look phenomenal (even without a bra), a slim silver choker, and red high heels.

Setting about doing my makeup, I had a flashback to when Anke had put her lipstick on in the mirror after kissing me. My fingers trembled nervously, but my black eyeliner somehow went on straight. I dabbed just a clear gloss on my lips, not wanting to get my makeup messy in case Anke kissed me again. And I definitely wanted to leave that possibility open.

When we were ready to leave, I called the phone number on the business card Anke had given me, just as she'd instructed.

"Yes, hi… someone told me to call this number?"

"Yes, Madam. This is the private car service. Just give me your address and someone will pick you up within the next ten minutes." I told her the name of our hotel, trying to pronounce the Dutch syllables. "Thank you, Madam. Have a pleasant evening."

As I hung up, I wondered what kind of people had private cars on standby. I was sure I would soon find out.

*   *   *

Tristan and I enjoyed the luxury of the leather backseat in the black Bentley, riding in style to our mysterious destination. Our driver, Tom, kept quiet the whole time, even when Tristan slipped his hand up my skirt and played with my clit in the car. Tristan was just teasing me to rile me up even more than I already was. I managed to contain my moans and my orgasm, finally moving his hand away to regain my composure.

When the car stopped, we were in what seemed to be an empty part of town. There was no sign out front, only metal doors that resembled an enormous meat freezer. Tom let us out of the car, then walked us to the door. There was only one person nearby, leaning against the building and smoking, looking at us.

Tom knocked on the door, and a large, tall man in a suit opened it. He greeted Tom in Dutch, and it was clear they knew each other. I didn't know what to say, so I just handed the man the card Anke had given me. Tom nodded goodbye at us and the bouncer, then left us there and walked back to his car.

The doorman examined the card, then handed it back to me; the way he looked at Tristan and I was as though he was sizing us up. He spoke Dutch again, this time into the headset he wore. When he received an answer, he stepped aside to let us in.

Industrial music was playing in the distance, but the path in front of us was nothing but a dark hallway with red lighting along it.

Tristan and I looked at each other. "Let's do this," he said, his eyes shining with excitement. I led the way into the place, knowing that he was just as intrigued as I was.

We didn't know what to expect or how we would even locate Anke and Stefan. The uncertainty of the entire situation scared me a little, which aroused the hell out of me.

The long red hallway twisted and turned, leading only to an elevator, with its doors already open. Waiting for us.

I grabbed Tristan's arm, a flicker of fear running through me. "What's the worst thing that can happen?" I asked him, pressing the single button inside the elevator.

Before he could reply, the doors shut, and I felt us go nowhere. But I heard the doors behind us open. Ah, tricky.

The music was louder here and gave us a better idea of the place's vibe, but we still didn't know what to expect. My heart fluttered with nervous excitement. I couldn't wait to see Anke and to touch her again.

We turned and both our jaws dropped. Near the elevator was a long walkway with a red carpet down the center of it. I was still holding on to Tristan's arm when we began making our way along it. Red velvet ropes adorned the sides of the walkway, and beyond those, we saw the club below.

Tristan and I peered over the edge, holding onto the metal rail to look down. The massive dance floor was completely packed with people dancing, drinking and flirting in the glow of the colorful lights. The guests were barely clad in latex, leather, lingerie, and some in BDSM fetish gear.

Several huge cages were suspended from the ceiling, each with people dancing erotically inside. A DJ occupied the main stage. I recognized him from his orange hair and white latex outfit as one of the most popular DJs in Europe.

Directly in front of us, at the end of the walkway, was a VIP area with couches and booths, and a bunch of very beautiful, well-dressed people. They laughed and flirted, sipping from their drinks. I had an urge to join them, to share in their joy and their sexual chemistry. Was this why Anke had invited us here, to indulge in this erotic decadence?

My heart raced as Tristan and I continued along the walkway, where a few other people were waiting in line behind the velvet ropes. A sexy blond-haired woman in a red latex dress and matching knee-high boots stood in front, flanked by two security guards. As she saw us coming, she walked up to us and greeted us personally with a smile.

"Hallo," she said. "Your hosts are expecting you. Right this way." She spoke into her headset and another gorgeous fair-haired woman, this time in a black latex bra and skirt, appeared out of thin air. What was this place? And why were we getting this all-star treatment? She smiled and led Tristan and I up a red-carpeted staircase.

Tristan and I exchanged excited glances as we headed into the inner sanctum. I was getting closer to Anke and to uncovering the surprises that lay within this club.

There she was, standing at the top landing with her hand on the rail. My pulse sped up, my pussy liquefying as my eyes soaked up her resplendence. Anke's succulent pink lips tormented me, and her perfectly coiffed blond hair invited my fingers to test its silkiness.

As we approached, her blue eyes glittered with mischief, looking like sapphires against her royal blue silk camisole. I was certain that she too was sans bra underneath, gauging by the way her nipples poked through the thin fabric. Her long, shapely legs were barely covered in her short white skirt. Among this crowd of dark-clothed, leather-clad people, she really stood out. And I think she wanted it that way.

Standing tall next to Anke was Stefan, this time wearing a sleek black suit and a red shirt with no tie. The two of them looked as though they could be models. Desire flooded between my thighs, my belly twisting with excitement. I wanted both of them. But *especially* Anke...

"Ivy," Anke greeted me, wrapping her arms around me in a full-body hug. She pushed herself against me, her vanilla musk dizzying me, her breath hot on my mouth. She leaned forward and kissed me hungrily, our tongues sliding together as we moaned against each other's lips. My hands roamed her back, my fingertips brushing her soft bare flesh. Her warm hands were everywhere at once — tangled in my hair, grasping my neck, roving over my back, squeezing my ass.

It was as though we were alone in the restaurant bathroom again. I was drowning in my own juices, my pussy thrumming more than the heavy bass of the club music. I craved her tongue and hands all over my body, her nakedness pressed against mine.

I didn't have the restraint to stop kissing and touching her. When she finally moved back, she smiled wickedly at me, taking my hand in her perfectly manicured one. "I am so happy you are here tonight. I would like you to meet my husband, Stefan," she said, gesturing to the man beside her.

Beside us, Tristan and Stefan had huge grins on their faces, no doubt entertained by the little show that Anke and I had just put on for them.

Stefan stepped forward, his hazel eyes gleaming with appreciation. "Ivy. You are just as breathtaking as Anke described. Welcome to my club," he said, leaning down to give me a warm kiss on my cheek. The slight stubble of his beard brushed against my soft cheek, and I imagined how his face might feel between my tender thighs.

"*Your* club?" Tristan echoed. "Wow, that's very impressive." Stefan smiled at him. I noticed they were both looking at each other with interest. "Oh, I'm Tristan, by the way." He extended his hand to Stefan to shake it.

"Stop this formal nonsense," Anke teased, laughing. Still

holding my hand, she brought me closer to her, pulling us into the space between Tristan and Stefan, wrapping one arm around Tristan's waist. "Group hug!"

We all laughed at her enthusiasm, gathering together to press our bodies up against each other. Tristan and Stefan each had one arm around Anke and I. The heat of their bodies against me like that, all at the same time, broke the ice between us. We moved apart, smiling at each other.

"Come with me. Let us get to know each other better," Anke said, her voice playful with promise. My imagination spiraled into dirty thoughts of finally being able to have her.

With Tristan and Stefan trailing behind us, Anke guided me by the hand and led me through the crowd towards the darkest corner of the VIP section. It was incredible to follow behind her and watch how other people reacted to her beauty. Her walk alone was infused with catlike grace, her sensuous, swaying hips threatening to seduce everyone in her path. I was truly hypnotized by her.

I immediately embraced the intimate atmosphere of this part of the club, the dim spot lighting over the luxurious black and red booths, with the club music playing at just the right level so that we could hear each other speak. People on all sides of us looked up as we passed by, saying hi to Anke and Stefan. I felt like we were in the presence of celebrities.

The four of us slid into the leather booth around a glass-topped table, with Anke and I in the center of the semicircle. Stefan sat next to Anke with Tristan by my side. The bass reverberated below my seat through every nerve ending in my body, magnified by the presence of all these sexy people surrounding me. My pulse fluttered just by virtue of being in Anke's presence, and my hunger was only increasing.

Anke folded one of her long, shapely legs over the other, revealing their perfection as her white skirt rode up her thighs. I admired the way her silver high heels laced up her ankle and calf in a sensual crisscross, making me want to untie them.

When I looked back up at her face, I realized Anke was watching me stare at her. Slowly, her beautiful lips formed into a secret, knowing smile. I couldn't help but grin back at her. She slid her hand over mine, which was resting on my bare knee, gently caressing my fingers.

Suddenly I remembered we weren't alone, and with some reluctance I tuned back into the frequency of our tablemates. Stefan and Tristan faced each other across the table, talking and making each other laugh as though they were old friends. Tristan was telling him about some of the amazing performers he'd booked at Aural Fixation.

"I still can't believe you own this place," Tristan said to Stefan.

Stefan grinned, a sexy dimple forming near his mouth. I had the urge to kiss it. "This isn't my only club," he said, without a hint of conceit to his tone. "But it happens to be my favorite." I could tell Tristan was impressed with Stefan's nonchalance about owning this obviously lucrative establishment, among others. "I get bored easily, so I like investing in new business opportunities. Keeps me busy." His entrepreneurial spirit enticed and inspired me. I could tell by the way Tristan was looking at him that he was also turned on by Stefan's ambition.

"So... is this a kink club?" I asked, hoping my question didn't sound stupid or obvious.

"In a manner of speaking," Anke laughed. "It's a club for open-minded people. A place for people to turn their deepest fantasies into reality." She turned to me. "What's *your* fantasy?" she asked, the corners of her mouth curling into a devilish grin.

"*You* are," I replied, slightly flustered by her question. Everyone laughed. "I'm just starting to explore," I added. "But I'm open to discovering new things." I didn't want them to think I was too vanilla and boring for them.

Anke's grin widened at my answer and reassured me of her interest. Tristan slid his hand over my thigh, smiling at me encouragingly.

Two young hostesses brought over a chilled bottle of champagne and four glass flutes, pouring for us. I admired the way their latex dresses perfectly outlined the hostesses' every curve, though they were no match for a beauty like Anke.

"This is the perfect place to explore," Stefan said. "Just look around you. Everyone here is in their element. You can do anything. And you haven't even seen all of it yet." He tried to hide his secretive smile behind his champagne flute as he took a sip.

"I've always wanted to own a place just like this," Tristan admitted, looking around and processing everything. "Where kinksters and swingers can drink and dance and really let loose." Wow, I'd had no idea that was the kind of club Tristan had envisioned opening.

Stefan raised an eyebrow and he smiled at Tristan. "Is that so? Tell me more."

"Oh *no*. We are *not* talking about work now," Anke interjected breezily, sliding her hand up my arm. "Tonight is all about relaxing, disconnecting... and maybe trying something new."

Stefan winked at her. "Ah, Anke. What I would do without you? Always making sure I'm not working too hard." He lifted his champagne, and we raised ours in turn. "Cheers to my perfect wife," he said, and the four of us clinked glasses, taking sips of the bubbly liquid.

I felt so comfortable with them, enraptured with Anke and fascinated by Stefan, surprised by how easygoing they were when they were clearly accustomed to living a completely unconventional lifestyle.

Our conversation was effortless. It seemed like we'd all known each other for years. We talked about music, art and philosophy. I admit, it was a challenge to focus on the discussion because I was incredibly distracted by Anke. As we spoke, her body kept inching closer to me on the leather booth, until her bare leg was touching mine. When she put her hand on my thigh, the heat of her fingers singed my skin, and I welcomed the burn.

I must not have been paying much attention, because I was caught off guard when Stefan asked Tristan and I, "so how long have you two been together?"

Tristan and I laughed. "We're just friends," we replied simultaneously.

Anke and Stefan exchanged amused glances. "You have beautiful sexual chemistry. You have had sex each other before, yes?" Anke asked. "I can usually tell these things."

"Well, you're right. We've had sex," I replied with a grin. I slid my hand over Tristan's inner thigh to emphasize my point.

"*Many* times," Tristan said, smiling at Stefan. I was thoroughly enjoying witnessing this attraction between both men.

Stefan looked over at Anke with desire, and they shared a brief yet succulent kiss. I watched in silence, all too conscious of how much I wanted to join them.

"So, you are not interested in a relationship with each other?" Anke asked, pointing her question at me. "Beyond the sex?"

"We aren't *in* love with each other," I replied. "But we love each other and respect each other."

"And we have a *lot* of fun together," added Tristan, making us all laugh.

"How long have you been in an open relationship?" I inquired, looking at Anke and Stefan for a response.

"We have been married for seven years, but we have been swingers for far longer than that," Anke shared, directing a seductive smile at me. "It keeps our relationship fresh," she added, turning to Stefan with a lust-filled look. "Opens up exciting possibilities with new people."

It was beautiful to watch them kiss. My sensitive nipples hardened painfully as Anke let Stefan sensually suck on her tongue. It almost seemed they'd forgotten about us, even though they were partly doing this for our benefit.

Tristan and I watched the erotic exchange between the two of them. Tristan's hand grazed my knee below the table, his fingers traveling upwards and teasing under the hem of my skirt. I jumped, looking over to see him smiling at me, watching me as his fingertips brushed against the warm skin of my inner thigh. The ache in my pussy intensified, anticipating his touch.

Stefan's hand cupped Anke's breast while they kissed, brushing his thumb across her nipple. Anke's hand found its way into Stefan's lap, rubbing against his bulge. I wanted to reach out and touch him, too.

Tristan's hand lightly brushed my swollen lips, my thighs parting to grant him full access. When I glanced at him, he looked as though he was frothing with lust. His fingers easily slid into me, my walls tightening around him as I moaned.

There was something mesmerizing about this place — about

Amsterdam, about Anke, Stefan, this club with Tristan as my partner in crime. Before our experience in the sex shop yesterday, I never thought I was capable of that kind of exhibitionism, without any self-consciousness whatsoever. Now here I was, in this public club, with this sexy couple, and Tristan's fingers knuckle-deep inside me. And I didn't even care who saw us. I *wanted* people to watch.

A new side of me was emerging. I didn't know what it was exactly, but I loved the way it felt. I had no idea where the night would take us, but I was ready for anything.

Anke peeled her lips away from Stefan's, and turned to look our way. Both of them clearly saw my bare, fully shaved, panty-free pussy through the glass top of the table. A thrill ran through me when Anke licked her lips, and Stefan leaned forward to get a better look. Now that we had an audience, Tristan was invigorated, and his fingers started to move faster inside me.

The music in the background didn't drown out my moans as I attempted to contain my building pleasure. Anke's gaze fixed on me, a naughty grin on her lips. Her arm moved beneath the tabletop, unzipping Stefan's pants. Through the table's clear glass, we saw Anke take out Stefan's impressive erection, starting to stroke him in front of us.

Tristan and I couldn't take our eyes off of them, and their gaze on us was just as intense. I squirmed in my seat as his fingers moved over my swollen clit. Anke watched me intently as she played with Stefan, whose cock beckoned to me.

I wanted to wrap my hands around him, to feel him stretch out both sets of my lips.

Craving a dick in my hand, I started unzipping Tristan's pants as he played with me. He smiled and he watched me free his bulge, surprising me with his lack of underwear. His erection sprang to life in my hands, and I squeezed him, rubbing him up and down in a twisting motion while he finger-fucked me.

Anke glanced hungrily at Tristan as she continued to pleasure Stefan with her hand. With her free hand, she pulled down the already low neckline of her top to show Tristan and I one of her perky breasts. My eyes widened at the sight of her perfect nipple, wanting to reach over and suck it, but she was too far away.

Tristan slipped his fingers back inside me as Anke circled her nipple, pinching it. She watched my hands moving on Tristan's cock, her blue eyes glinting devilishly. Anke lifted her little white skirt to show us her bare pussy, shining invitingly with her wetness. My mouth watered, thirsty to taste her.

Tristan's fingers moved faster inside me, my walls spasming around him. I knew I was soaking through the back of my skirt, but I didn't care. As Anke's fingers glided between her perfectly pink lips, I came suddenly, my hips bucking against Tristan's still-moving hand, drenching him with my orgasm.

The three of them smiled at my visible satisfaction as I caught my breath. This was the first time I'd ever had an orgasm in such a public place. And I loved it. What an incredible rush.

I leaned back in the booth to recover, idly stroking Tristan's cock while he brought his hand to his lips, sucking my liquid sex from his fingers. Stefan gently pushed Anke's hand away and was doing his best to zip up his pants over his raging hard-on. He murmured something to Anke in Dutch, and she smiled wickedly at him and nodded.

"Come with us," Stefan said suggestively. "Let's clean up. And then there's something we want you to see." Tristan barely managed to zip up his pants over his erection while Anke and I adjusted our skirts over our thighs. I caught another flash of her bare pussy lips. I needed to have her.

We stepped out of the booth, and I let Anke take me by the hand again to lead us through the club.

The music thumped in rhythm with the erratic pounding of my heart as I followed her down the stairs and onto the dance floor. We wove our way through, people parting the way for us — or should I say, for Anke, who was clearly the Queen of this place. I briefly registered how beautiful the people all around us were, dressed in all manner of lingerie, latex and leather. But my focus was on Anke's back, the curves of her slim hips and rounded ass, and those perfectly shaped, long legs. I was dying to touch and taste what was in between them.

At the complete other end of the dance area was what appeared to be an elevator with a security guard standing in front of it. When he saw the group of us coming, he stepped aside. I noticed a security panel for a handprint and wondered why this kind of protection was needed. Where were we going?

Anke placed her hand on the reader, and the steel doors slid open for us. She stepped in and I followed her, as did Stefan and Tristan.

When the elevator closed, Anke slid her arms around my waist and kissed me deeply, catching me off guard with the intensity and sweetness of her tongue in my mouth. Then, just as quickly as the kiss started, the elevator chimed to indicate we had arrived.

The doors opened into a dark hallway patrolled by another security guard, who looked ready to pounce. I was a little uneasy, but he nodded his head respectfully when he saw Anke and Stefan and moved out of the way.

The hallway reminded me of an underground stone passageway you'd find in Medieval castles. A cool, damp feeling lingered in the air. Although it felt similar, this one had some modern upgrades. Electric torchlights were mounted on the walls to illuminate our way down the red carpeted path.

We walked in silence. The sexual tension between all of us was vividly real, and I was ripe with anticipation that I might be able to fulfill my fantasy to have sex with more than one person at a time. Would that finally be possible to do tonight?

At the end of the long passageway was another set of steel doors with a handprint lock. This time, Stefan used his hand to open it, then stepped aside to let us pass. The security guard on the other side of the door nodded at Stefan and granted us access.

I was completely fascinated. The vintage chandelier dangling from the center of the high ceilings over us in the center of the marble foyer gave just enough light for me to take in the grandeur of it all. I noted original moldings, black marble pillars, and a burgundy-carpeted winding staircase that revealed there was much more upstairs. This place was a palace.

"You *live* here?" Tristan asked skeptically.

As Stefan steered us through the foyer, he explained about the house. "It was my late uncle's," he said, opening another set of large wooden doors, this time walking us through a beautifully decorated room in burgundy, mocha and ivory tones. My heels sank into the plush carpet, and I examined the art hanging on the walls. "He left me everything in his will."

Tristan and I admired our surroundings. There was no one else around except for us and the occasional security guard passing by. I wondered how many guards there were on the grounds... and exactly what — or who — they were guarding.

We passed through a dining room with a table large enough to accommodate fifty people — an extravagance that would have been well-suited for Buckingham Palace. I wondered what kind of guests he and Anke would host at a dinner party like that.

In a private room off the dining hall was a set of heavy wooden doors, engraved with erotic figures of intertwined men and women in sexual positions. There was a large vintage lock, interestingly out of place with all the modernity we'd witnessed so far.

Stefan pulled an old-fashioned metal key from his pocket and inserted it into lock, turning it until it clicked open. The doors opened with a creak to reveal a torch-lit stone tunnel leading underground.

My need and curiosity heightened. What would they show us next?

Anke joined Stefan, sliding her hand into his. Tristan reached for my hand also, intertwining his warm fingers with mine. We followed them through the tunnel until they stopped walking.

"Are you ready?" Anke asked, turning around to look at Tristan and me.

Before we could answer her question, they opened the double doors to reveal a scene that was so raw, so erotic, that I could never have dreamed I'd witness it. I gasped in surprise, awe, a little bit of shock, and a lot of arousal.

"It's extraordinary, isn't it?" Anke whispered in my ear. Her breath was hot against my neck, sliding her hand on my back.

There were at least fifty people at the center of the dimly lit dungeon chamber, their expressions filled with rapture. The stone-walled room was surprisingly warm and seemed to heave with every breath, every thrust, every movement of the swelling mass of beautifully naked bodies. A symphony of moaning and groaning was punctuated by cracks of a paddle or whip or flogger against someone's flesh, followed by pleasured cries and louder moaning.

All of my senses were completely overwhelmed. The air was redolent with sex, leather and wood. Deep, dark music created the perfect backdrop to the carnal orchestra. I didn't know where to look first. My eyes roved over all the people, the St. Andrew's Cross with someone strapped to it, the leather and wood benches, flogging posts, and cages. There was also luxurious vintage furniture, all of which were being used as props by Anke and Stefan's guests.

Among the furniture were two ornate thrones, which sat empty. I imagined how many nights Anke and Stefan must have sat there, possibly using willing slaves as footstools, their every desire being served. Or simply choosing to watch at their leisure as their guests indulged in pleasure in front of them. I couldn't even imagine the things they'd seen and done.

As the kink orgy raged on, my entire being burned at the prospect of stripping my clothes off and partaking in ecstasy with all these beautiful strangers. But it was Anke I wanted above all, and I needed a more private and less distracting space to be able to focus on her.

I stood on the fringes of the crowd, enthralled by the action, with Stefan and Anke flanking my left and right, and Tristan standing next to her. Anke took my hand and slipped it up her short skirt. My fingertips brushed against her sparse hair and against the delicate wet folds of her pussy. She felt as soft as she'd looked when she'd exposed herself to us earlier.

Anke smiled and slid her hand under my skirt to touch my sensitive lips. I quivered, wondering how much longer I could take this torment.

In front of us, a woman with black hair as long and wavy as a mermaid's was being spread out on top of a torture table by two men, her hands and ankles bound at each corner. One man straddled her face and pushed his cock into her mouth while the other grabbed her thighs and thrust deeply into her slit.

As a novice, it was difficult for me not to feel overly excited at being part of this kinky underground sex experience. Anke and Stefan seemed so advanced in their carnal knowledge it was almost intimidating. Clearly, this was their playground. It was surreal to me that they'd invited us to be their playmates for the night.

I couldn't hear Anke's moans, but I felt the vibrations through my body as I played with her. We were side by side, stroking each other's pussies with our fingertips. When another hand touched mine between her legs, I looked over and realized that those fingers belonged to Tristan, with Anke's hand guiding his arm. Tristan caught my gaze and smiled wickedly at me as we made her moan together.

Stefan came up to me on the other side, his hand drifting between my thighs, too. My legs weakened at the feel of Anke's soft fingers and Stefan's slightly rougher touch playing with me at the same time.

Soaking up the erotic scene in front of us, I swooned over a gorgeous flogger-wielding domme who had two slaves clad in black latex gimp outfits with leashes around their necks. She was making each of them take turns licking her pussy. Near them, a dominant in a black studded leather harness, had two male slaves bent over in front of him, the whips of the dom's flogger kissing each of their bare asses in turn.

I was curious about how it would feel to be in such a submissive position. I'd never played in the BDSM space before, and the idea of it had always awed me. But right now, what I wanted even more was to go somewhere with my partners, indulge in their skin, and explore all of the new feelings and sensations flowing through me.

Anke's hand moved faster on my clit, using her other hand to turn me to face her. Her silken tongue explored my mouth while her fingers caressed my trembling pussy. I groaned, pushing my body into her. Stefan came up behind me, his erection pressing into the small of my back. Tristan buried his hands in Anke's hair as he approached behind her, kissing her neck while she kissed me. Knowing that all four of us were connected in this moment of pleasure heightened my sensitivity.

Stefan lifted the back of my skirt and spread my ass cheeks apart with his big hands while Anke slid her fingers over my clit. Moaning, I matched the intensity of her touch between her slippery thighs. Tristan's hand brushed against mine between her legs as he penetrated her with his fingers. Anke moaned into my shoulder, her breath hot on my bare skin.

My core burned with desire between Stefan and Anke's bodies while Tristan and I played with her. Nothing could prepare me for the beauty of Anke's face as she shuddered and moaned, her lips parting in pleasure. She soaked my fingers with her juices, her pussy shuddering in my hand, satisfying me.

Even in her heady, post-climactic state, Anke kept working my clit as my hand remained between her thighs, soaking up her warmth. Stefan slid two fingers into my tightness at the same time, working me from inside. I began to tremble against both of their hands, the buildup too much to take. Heat spread throughout my body as I came, gripping on to Anke's arm as they teased the orgasm out of me.

Anke slid her wet fingers into her mouth to taste me, and I slipped my hand from between her legs to do the same. Her sex tasted faintly sweet and made me want to delve between her thighs for more. She smiled seductively, then grabbed me and kissed me, the sweet combination of our juices arousing me anew.

"Come with us," she whispered in my ear. With a satisfied expression on her face, Anke grabbed my hand and led the way to yet another door. My pulse quickened as I imagined the four of us exploring our exciting new attraction.

The guard gave us a brief nod as we approached, recognizing Anke and Stefan, allowing us to go through. This time, the hallway was more modern and slightly better lit than the other passages we'd walked through before. In the sensual lighting of several crystal chandeliers, we padded along the plush black carpeted corridor. Closed white doors lined the walls, each with a number on them. I wondered who and what was inside them, fighting the urge to turn one of the doorknobs to discover for myself.

As we followed her down the hall, we heard moaning emanating from within the rooms, and understood that each one was occupied with lovers. At the end of the corridor, she opened the tall double doors marked RESERVED, leading us into a large bedroom.

I admired our surroundings, lit by several dim lamps that created a sensual atmosphere. At one side of the room was a beautiful King-size bed with a gold and vermilion embroidered coverlet, and a dozen plush gold pillows. Glass bowls of gold-wrapped condoms were placed on the night tables by the bed. On the other side of the room was a heavy antique mirror with a bronze frame perfectly showcasing the bed, and a vintage red fainting couch with dark wooden edges. There were no windows in the place. It was perfectly private.

The door clicked shut softly behind us. Stefan strode confidently into the room, his fit physique perfectly outlined by his lavish suit. My pussy tightened and ached, restless for release.

"Welcome to the our lair," he said with a smile.

"You can freshen up in there," said Anke, pointing to the washroom off to one side.

"Thank you," I told her, ducking into the room. I leaned against the marble countertop and washed my hands at the double sink, looking at my elated reflection in disbelief. Was this *actually* happening?

Tristan joined me inside. "Are you having fun tonight?" he asked wryly, washing his hands as I dried mine.

"Can you *believe* this place?" I asked excitedly in a hushed tone, handed him the towel, then grabbed him by the front of his shirt to kiss him.

He pulled back and smiled. "Let's join our perverted hosts," he joked, placing the towel on the counter.

When he opened the bathroom door, Anke and Stefan were standing there with amused smiles, waiting for their turns to wash up. It was clear that they'd heard the whole thing.

"Perverted, you say," Anke teased, stepping past me to soap up her fingers in the sink. "We have barely even started yet."

"But it is good to know you're enjoying yourselves so far," Stefan added, exchanging a knowing glance with Anke in the mirror as they rinsed and dried their hands.

"We were trying to be discreet," Tristan said, then looked at me and laughed.

"Come. Relax," Anke smiled, guiding us back into the bedroom. "Have a seat and let me make you a drink."

Tristan perched on the arm of the fainting couch, and Stefan and I took the soft velour seat. The three of us watched Anke's gorgeous curves as she poured our drinks with expert precision. I had no idea what she was making, but I was sure it would help soothe my nerves. My mind raced back to the scene in the other room: Anke exploding onto my fingers, the feel of her and Stefan's hands between my legs...

Tonight, I was fully ready to take on three lovers simultaneously, even though I'd never been in a scenario like this before. I was a bit shy, because it seemed everyone else here was far more experienced than me, including Tristan.

Anke smiled at me reassuringly over her shoulder, as though she understood my trepidation. "Just so you know, we have no expectations. Stefan and I like to go with the flow. Isn't that right, my love?" she asked him.

"We can stop at any time," Stefan added. "We just want to make sure you are both comfortable and well entertained."

"Oh, we definitely are," I said, and we all laughed, easing any remaining tension in the room. Anke brought Tristan and I our drinks first before serving herself and Stefan.

"Proost," said Anke, and we all raised our glasses to clink them together.

"To a pleasurable evening," said Tristan, winking at me as we sipped from our drinks.

The alcohol warmed its way down my throat and lit up my belly. I instantly felt a bit more at ease. I slid off my high heels and tossed them to the side and out of the way, stretching out my toes.

After another sip of his drink, Stefan's hand rode up my bare thigh. Afraid to spill anything on the lush furnishings, I handed him my glass to set down on the small table near him. With our hands now free, Stefan turned to me and covered my lips with his, kissing me with the same thirst as Anke had, but with more roughness. His stubble lightly scratched my chin, but it felt too good for me to care. My hands gripped onto his strong back and shoulders, his musky cologne making my head spin.

Stefan pulled away from me a moment, turning us towards Anke and Tristan, who had started kissing each other next to us. Tristan's hands roamed her body as she pressed herself against him, and Stefan began to unzip the front of my top.

Tristan's eyes widened at the sight of my skin being revealed and came to sit on the other side of me. Anke sat on the bed across from us, watching us with dark eyes and an amused smile as she casually sipped from her drink.

I smiled at her as these two beautiful men slowly undressed me, dragging their warm lips over every inch of newly bared flesh. My top and skirt were discarded on the soft carpet, leaving me sitting naked with both men exploring my body. I reveled in the roughness of their touch, while also craving Anke's softer hands on me.

As Stefan knelt on the carpet in front of me, I slid down on the fainting couch to let Tristan worship my breasts, running his tongue around my nipples before sucking them. The soft velvet was cool and comforting against my back as I gave my body to them. When I glanced up, Anke was smiling at me approvingly from her seat on the bed.

Stefan gave me a wicked grin as he lowered his face between my legs, lapping up my continuing flow of warm juices. Tristan moved his mouth from my breasts down my belly, down to where Stefan was sucking on my clit. I watched Stefan and Tristan kiss, incredibly aroused to see these sexy men sharing my taste between them.

Each man grabbed one thigh to spread me even further apart, all while they both licked and sucked attentively on my quivering snatch, their hungry mouths working me into a pleasurable rhythm.

I met Anke's eyes across the room, smoldering with a thirst that surprised and delighted me. She stood from the bed, removed her heels, and walked over to me barefoot. Once in front of me, she nudged her way between the men to taste me for herself.

I moaned as her tongue explored my clit, all three of their tongues working together on my swollen clit and my ass. I couldn't tell whose mouths were whose as they danced their way across my most sensitive parts. Their hands roamed over my inner thighs, my belly and my breasts as they covered me with their combined touch.

My moans were wild, and I knew I was on the brink of yet another orgasm. It was unbelievable to have so many people simultaneously snacking on me this way, with so much attention paid to my pleasure.

My pussy twitched as though I was about to cum, my hips raising slightly off the couch. But my trio of lovers read my body language and collectively slowed down the pace of their mouths, seeking to prolong my torment. Anke removed her lips from me, but not before gently sucking my clit and giving me an impish smile.

Stefan held down my thighs as he continued to tongue me with a delectable slowness, the tension between my legs mounting even more. When I leaned up to watch him, he was slowly stroking his massive cock in one hand. I craved him between my lips.

Suddenly, their mouths stopped, my thighs missing their heat between them. They had paused their pleasuring for now so they could strip off the rest of their clothes. I slid my hand between my thighs, masturbating slowly while I watched them all remove whatever they wore, feasting my eyes on all of their sexy bare skin. My clit throbbed with need, ripe to feel their touch on me again.

Tristan hurriedly discarded his shirt, removing his pants and shoes, tossing everything aside. Stefan did the same, although he was a bit neater and more patient about it, folding his suit over the side of the couch.

The men helped Anke undress, casting off her camisole and skirt. She stood before us in her natural state, and I basked in this long-awaited view of her body. I gazed in awe at her petite form, her small, pink nipples and round breasts, her flat belly, the perfect triangle of hair between her thighs with her pouty pink nether lips. I had to stop masturbating, because I was too close to orgasm again, and her sexiness was about to send me over the edge.

Anke took a few steps toward me, then grabbed me by the hand to help me off the couch and led me to the bed. She lay me down on the cool bedspread, draping her body over mine and kissing me. Our arms wrapped around each other, pressing ourselves closer together. Both men approached to find their places in the mix as her pussy grazed against my thigh, leaving behind her hot, wet trace.

Tristan and Stefan stood next to us, their hard cocks ready, their hands running over Anke's back as she kissed me. When she finally looked up, she smiled up at both of them.

"Come here, Tristan," she instructed, gesturing for him to join her. She shimmied her delectable body up my torso until her knees were spread on either side of my face, with her silken slit in full view. Finally.

I hungrily pressed my mouth into her perfect pink lips, reveling in the taste of her and breathing in her clean musk. When I opened my eyes, I witnessed the incredibly sexy sight of Tristan pushing his thick cock into Anke's luscious mouth.

With her body on my face, I couldn't see Stefan, but I felt his hands between my legs, spreading my thighs. Anke rode my face, and I spread her glorious ass cheeks as far apart as I could. I filled her pussy with my fingers, as Stefan's fingers did the same to me, making me moan.

Anke's body moved with the strokes of Tristan's hips as he shoved himself deeper down her throat. I watched the impressive show, Tristan's girthy erection repeatedly disappearing into her mouth. Desire mounted faster in me with Stefan's fingers sliding over my aching clit.

Stefan stopped suddenly, coming up to where all the action was happening, bending his head to mine. "Are you ready for me, Ivy?" he asked seductively, unwrapping a condom.

I moved my mouth from between Anke's thighs for a second to reply yes. He lowered his face to mine, kissing me, briefly dipping his tongue into Anke's slit. She moaned on Tristan's dick, and Stefan smiled before standing up to open my thighs with his strong hands.

Stefan lifted my hips onto his thighs and began to feed the head of his cock into me, slowly spreading me apart, inch by inch. I groaned as he filled me, my warm juices squirting down the crack of my ass. He eased his way inside until his balls rested against my tight asshole.

Anke choked gratefully on Tristan while muffling her cries of pleasure as I slid my tongue over her slit. I caught Tristan's eye as he pulled himself out of her mouth.

"Turn around," he guided Anke, and she smiled and carefully spun on my face. I could now lick her clit while giving her a view of Stefan fucking me. Tristan grabbed a condom from the bowl, rolling one on carefully before positioning himself behind her. When I opened my eyes, I had the perfect view of him slapping her pink folds with his dick to torment her a bit before entering her.

The slick sound of Tristan fucking Anke made me thirsty to lick him clean too, so I alternated my tongue between Anke's quim and Tristan's shaft and balls. They both groaned as he pushed his cock into her, his balls just inches above my face.

The angle of my view was incredible. I reached up to rim her ass with my wet fingertips as Tristan spread her cheeks.

We became a quartet of moaning and groaning naked limbs, moving around in unspoken synchrony. Anke angled her body downward, leaning to suck Stefan as he slipped out of me. As though she didn't want me to be absent pleasure for even a second, her hand stroked my clit as Stefan fucked her mouth. He groaned and plunged back into me, fucking me harder.

Anke's tongue covered my slit, her soft hair tickling my inner thighs, inflating my arousal. My cries were muffled between her thighs. I lost track of time, dizzied by the scent of her pussy as my orgasm built up. Stefan didn't stop thrusting into me until Tristan asked him, "Do you want to switch?" followed by Stefan pulling out of me.

I missed his dick already, but it was about to be replaced by Tristan's. Anke dismounted my face, leaning down to kiss me and suck her taste off my tongue. The men repositioned themselves so they could put on fresh condoms before swapping between us.

Stefan lay back on the bed, and Anke faced me and began to straddle him. "I want to watch Stefan eat you," she said before sliding him inside herself. I obliged her, facing her as I covered her husband's mouth with my pussy. It was only then that I noticed we had a spectacular view of ourselves in the large mirror in front of the bed. I could see almost everything we were doing to each other. I glanced at our reflection and began to ride Stefan's face at the same rhythm as Anke impaled herself upon her husband's cock.

Sliding into my pussy from behind, Tristan gave Stefan the same view that I'd enjoyed when Tristan had fucked Anke just moments ago. He grabbed my hair roughly as he thrust hard into me, all while Stefan busily sucked on my clit.

Tristan pulled out of me for a moment, covered with my wet sex, and Stefan took Tristan's dick into his mouth to suck him. Tristan groaned deeply, his eyes rolling back with pleasure. Watching these sexy men together only intensified my arousal, and looking at Anke's hungry eyes, she felt the same. Then Stefan moved his mouth back to my clit and Tristan's cock split me open again.

I heard Tristan spit and felt a trail of his saliva between my ass cheeks. Stefan raised his head to lick my ass, spreading the wetness around. Tristan slowly slipped his finger into my tight hole, massaging his dick on the other side of my tight walls. My pussy clenched and threatened to burst again.

Anke leaned forward over Stefan to kiss me and play with my breasts. When her tongue entered my mouth, I couldn't control my climax anymore, and I grabbed onto Anke's back as I began to tremble violently. My screams were muffled against her lips as I dripped onto Stefan's awaiting tongue, my juices coating Tristan's dick and balls. I felt Anke climax too, grinding herself harder against Stefan's thickness, digging her nails into my shoulders as her head fell back in pleasure.

She and I were still catching our breaths when Tristan withdrew from my pussy with a slick sound, slowly working his finger out of my tight ass. I detached myself from Stefan's tongue, moving off of him and onto my knees on the bed again.

Anke dismounted Stefan's still-engorged cock, cleaning him of her cream. She crawled over to us with a naughty smile.

Reaching into the first drawer of the small night table by the bedside, Anke extracted a few toys, setting them down onto the table. I noticed a steel butt plug, lube, and a harness with a fake black dildo dangling in the front — reminding me of the one that Tristan and I had seen at the sex shop the other day.

"Get on your knees with your back to me," she told me. I quickly moved to comply, my body trembling with excitement as I brought my ass closer to the edge of the bed.

Stefan and Tristan stood in front of me, kissing each other while they stroked each other's dicks. They pushed themselves closer to my mouth, and I started sucking each one of them, pressing their cocks together and alternating between them.

"You filthy woman," Anke teased as I devoured both men. She thoroughly lubed up my ass and slowly, gently inserted the butt plug, stretching me out. I moaned around Tristan and Stefan's dicks, fired up to see them stroking each other's shafts while I sucked their heads into my mouth. The butt plug slid into place inside of me and I reveled at the fullness in my tight ass.

"Now put on that harness and get up," Anke instructed me, "you're the only one here who hasn't fucked me yet." She sat on the edge of the red coverlet, spreading her legs with her swollen pussy lips open and waiting for me.

I was thrilled at the idea of being able to penetrate her with something other than my fingers and hands. I pulled myself away from the men, standing up in front of Anke. Stefan helped me put on the harness, the straps framing my ass as I tightened them around my waist and thighs. I laughed when I saw my reflection in the mirror. The big black dildo dangled from the front of it, beckoning to be played with. The size didn't even compare to Tristan's or Stefan's, but I hoped I could make it hit all of Anke's most sensitive spots.

Anke handed me the lube and I squirted some of it onto the dildo, as though I was jerking it off, warming up the silicone toy to make it as comfortable for her as I could. She lay back on the bed with her legs spread for me and I positioned myself between them.

I started playing with Anke's clit with the head of my black dong, torturing her and slipping into her for a brief moment before pulling out again. One inch at a time, the same way Stefan was suddenly sliding into me from behind. When I plunged my entire length into her, Stefan shoved himself into me completely, occupying my pussy again. I was narrower than usual because of the butt plug inside me. I cried out in pleasure at the feeling of being stretched apart.

Tristan had come up onto the bed on the other side of Anke. She feasted on his cock while he played with her small pink nipples. It was so sexy to watch Anke not only take all of him inside of her mouth and throat, but invite him to go as deeply as he dared. As he carefully abused her mouth, I thrust into her at the same rhythm.

Every nerve ending in my body was on fire. Stefan's hips moved faster, his hand pushing the butt plug as deeply as he could into my ass. I pumped into his moaning wife, matching stroke for stroke. Stefan grabbed my breasts, pinching my nipples almost savagely and evoking pleasure throughout my body. I held Anke's shapely long legs open, getting a glorious view of my black phallus disappearing inside of her, with Tristan's dick fucking her throat at the same pace. The stunning reflection of the four of us in the mirror could barely capture the beauty of our intertwined bodies.

Anke quivered as I pumped the dildo deeper into her, just as Stefan drove himself into me with more ferocity. I moaned with pleasure, trying to focus on rubbing her clit in circles with the pad of my thumb, parting the lips so she could feel even more of my touch on her most sensitive flesh. She writhed under me, reaching out to grab my ass to pull me closer.

The harder Stefan fucked me, the harder I thrust into Anke, and the harder Tristan fucked her mouth... all of us penetrating and pleasuring each other. The tension between my legs mounted, threatening to snap. Another orgasm was rising inside of me, weakening my knees and making my thrusts falter slightly.

Stefan fucked me powerfully, gripping hard onto my ass and lifting me slightly off the floor. With his strength as a guide, we fucked Anke with a roughness that she and I both wanted, her cries muffled by Tristan's dick in her mouth. She dug her fingers into his thighs as she began to shake, bringing on my own violent climax.

I fell into her open arms, my silicone dong still moving gently inside her. Stefan thrust a few more times into me, then slowly pulled his cock out of my soaked hole. The plug remained in my ass, reminding me that there was more to come.

Tristan and I slipped out of Anke's mouth and pussy, respectively. She rose to her knees on the bed, bending to lick her juices off the dildo I wore, while Tristan knelt to suck my liquid sex off Stefan. He held the back of Tristan's head as Tristan took him fully between his lips and worked him into his throat. But it seemed that Stefan was close to exploding, and could only handle a few deep thrusts before he reluctantly withdrew himself from Tristan's mouth.

"Lie on your back on the bed, Tristan," Anke said, tossing him a fresh condom. "And you, Ivy, get on top of him with your back to him." I loved the way she took control of us, like she was directing a porn scene.

Tristan reclined on the bed, grinning at me wickedly. "Are you ready for your little ass to get fucked?" he asked, preparing himself.

"Mmm, you know I am," I said, getting up on the bed to face Anke as I began to straddle him. I was too excited and focused on watching Anke clean off the black dildo and put on the harness to see what was going on behind me.

I couldn't tell whose hands slowly removed the butt plug, but my pussy dripped onto Tristan's hard cock as the plug was pulled out of me, leaving me empty again. Someone then squirted cool lube into my ass, massaging my tight hole and stretching me out with their fingers. I groaned with pleasure, watching in the mirror as Stefan took Tristan's dick in his hand and helped him into my ass.

Tristan and I moved together slowly to fit him inside me, letting my body grow accustomed to the feeling of his size in my tight ass. This wasn't my first anal session with Tristan, but it had been awhile since I'd been stretched out like this. I leaned back onto his powerful chest and forearms, letting him pump into me gently.

Waiting for Tristan to be able to fit his whole length into my ass, Stefan got to his knees in front of me on the bed, his erection edging between my thighs. Anke leaned down and sucked her husband briefly, then guided Stefan into my pussy. This time, he was met with even more tightness than when the plug was inside my ass.

It took a few minutes of slow thrusting until they were both completely inside of me. I was impressed that my holes were able to handle them. This was my first time ever being double penetrated by two cocks at the same time. The fullness of them inside me, the intense pressure created by them pushing against each other through the thin wall between my pussy and my ass, was a pleasure unlike any I'd ever known.

As the men found their rhythm inside me, Anke was ready with the strap-on and positioned herself behind Stefan, rolling a condom on her dildo. She'd put her heels back on so that her hips were at the same height as his. After lubing up her black dong, she played with his ass a bit before easing in the tip of her dildo. Stefan muffled a cry and paused his thrusts inside of me for a moment to let Anke get a little deeper inside of him.

And then, there was thrusting all around. Tristan fucking me in the ass from below me, Stefan from in front of me while he played with my clit. As Anke moved deeply within Stefan's ass, he in turn pounded that level of intensity back into me. It was like she was really the one fucking me.

Heat and pleasure overcame me and I started to quake. I was lost in a cloud of elation until I burst, seeing stars behind my eyes as my partners all kept on moving inside me, forcing the final spasms of my climax.

Prompted by my convulsing pussy, Tristan lifted me slightly off his body to pull out of my ass, looking ready to explode. Stefan and I brought our hands to Tristan's cock, removing the condom and stroking him until he erupted with orgasm all over the front of me and Stefan. His cum slid down my belly and between Stefan and I, a decadent mess I was dying to taste.

Stefan pulled out of me, aroused by the sight of Tristan's cum on my flesh. As Anke kept fucking his ass, translucent white juices spurted out of Stefan's dick, mingling with Tristan's cum on my belly.

I was completely covered with sex, and I absolutely loved how filthy it made me feel.

Anke slowly withdrew herself from Stefan's ass and removed her harness and the condom from the dildo with expert quickness. She set it aside on the table, using a wet wipe on her hands before coming to lick all the copious juices off my body.

"I want to taste, too," I told her, and when she was done, she kept some fluids in her mouth and kissed me to swap their delicious taste with me.

The four of us collapsed onto the bed together in a sticky, satisfied mess, limbs intertwined. I couldn't believe we'd just done all of that, how many firsts I'd experienced in just one night.

"How about a shower and a sleepover?" Anke suggested, making us laugh. "We have some other friends we would love you to meet tomorrow."

Tristan and I glanced at each other, already knowing our answer.

After all, our sexual enlightenment was only just beginning.

ABOUT THE AUTHOR

Lexi Sylver is the Montreal-based erotica author of *Mating Season* and *All the Queen's Men*. She enjoys sharing her stories and experiences living an unconventional and kinky lifestyle. As an entrepreneur, advocate, educator, podcast host and producer, media personality, public speaker and coach for consensual non-monogamy, she journeys the world to attend travel events and conferences. She regularly contributes articles about sexuality and relationships to Pornhub's Sexual Wellness Center, ASN Lifestyle Magazine, SDC.com and her personal blog. Her mission is to promote empowerment and education by guiding you to shamelessly explore your Lexuality. Find out more at LexiSylver.com.

Get Lexual

Subscribe to Lexi's newsletter and connect with her on social media for more Lexual updates!

Website & newsletter signup:
https://lexisylver.com

Twitter:
https://twitter.com/lexisylver

Instagram:
https://www.instagram.com/lexisylver

Facebook:
https://www.facebook.com/getlexual

Author Photo Credits:

Model: Lexi Sylver

Photography by Fabrice de Bray's Indiscreet Arts | fabricedebray.com

© 2019 by Fabrice de Bray. All Rights Reserved.

Lexi Sylver

Made in United States
Orlando, FL
06 August 2023

35829718R00161